I0461105

# LADD
# HAVEN

Dianne Venetta

LADD HAVEN
Book #4


Ladd Springs Series:

LADD SPRINGS ~ #1
LADD FORTUNE ~ #2
HOTEL LADD ~ #3
LADD HAVEN ~ #4
LOSING LADD ~ #5




Other novels by Dianne Venetta

Romantic Women's Fiction
The Gables Trilogy:
JENNIFER'S GARDEN
LUST ON THE ROCKS
WHISPER PRIVILEGES

Women's Fiction
CONDEMN ME NOT

Copyright 2013 by Dianne Venetta
All rights reserved
ISBN 9780988487185

Ladd Haven
Copyright 2013 by Dianne Venetta
ISBN: 978-0-9884871-8-5
Publisher: BloominThyme Press
Editor: Best Foot Forward
Cover Design: Jaxadora Design

This book is a work of fiction. Any references to historical events, real people, or real locales are used fictitiously. Other names, characters, places, and incidents are the product of the author's imagination, and any resemblance to actual events or persons, living or dead, is coincidental. This book is licensed for your personal enjoyment only. All rights reserved. Without limiting the rights under copyright reserved above, no part of this publication may be reproduced, stored in or introduced into a retrieval system, or transmitted, in any form, or by any means (electronic, mechanical, photocopying, recording, or otherwise) without prior written permission from the copyright owner.

# Acknowledgements

As an animal lover, I find any and all abuse of animals abhorrent. Doesn't matter how big or small the creature, animal cruelty is senseless and repulsive. Troy Parker, the hero in Ladd Haven, is a young man who has dedicated his life to working with horses, turning a childhood passion into his career. Rough and tumble country boy on the outside, Troy's a man with a gentle heart. Especially when it comes to those he loves, including his horses.

Many of you might be familiar with a horse trainer by the name of Monty Roberts. I was introduced to his work years ago via a novel I read, written by Nicholas Evans. An unforgettable read, *The Horse Whisperer* is one of those books that breaks your heart, then turns around and mends it by weaving a story filled with incredible acts of kindness.

Many of the horse training moves my character demonstrates are rooted in the principles emphasized by Monty Roberts: a gentle tone, non-verbal communication, and patience. Translated: Never push an animal to do what it's not ready to do. Mr. Roberts developed his approach after witnessing the violent training methods of his father. I imagine watching a man tie a helpless animal and almost torture him into submission would change a person. It would me.

If you ever get the opportunity to see a live demonstration by Monty Roberts, don't miss it. Years ago I watched him perform in Ocala, Florida and walked away from the event amazed and joyous.

## Dedication

This book is dedicated to horse lovers everywhere.

*Meet the cast of characters of Ladd Haven...*

Ernie Ladd – Original owner of Ladd Springs
Albert Ladd - Ernie's brother
Jeremiah Ladd - Ernie's son, forsaken by the family
Susannah Ladd Wilkins – Ernie's sister (deceased)
Delaney Wilkins - Ernie's niece, daughter to Susannah
Nick Harris – Owner, Hotel Ladd, Delaney's husband
Felicity Wilkins - Delaney's daughter
Casey Owens – Jeremiah Ladd's daughter
Troy Parker – Casey's boyfriend
Jimmy Sweeney – Friend and co-worker of Casey
Annie Owens Foster -- Casey's mother
Calvin Foster – Annie's husband, Foster son
Jack Foster – Cal's brother & Delaney's ex-husband
Gerald and Victoria Foster – Parents to Cal, Jack, Beau & Clint
Travis Parker – Twin to Troy, boyfriend to Felicity
Malcolm Ward –Business partner of Nick's
Lacy Owens Ward – Annie's sister, married to Malcolm
Ashley and Booker Fulmer - Ernie's sister Susannah's best friend & her husband
Candi Sweeney - Annie's best friend, Jimmy's aunt
Fran Jones - Owner of Fran's Diner, aunt to Annie
Hank Dakota – Town lawyer

## Chapter One

"So they can't take a honeymoon?" Seated across from Casey Owens in a red-vinyled booth at Fran's Diner, Jimmy Sweeney shook his head. Bright light flooded in through the pane of front windows, red-checkered curtains serving to cast his fair complexion in warm shades, accentuating the naturally red highlights in his brunette hair. Casey noted most of the black hair dye had grown out, the dark ends the only visible hint of Jimmy's Goth stage. He refused to cut his hair short which would have eliminated the color altogether, claiming he wasn't comfortable with short hair. Too mainstream. At least it was only the tips, Casey mused. The brown hair made him appear semi-normal and not half-bad looking, no longer sullen, brooding and rebellious.

Jimmy was a loner at school, torn between his desire for attention and his debilitating shyness. He couldn't make the first friend yet it was all he longed for. Friends, people who understood him, accepted him. He was a little on the quirky side, but Casey had come to learn it was due to his extreme intelligence. Jimmy was a brainiac born to a family of dysfunction. His aunt Candi was Casey's best friend, a thirty-eight-year-old woman who still lived at home. His Uncle Clem was a no-good bum, a man who tried to loot gold from Ladd Springs, land that now belonged to her thanks to her mother's vigorous battle to prove paternity. A victory Casey had only recently come to appreciate. While she was glad to own part of Ladd Springs, Jeremiah Ladd was a dirt bag. Could anyone expect her to celebrate the fact he was her father?

Her change in attitude was due in large part to Jimmy. He'd convinced her to see the positive in owning half of Ladd Springs, as opposed to the negative. Forget the reason she had the land and focus on what it meant going forward. But that was Jimmy. He was her constant. The guy who'd been there for her when everyone was else was too busy with their own lives. The two struck up conversation one night while rolling silverware after working a shift at the diner. Going through troubles of her own at the time, she'd needed a friend and was willing to chance a conversation with the extremely odd Jimmy Sweeney. Turns out, he wasn't so weird once you got to talking to him. He was smart, generous, and a good listener. They even had a few things in common. Peering into his dark eyes, eyes that held affection, friendship, she sighed. If it hadn't been for Jimmy and his friendship, Casey would have lost her mind. Lost her life, really.

"It doesn't seem right," Jimmy said. "If I were newly married I'd want one."

Staring at him, a part of her knew Jimmy wouldn't mind that marriage to include her. Only she wasn't interested. "They're too busy with opening the hotel," Casey replied, picking at a biscuit on her plate, one of two her Aunt Fran had delivered along with a cheese sandwich, none of which she'd ordered. She didn't want biscuits or sandwiches or her customary cheeseburger and fries, but if she didn't eat, Fran would get on her and she wasn't in the mood for another lecture. *Now fill up, sugar, you're eatin' for two. Don't go starvin' that baby or I'll report you to your doctor.* With the amount of food Fran was trying to pile down her throat, one would think Casey was eating for two hundred! She was pregnant, not vying for an eat-a-thon.

"But no honeymoon?" Jimmy pressed. "I thought that's what newlyweds were supposed to do."

"Eventually they will." Swiping a finger against a thick drip of honey, Casey sucked the sweet substance from her fingertip. "My mom wants to go to Bermuda for her honeymoon."

Jimmy gaped. "Bermuda?"

Casey nodded. "Says it's the closest exotic destination she could think of."

"What—she afraid to go far?"

"She's not sure about flying." Annie Owens was almost forty years old and had never been on an airplane. Casey would say that was weird, except she hadn't been on one either. Growing up in a small town with little money to their name, they never had reason. Now that her mom had married Cal Foster, things were different. He had money—lots of it—and he was more than willing to share, offering to build her a small house of her own on the land her mother had secured for her. Warm feelings washed over her. Mr. Foster was a good man. A loving man. Casey was glad her mother had married him. Better yet, the marriage came with a new stepsister, one she hadn't met yet. Cal's daughter, Emily, was eleven and lived in Arizona with her mom. Unable to attend the wedding, Emily was scheduled for a visit later in the summer and Casey couldn't wait. With no siblings of her own, Casey thought it would be neat to have a kid sister. Cal said if things went well, Emily might be able to spend summers here. Well, if Casey had anything to say about it, Emily's first trip to Tennessee would be memorable.

Jimmy nodded, as though flying anxiety were completely normal. "Cool."

Casey smiled. So easygoing. Jimmy accepted life as it came. He was smart, wise. It was Jimmy who was able to convince her of the futility in taking drugs. There'd been a time when she was so unhappy, so miserable, life didn't seem worth living. But he made her see there was hope over the horizon. Change, freedom. Despite the people around you, life could be enjoyed. And Jimmy knew what he was talking about. His parents fought non-stop. They were loud and obnoxious but refused to get a divorce. His grandparents took him in but they weren't much better. They were miserable. Yet throughout it all, Jimmy said he never gave up hope. He hid behind a wardrobe of black for a while but said he always believed in himself and his future. Today he lived on his own in a cute apartment downtown, drove a nice car and was taking classes to earn his degree. He didn't know what he wanted a degree in yet. Only that it would be something that would get him a good job and get him out of this town.

Unfortunately, Jimmy wasn't her type. He was too tall, too skinny, but he was nice and he was her friend. Casey set a hand on the enormous swell of her stomach. Two things she had come to appreciate after Troy Parker left town. The love of her life, and father of her child, had deserted her. By the time he finally got around to telling her what he'd done, where he'd gone, she'd been so mad she refused to take his calls. He'd moved to Kentucky. Took a job on a ranch there and planned to settle down. Troy didn't ask her to come with him. He didn't insist they never spend another night apart. Nope. He up and left and didn't call her for a week.

A strange sensation pushed into Casey's stomach. It wasn't nausea, it wasn't a cramp. Pushing back in her seat, she slid a hand over the rise of her belly, rubbing in a circular motion as she allowed the feeling to pass. They seemed to be occurring more often these days, feelings in and around the baby inside her. They were physical sensations, but she was beginning to have emotional ones too. An intuition she never had before. Too bad it didn't exist before she started dating Troy. Maybe then she would have seen him for the train wreck he was.

Jimmy looked down at her stomach as though it were a ticking time bomb. "Are you all right?"

"Fine."

"Are you sure?"

She nodded. Like everyone else, Jimmy was a worry wart when it came to her condition. There was nothing wrong with her. It was just a feeling. Continuing to caress her belly in a rhythmic motion, calming, Casey wondered if it could be indigestion. Staring at the tall glass of half-drunk coke, she wondered if it might be the carbonation unsettling her stomach. Or maybe the biscuit drenched in honey butter. Strange how pregnancy changed things. Not only was she experiencing new sensations and feelings, but her tastes had changed. She used to love French fries, but now they soured her stomach. Too greasy. Same with cheeseburgers. She could no longer eat the two staples of her diet. She glanced around the restaurant, her gaze landing on a waitress carrying a heavily loaded tray of food through the diner. Circling a table, she delivered fried chicken, fried okra, fried tomatoes and cornbread. Casey frowned. Practically everything in the restaurant was fried, which made her cringe. Good thing she only had another two months or so. She wasn't sure how much longer she could tolerate it!

The front door opened, the clang of bells reverberated in her heart.

"Casey?" Alarm careened into Jimmy's gaze. "What's a matter?"

Panic closed her throat. She couldn't speak. She couldn't move.

Troy Parker, in the flesh, was standing by the hostess stand.

Jimmy whirled around at the same moment Troy spotted them. Removing his black hat as they made eye contact, his familiar brown eyes latched onto Casey like a bee on a blossom. Her heart squeezed, her legs dissolved beneath her. Troy was here.

*But why?*

He hesitated, glanced around tables and booths in the crowded diner. Even from ten yards away, partially concealed beneath those long brown bangs of his, she could see his anger flash hot. Troy clenched his jaw and headed straight for them. Instinctively, she jammed elbows to the table and leaned forward, crossing her arms protectively over her stomach, catching the edge of her plate which toppled, then spun loudly back in place. Casey's pulse shot wildly out of control—thudding so hard—she feared it would break loose from her chest.

Troy's long jean-legged strides closed the distance in seconds. Jimmy turned back to face her, the full impact of what was coming gripping his expression steps before Troy made it to their table, arriving in a sweep of tension, emotion churning the air around him. He stared down at the two of them, eyes darting between her and Jimmy, hostility pulsating beneath his surface of calm. Casey gulped. "Casey," he said tersely.

"Troy," she returned, scratching out the single word.

Jimmy sat pensive, clearly unsettled by the surprise appearance of her ex-boyfriend, a position he'd been vying for himself of late. Jimmy wanted to give her baby a name. He wanted to support her, be there for her where this man had not. It was a gesture she appreciated but declined. She couldn't be with Jimmy. She wasn't interested.

There was only one guy who held her interest and he was standing before her very eyes, glaring at her like she was a traitor or something. He stood bolted in place, looking between the two of them, as if waiting for Casey to fill the void. "I thought you were in Kentucky," Casey sputtered, even as she battled a chest full of nerves and her heart sang, *Troy's home.*

"I'm not," Troy replied. "I'm here."

"We can see that," Jimmy wisecracked, swiping Casey with a sidelong gaze.

Troy's hand flinched, giving Casey a start. "Why are you here?" she asked quickly, diffusing the powder keg between the two. Troy didn't care for Jimmy and the feeling was mutual.

"I quit."

Her spirits burst like a balloon. Troy quit. *Of course.*

It's what he did.

"It's not what you think."

"We don't have to *think*," Jimmy said, surprising Casey with his show of nerve. "It's what you do. It's expected."

Troy turned on him. "Why don't you hold your tongue before I rip it out of your mouth?"

Casey jumped at the sheer nastiness he was displaying. "Troy!" He could break Jimmy in two and probably love the chance to do just that. "Please!" she cried. A few nearby diners were taking in the trio, but none with any knowledge as to the significance of what was happening.

"Why don't you get lost?"

Casey stared across the table. This was a side to Jimmy she had yet to see. Usually he preferred to hang on the sidelines, avoid confrontation altogether. He did it the last time he and Troy faced off, did it with their professor at school...

"You first," Troy spat.

"Stop it," Casey thrust between them.

Troy tossed a fiery glare her way but quickly extinguished it. "I don't need him interferin'."

"Interfering with what?" she asked, annoyed and disconcerted at the same time. Troy was back. He was fighting with Jimmy. Continuing to conceal the round of her stomach, she smacked, "You're the one who walked up on us, remember?"

Taken aback by the edgy response, he gave her a double-take—which gave Casey a warped pleasure. *That's right, Troy. You're the one interfering. We don't want you here.* But for some reason Casey couldn't give voice to the first word. She was too happy to see him.

Troy straightened. He pushed back his muscular shoulders and announced, "I came by to tell you I'm back. For good."

Casey laughed, but it was strangled, ineffective. What she intended to be hurtful fell short. She couldn't look at Troy and instead sought refuge in the safety of her friend and supporter, Jimmy Sweeney. His Adam's apple rose and fell as he accepted her lead. "Sure you are," she muttered, wishing his return wasn't on public display. There were so many things she wanted to say, to know. Troy was home. He'd quit. What would he think about the baby?

"I am, Casey." Appearing to dull the blade of his attack, Troy shifted weight from heel to heel, holding her steadily in his gaze. His eyes were molten with emotion, his surprise discovery of the two of them together surely unsettling. Troy was the jealous type and, worse, had always suspected Jimmy of being interested in more than friendship. To find them together had only underscored that suspicion. "I made you a promise when I left here and I aim to keep it."

"Too late. You already broke it." Uttering the words broke her heart all over again. On their last night together, the most beautiful of her life, Troy had promised they'd be together forever. He was talking future and family. Her heart pinched at the memory. Stupidly, she'd believed him. Tearing her gaze from his face, she sought the safety and security of Jimmy.

"I didn't break anything," Troy countered. "I quit drinking, I'm on a better road..."

But the fight had left him. From the corner of her eye, she could see him waver. Troy wasn't sure what to do. She understood his instinct was to stay and argue, but her voicing her position in no uncertain terms seemed to undermine him. He wasn't sure how to proceed.

From across the table, she could feel Jimmy's displeasure. He was mad—at her, at Troy—at the whole situation. He'd been warning her about this day, warning her that Troy might come back and try to convince her to give him another chance. As if she'd forgotten, Jimmy constantly reminded her how Troy had run around with Jeremiah Ladd's girlfriend, flirted with Jillian Devane, all while professing he cared for Casey. Then dumped her, ran off and left her pregnant.

Casey didn't need reminding. She lived with the pain every day of her life. At the moment, it was dulled in comparison to Troy realizing she was pregnant. That conversation was sure to stir up a hornet's nest of trouble. Glaring at Jimmy, she needed Troy to be gone. She could only sit hunched over the table for so long before it became awkward and he saw the size of her stomach beneath the flimsy cotton dress.

"I'm finished with it all," Troy said. "No more."

"Yeah," Jimmy replied snidely, "until the next eighteen-wheeler pulls into the lot with a case of Jack Daniels."

"Jimmy!"

Troy glowered. "Why don't you shut your mouth before I knock your skull into next week?"

"It's the truth," Jimmy continued, angling his shoulders to face Troy. "You're a waste of breath."

Ignoring him, Troy thrust angrily to Casey, "We need to talk. This isn't over 'til we do."

"What isn't over?" Jimmy asked. "You already dumped her. What more do you have in store?"

Troy stood rigid, his wrath aimed squarely at Jimmy. "This ain't none of your business."

"It is my business when you're standing here talking to my girlfriend."

Casey gasped. Troy froze. He locked onto Jimmy. "*What did you say?*"

"You heard me," Jimmy repeated.

Gawking at Jimmy, Casey was met by a challenge. *Tell him the truth.* Fastening his gaze to hers as though daring her to say otherwise Jimmy hitched his chin toward Troy. *Go ahead. Tell him you're pregnant.*

Casey freaked. Did he think he was helping? Did he think taunting Troy with a statement like that was going to settle the matter?

Troy pounced on her, his brown eyes searching. "Is this true? Is what he said true? You two are dating?"

Fear zipped up and down her spine as she evaded his question. No—it wasn't true—but maybe Jimmy was right. Judging by Troy's reaction, maybe this was *exactly* what he needed to hear to get a taste of how it felt to be dumped—flat on his face.

"Answer me."

"I don't answer to you," Casey defied. Drawing strength from Jimmy's presence, Troy's anger, she flipped her gaze up to meet his and nearly fell out of her seat. Instead of angry, the upheaval in Troy's gaze undid her. He wasn't angry. He was crushed. Guilt washed over her in a flood of surprise. But if he was here because he quit, he sure as heck wouldn't be happy to hear she was pregnant with his child!

Nerves pushed in at her stomach. Uncertainty flapped in her breast. Pregnancy changed everything. Things were dif-

ferent. She couldn't dash out on a last minute picnic or hike
along the river's edge. They couldn't lie around in a field late
at night, stargazing until the wee hours of morning. Pregnancy meant bills, diapers, a screaming baby... It meant responsibility. Stability. Troy couldn't quit work on a whim or get
fired for impulse decisions. Being a father meant a whole new
lifestyle, one that didn't suit Troy's temperament. No matter
what he promised that night, that beautiful, wonderful night,
reality would prove different. Casey struggled against tears. It
was *her* reality now. Something he was going to have to get
used to. "When you left me, Troy, you gave up your right to
have a say over what I do, or don't do."

"I never left you!"

The outburst drew curious stares as Jimmy retorted,
"Could'ave fooled us."

Troy plastered his hat onto his head. Without making a
move for the door, he stared at Casey for the longest minute.
It was a look that erased people and time, months and doubt,
and replaced it with longing. There was so much left to say,
so many questions, feelings, but neither uttered the first one.
Too much needed to be said. Jimmy was wedged between
them. It was awkward. Troy turned on his heel and strode out
of the diner, dragging Casey's heart behind him. Her gaze
trailed him as he shoved open the door and disappeared from
her sight. He was gone. It was over. In a rush of rage, she
turned on Jimmy, smacking a hand to the table. Silverware
bounced as she demanded, "What the heck was that about?"

"What?" he asked dully.

"You telling him we're boyfriend and girlfriend!"

"Well, we should be," Jimmy mumbled.

"But we aren't, Jimmy! Now he thinks we are!"

Met by a vacant stare, Casey could kill him. With one
stupid statement Jimmy ruined her opportunity to understand
what had happened. Why did Troy leave? Why was he back
home? What happened between them? Was it her fault? His?
At this rate she'd be lucky to ever see him again, let alone
speak to him.

"What am I going to do?" she wondered aloud.

"I thought you said he was a thing of your past." Dark brown eyes grew still. "Sounds to me like you want to pick up where you left off."

About to tell him exactly what she thought, Casey stopped herself. It was clear how she felt—to Jimmy, herself—to everyone but Troy. A ripple of spasm crawled slowly across the side of her belly, reminding Casey of someone else who didn't know, might never know, especially now that she had just run him off. Troy was probably gone for good this time. Knowing his obstinate temper as she did, he wouldn't give her a chance to explain about Jimmy. He hated the guy. Troy would assume it was true and cut her from his life.

"I was only trying to help you," Jimmy said. Sliding his glass of coke to him, he pulled a long sip from his straw. He didn't look at her. He drank. Purposefully, mindfully, he ignored her.

Dropping her gaze to the table, Casey was torn. She couldn't be mad at him. Jimmy was only acting based on what she'd told him. She never wanted to see Troy again. Never wanted to hear his name. She'd never expected to see him again, especially not making statements like he had. *I made you a promise when I left here and I aim to keep it.* Did he mean it?

Visions of him storming out tumbled through her. Angry, hurt, Troy wasn't interested in explanation. Consumed with thoughts of him, she tried to convince herself it was for the best. Men disappeared when they heard their girlfriend was pregnant. It meant obligation, commitment, two important traits Troy lacked. *I quit.*

He couldn't even hold down a job. How was he going to support a family?

At a quiet slurp, Casey's thoughts reverted back to Jimmy. Unlike him. He worked two jobs to pay for his apartment and college classes, plus the occasional money he slid to his mother on the sly because his dad was a bum. Jimmy didn't run from responsibility. Casey's spirits slumped. He begged for it.

## Chapter Two

Troy thundered into his parent's home, anger and jealousy tearing through his heart. Jimmy and Casey? How could she? And with him of all people? Stomping up the stairs, he headed straight for his bedroom, his mind warring for reason. The guy was nothing but a weasel—a slimy, slithering, no good snake. He had no right to be with her. She was *his* woman, not Jimmy's.

But despite Troy's every protest, the pain of reality continued to slice him with every step he took. Jimmy and Casey seemed real cozy tucked away in that booth in Fran's Diner. The homecoming that he expected to be rocky turned out to be a dad gummed bald-faced cliff hurling him over the edge. *How could she have moved on so easily? How could she have forgotten their night together?*

It was the most beautiful night of his life...better than any they shared before. Casey had run away to be with him in Murfreesboro, but it wasn't the same. The night in the field beneath the stars had been special because she'd forgiven him. She'd forgiven him, when even he knew there was no reason she should. It was a grace he didn't deserve but one she had given whole-heartedly. That night had meant more to Troy than anything in his life. Casey Owens was the only person in this world who believed in him and him alone, willing to overlook his stupidity. Could she really have changed so drastically?

*When you left me, Troy, you gave up your right to have a say over what I do or don't do.* The scene at the diner felt unreal, like he was walking through a nightmare. Didn't their love mean anything to her? Was it so easy for her to forget the words they said, the promises they made?

*When you left me, Troy...*

Anger surged through him. Why did she say that? He didn't *leave* her. He told her he needed to get a job and make something of himself, prove to everyone he wasn't a loser. Just because he was doing it in another town didn't mean he'd left her. He couldn't. He could never leave her. The night they shared together and everything it meant lived and breathed in him, every hour, every second. It gave reason to his days, gave comfort to his nights. It was his reason to stay sober, to keep out of trouble and on target with his job. Casey had forgiven him and he wasn't going to let her down—ever.

Troy's heart wrenched as he envisioned Casey lying in Jimmy's arms. He could see her pale white skin, her delicate curves, her tender smile—could recall the scent of her with painful accuracy—and she had revealed it all to Jimmy. Busting into his bedroom, he slammed a fist on the dresser. "Dammit!"

Visions of Jimmy Sweeney sitting across from his woman roused a hatred that unnerved Troy. He'd wanted to lash out and punch the kid in the face. Flatten him. It was probably *his* fault Casey didn't return any of his calls. Originally Troy had blamed Casey's lack of response on her mother but now...

Thoughts of Jimmy and Casey together swirled in a sickening mix of disbelief and jealously the likes of which he'd never felt before. It had probably been Jimmy who convinced her not to talk to him. Troy knew the guy had been waiting to get his hands on her. Probably snuck in the second he left town to grab his opportunity.

But Casey was Troy's woman and only his. She told him so. Promised it would always be that way. She couldn't love Jimmy. She couldn't get over him that quick—it was impossible.

Had been impossible for him. Every day on the job became harder and harder, his mind split between thoughts of Casey and the horse he was working. He couldn't focus and the animal knew it, fought him every step of the way. The head rancher thought he was a loser. Thought his talk of training and experience was nothing but bull. It wasn't. Mr. Foster had backed him up with a phone call. But in the end it didn't matter. Troy couldn't focus, couldn't perform his duties. He couldn't do anything without Casey.

Raking a hand through his hair, he pulled his bangs tight. Sending his gaze fitfully about his room, his bed untouched, his suitcase unpacked, he wondered what next? Should he leave town? Should he give up and move on, accept that Casey had done the same? Settling on her vision, remembering blue eyes that cradled him with more love than he had ever known, a heart that encouraged him with a voice more certain about his future than even his own, Troy knew he couldn't leave. He couldn't give up. As sure as he was standin' here, his gut clenched tighter than a dog on a bone, he couldn't leave. Not until he was sure. Not until Casey told him to get out of town pointblank would he leave.

He'd stay. He'd stay and wait her out. Maybe she'd realize what a mistake she was making by choosing Jimmy. Maybe after she had time to think about it, she'd change her mind and come back to him. His heart sank into his boots. She had to. No other girl but Casey would do.

Travis Parker appeared in the doorway to his bathroom. "Whoa, brother. What's got you so riled up?"

"None of your damn business," Troy fumed, hardly able to manage the rage and suffering streaming through his veins without the presence of his self-righteous brother. Travis always acted like he knew better than Troy. Like he was superior. Well, he wasn't. Even dressed in his uppity jeans and designer T-shirt or with his first year of college behind him, his twin brother was no better than Troy.

Travis smiled, his eyes dripping with self-importance. "Sure doesn't look like nothing to me."

"Well, it is."

Travis leaned against the doorframe, his gaze matching the smug smirk on his lips as he crossed arms over his chest. "Get turned down?"

Troy wanted to rip that smile right off his mouth. Instead, he yanked the hat from his head and tossed it to his bed. Pulling the wallet from his back pocket, he chucked it to the bureau. It slid into a picture of his parents, sending the frame crashing to the ground.

Travis chuckled as though he knew exactly what was going on. "Shouldn't have left her in the first place."

Troy whipped a finger toward his brother. "Back off, Travis. This ain't none of your business and I ain't in the mood to mess with you." Troy yanked off his T-shirt and threw it to the floor.

"None of my business? I'd say it's everybody's business now."

"Is not."

"How do you figure?"

"What I do with my girlfriend has nothing to do with you."

Travis pushed off from the door and walked closer. Spearing him with a spiteful gaze, he said, "It does when you leave me to pick up the pieces of your mess."

Troy stopped dead center of the room, his bare chest heaving in the heat of anger. Shoulders back, fist clenched, he was ready to lash out if need be. "What the hell are you talking about, 'pick up the pieces of my mess'?"

"What do I mean?" Travis raised his eyebrows, lines forming across his forehead as he asked, "Isn't it obvious? Do you need me to spell it out for you?"

Troy honed in on him. "What's obvious?" Was he trying to rub it in? Did Travis know something he didn't? A sharp dread stabbed at him. *Were Jimmy and Casey more serious than he realized?*

"I thought you went to see Casey."

"I did."

"And?"

*And she's hooked up with Jimmy*, Troy admitted silently but couldn't bring himself to say the words. *Hooked up with*

*Jimmy*. They were words he never thought he'd have to think let alone utter.

Clipped to his jean waistband, Travis' cell phone rang. He plucked it free and pressed the call button. "Hey, Felicity."

Hearing her name only added to Troy's misery. Felicity Wilkins was a childhood friend of the brothers, the three a best-friend trio since grade school. For a time Troy had designs on getting together with Felicity. Seemed Travis did, too. The rivalry stirred up a lot of trouble between them until she made her choice during high school—Travis would be her boyfriend leaving Troy to find his own love. At the time, he'd been hurt. But life was weird that way. If it weren't for Felicity's decision, he would never have found Casey.

Turning away from Travis and his happy phone call, Troy felt the blow. Travis and Felicity were happily together, the way he and Casey were supposed to be. Dad *gummit*—he should never have left! If he'd stayed in Tennessee, none of this would have happened. Tugging his belt buckle loose, he hauled it clear of the belt loops.

Travis chuckled. "You don't say. He has no idea? Huh," he replied, shooting Troy a know-it-all smirk. "If you insist, I'll keep it to myself." Ending the call, he smiled. "Never mind."

"Never mind what?"

"It's a private matter," Travis replied, barely able to keep a straight face.

Troy couldn't care less about his and Felicity's private matters. He only wanted his brother gone so he could take a cold shower and get these rabid thoughts and visions out of his head. When his mind was cooled, he could plan his next step.

Travis re-clipped his phone and gathered himself into a half-serious expression. "Though in all honesty, there's nothing funny about it."

"About what?"

Travis stilled. "About you and your lack of judgment."

"Get out of my room, Travis, before I throw you out."

"No problem."

At the sudden disgust in his brother's eyes, Troy wondered what the phone call from Felicity was about. *He has no idea*? *Who* has no idea? About what?

Shoving the thoughts from his mind, he growled under his breath. Whatever. His brother was gone and that's all that mattered. At the moment he had bigger problems to deal with and they didn't include Travis.

Two hours later, Troy had switched gears from hurt and anger to reason and determination. Jimmy might think Casey was his girlfriend but she wouldn't stay that way. She was in shock, is all. She didn't expect him to show up, didn't know what to say to him when he did. Hell, could he blame her for falling for the guy's sneaky ploy?

She'd been on the rebound. She was hurt. Obviously, she didn't understand what he meant when he told her he was going to prove himself, though how she could have misunderstood was beyond him. There was no place around here where he could work to make it up to her. He had to go somewhere else. He had to go where people didn't have preconceived thoughts about him. Around here, no one believed in him. They all thought the worst, except for Mr. Foster. Cal Foster was decent, understanding. He didn't leap to judgment like everyone else did, painting him into a corner and hanging an "I'm a no-good drunk" sign from his neck. After working with him at his family's ranch, Mr. Foster said Troy was one of their best ranch hands, ever. Said he was real impressed with Troy's performance.

Until he blew it by showing up with a hangover. Cal's daddy, Gerald Foster, had a zero tolerance policy for drinking—on the job and off. Rumor had it was due to the fact his four sons had blown through more bottles of bourbon than a whiskey-soaked river, souring the old man on alcohol use of any kind. Troy should have known better than to go anywhere near the place with a hangover, but he thought he could avoid the old man for the day. The only reason the senior Mr. Foster came by was to pay Troy a visit, commending him for a job well done with the foal delivery. It was a job that ended five minutes later.

Slowing down for the turn to the Wilkins' place, Troy knew if anyone was going to give him a chance, it'd be Cal Foster. Not that Troy could work for his daddy again. Old man Foster didn't give second chances. But with Cal in charge as General Manager of the new Hotel Ladd, Troy might have the opportunity to work their stables, maybe train their horses. Hell, at this rate he'd be happy to pick up their *crap* if that's what it took to get a paying job with the animals he loved. He would've done a good job at the ranch in Kentucky if it hadn't been for missing Casey. He'd thought he could do it. He thought as long as he told himself it was temporary, he could manage the separation and make a name for himself. Then, he could return home with his head held high and proof behind his claims. *He'd quit drinking. He could work with horses.* But try as he might, he couldn't manage. The ache in his heart had been too strong, even the dad gum horses were beginning to feel it!

Rolling over the bridge, sunlight glittering in the river stream below, Troy was astonished by the transformation of Ladd Springs. Slowing, his gaze roamed over buildings and trails, cars and signs. If he didn't know his way here by heart, he wouldn't have recognized the place. Ernie Ladd had been the owner before Felicity and Casey, living here until his dying day about a year ago. His dilapidated cabin used to sit along the creek but had been replaced by a custom log cabin. It was a small structure but quality built with its thick log walls and river rock base. It had clean lines, a tin roof and nice patch of grass around it, complete with a wishing well off to one side. Automatically, Troy checked for the original well that used to be here and found it, located off a manufactured path leading up into the mountain. Did that lead to the stables? But they couldn't have left Miss Delaney's old stables intact. Delaney Wilkins had lived here as a child and moved back with her daughter ten years ago. The stables had been built years before, about the time Miss Delaney was a kid. If they bulldozed old man Ernie's house they wouldn't leave her stables. They were in about the same condition.

Parking near a line of cars, Troy climbed down from his truck and trekked up a trail toward the hotel. Up the mountain—practically wedged into the rock and trees—was the main building. It wasn't very big, from what he could tell, but it was damn fine with floor to ceiling windows. Nearing the hotel, he could see massive interior wooden beams, leather furniture and recessed ceiling lights, in addition to a huge metal chandelier, round in shape with candle-shaped lights on it. There was also a fountain inside. Outside, stone steps lead up to the entrance, heavily landscaped with native rhododendron and colorful hydrangea.

Troy let out a low whistle. "Dad gum, this must have cost Mr. Harris a ton of money." According to his mother, the inside was even nicer than the outside. She was here for the double wedding ceremony between the hotel's owner Nick Harris and Miss Delaney who got hitched alongside Cal Foster and Casey's mom, Annie Owens. Afterward, Troy's mother took a tour of the property, claiming the décor was straight out of a fancy designer home magazine, complete with huge river rock fireplaces and four-poster beds in every guestroom. Troy bet they were charging a bundle for people to stay in that place. He laughed under his breath. To stay in Podunk, Tennessee, no less. Who would have guessed it? While he loved his hometown, Troy never imagined anyone paying top dollar for the chance to hang out around here. Until now, the local two-story hotel downtown was the fanciest thing they had going.

Cal Foster came into view. An elegant man with fair-skinned looks and mild-mannered behavior, Cal appeared every bit the professional in his khaki dress pants and pale green button-down shirt. Pushing out through the entrance, he jogged down the natural stone stairway.

Troy's heart pitched. Time to call in a favor.

Taking a deep breath, he waited for Mr. Foster to notice him. When he did, his face lit up. "Troy!"

The warm welcome loosened the knot twisting in his chest. "Mr. Foster," Troy called back and hurried over.

Cal greeted him, hazel eyes dancing as he dove a hand in for a firm handshake, followed by another hand to Troy's shoulder. He squeezed. "How the heck are you doing?"

Heartened by the familiar tone, he replied, "Fine, sir. Real fine."

"When did you get back in town?"

"Yesterday."

"Travis tells me you've been working in Kentucky."

"Yes sir, I have.

"Did you come home for the summer?"

Troy stumbled and replied vaguely, "Taking a break."

To his relief, Cal didn't question him further. "Have you seen the new hotel?"

"I haven't sir, but my momma told me all about it. Said it's the nicest one she's ever seen."

Cal accepted the compliment easily, satisfaction glimmering in his eyes. "Malcolm and Nick do top-notch work, there's no question. Would you like a look around?"

Standing beneath the shade of trees, Troy removed his hat, brushed the hair from his brow. Malcolm Ward was Nick's partner in the hotel business. Originally he came to Tennessee to help Mr. Harris get the rights to use the property but stayed on after he met and married Casey's aunt, Lacy Owens. Troy didn't know him that well, but he seemed like an allright guy. "Well, I'd like to, but I don't want to bother you, sir."

He patted Troy's shoulder and said, "It's no bother at all."

Troy hesitated. He had more pressing issues on his mind than touring the new hotel. "Actually, I'm here to see about a job."

"A job?"

"Yes, sir."

The hand slipped free from his shoulder. Hesitation entered his friendly gaze. "What kind of job?"

"With horses, sir. I understand you have some mighty fine stables, and I'd like to see if there's a space for me."

"Well, actually," his expression closed a shade, nipping at Troy's confidence, "Delaney's in charge of the stables."

Troy could feel him slipping from his grasp. "Miss Delaney?"

"Yes, but..." Clouds gathered in his gaze. "Have you talked to Casey?"

"Yes, sir. Saw her at Fran's Diner earlier today." Cal didn't say anything, evidently waiting for him to elaborate. When he didn't, the older man simply nodded, as though turning it over in his mind. Once again, Troy was struck by the nagging sensation there was more to the question. "Well, like I said, I'm here to see about a job."

Cal looked at him queerly, as if Troy had morphed into some kind of weird creature. It was beginning to grate on him.

"Mr. Foster?"

Chapter Three

Cal Foster shook whatever fog had overcome him and snapped back to his senses. "Well, you'll have to speak with Delaney about a job in the stables. I don't have any say over the hiring and firing when it comes to the horses."

Troy didn't understand. "But you're the boss, aren't ya?"

"Not over Delaney, I'm not. You want a job working the stables, you'll have to go through her."

Troy sensed Cal had been trying to crack a joke, but the humor never made it to his eyes. All of a sudden, the man seemed uncomfortable to be around him. His biggest ally in the past was paddling backwards at a hefty pace. Which was strange. Only minutes ago Mr. Foster seemed real pleased to see him. Troy shifted restlessly. "Well, is she here?"

Cal pointed a finger behind him. "That trail over there will take you straight to her. She's in the stables."

Troy followed his line of sight and saw a trail. Familiar with the property, he knew it led to the original Ladd homestead, the one that existed a hundred years ago. When they were riding horses one day, Felicity had showed it to him and Travis, explaining how it had been home to her great-grandfather. There was nothing to see when they rode through, except for a few piles of old bricks and rotten logs. Troy remembered an eerie feeling as they walked the area, like maybe there were ghosts or something lurking in the woods, watching them. He shook a mild shudder from his body and firmed his resolve. Miss Delaney liked him. If Cal wouldn't give him a job, she would. "Thank you, sir." Troy slipped his hat in place. "I'll go and talk to her right now, if you don't mind," he added, inferring that he couldn't go on that guided tour of the hotel.

"Listen, Troy. I don't know if she'll give you a job, but if she does, make her see what I see." Surprised by the seriousness in his voice, Troy idled in place as Mr. Foster added, "Don't let her down."

A little more than insulted, Troy rebuffed, "I don't intend to, sir."

"I know you don't," Cal replied quietly. "But you have a lot riding on this. Don't blow it. You know I'll give her my best recommendation if she asks, but it's up to you to prove your case."

"Yes, sir. I understand." Troy assumed he was referring to the drinking episode, yet he couldn't shake the feeling there was something else at play. Something deeper was ground into the brown-eyed gaze staring back at him.

Cal placed a hand to his shoulder and squeezed. "I hope you do. For all our sakes."

Troy straightened, pulling himself a little taller. "Mr. Foster, I'm good with horses. I know I've made mistakes in the past but I don't aim to repeat them. I'll make Miss Delaney the finest ranch hand she's ever seen."

"You're preaching to the pastor, Troy. I believe in you." His gaze softened. "I'm glad to see you still do, too."

Troy took the trail as instructed, hiking the newly graded terrain in the direction of the stables. Gone were the uneven rocks and roots, the hard clay smoothed for easier passage and lined by a sparse covering of meadow grass. Overhead, trees provided a canopy of shade, the air temperature several degrees cooler than in the open sunshine. It was a tranquil walk, but Troy couldn't shake the sudden change in Mr. Foster's demeanor. He said he believed in him, enough to give him a second chance if the choice were his. Said he'd give Miss Delaney a good recommendation if she asked. Why so many ifs? It was the uncertainty that was driving him crazy. First Casey, then Travis and now Mr. Foster. It was like the world had flipped upside down and people had lost their marbles. Like their brain cells had dribbled out of their heads into a sea of nothing. Everybody started off normal enough and then switched, like a light bulb had been turned off—or on—Troy couldn't figure out which. They acted weird, like they didn't know if they were coming or going or if they even should.

Troy shook his head. No matter. Miss Delaney wasn't like that. She was a straight shooter. Damn accurate, too. If something was going on, she'd tell him straight up. As the trail opened up into pasture, Troy looked uphill, struck by the sight of brand new stables he took a step back. *Whoa*. He surveyed the wide open space of rolling green, the brand new fencing that led up to a distant line of stables. He tipped his hat back and couldn't believe what he was seeing. Stables as nice as any he'd seen. Murfreesboro had been a top notch operation, the group out of Kentucky a step above most, but this? Seemed Miss Delaney had a top of the line establishment on her hands. He could only imagine what it looked like up close.

Avoiding further thoughts of Casey and Jimmy creeping into his mind, Troy hiked up the hill. He couldn't stand to even consider the two of them as a possibility. It was probably all the talk about the recent double wedding. His parents had gone and it was all his momma could talk about, other than lecturing him on his decision to return home. She'd never once mentioned Casey. After Jimmy delivered the news, he could see why. His momma might not be happy about him skipping college to work with horses, but she sure as heck wasn't gonna upset him with the news his girlfriend had hooked up with another guy.

Halfway up, Troy wondered how the guests were going to manage the trip. For him this walk was nothin' but for folks that weren't used to hiking, he could see it as an issue. Horses grazed to either side of him, their lazy swish of tail a sign of contentment. The hotel probably had some horse and buggy lined up to transport them. From what Felicity said, Mr. Harris had tons of money and built expensive hotels all around the world. He was leasing Ladd Springs land for his hotel. He didn't own it. Felicity did—a fact that still seemed incredible to Troy. Nineteen-years-old and Felicity Wilkins was earning thousands of dollars, maybe hundreds of thousands. Troy didn't know any of the details. All he knew was after Ernie Ladd died and willed the property to Felicity, she was free and clear to make a deal with Mr. Harris and allow his hotel to be built. Didn't hurt that her mother was engaged to the man.

Casey owned the other half. Thanks to the fact her mother slept with Jeremiah Ladd eighteen years ago. The man was a no-good dog, but as Ernie Ladd's son he and his heirs had rights to the property. Or so Casey's mom believed. She was the one who fought for Casey's rights and won. Right after Felicity received title to Ladd Springs, Miss Delaney signed over half of it to Casey. Not only a straight shooter, but she was a fair woman with a big heart.

Nearing the stables, Troy slowed his pace. Beyond the stables were three pens and a huge granddaddy of a barn, everything brand-spanking new. So new, it looked more like a picture ad than a working horse operation. Venturing inside, Troy was hit by the thick scent of sweet feed and freshly oiled leather. A tack room sat to his right, a line of saddles set out front of it. Down a wide center aisle there was a dual line of stalls. He didn't see any animals. Were there any horses?

"Hello?" he called out, looking for signs of Delaney as he continued in. But there had to be. He could smell them. He walked over to a corner and peered through a plate glass window. There was a desk, cabinets, several pictures on the wall but no Delaney. Continuing toward the stall corridor, he glanced overhead, admiring the tongue and groove ceiling, the exposed wooden rafters. Troy figured it must have cost some serious dough to build this place. Coming upon an oversized stall, large by anyone's standards, he deemed it to be a foaling stall. Instantly he recalled the foal he helped Mr. Foster deliver a little black beauty named Vegas. Looking back, that had been one of the best days of his life. Not only had he taken part in saving the life of an animal, but he earned the recognition from someone other than his father. Troy's heart skipped at a low whinny from a horse. Drawn to the sound, he looked into the adjacent stall and saw a beautiful chocolate brown Arabian.

Pulling up to the wooden barrier, he reached a hand through the metal grill of the sliding door. "Aren't you a beauty? C'mon here, baby." Ears perked at the sound of his voice and the horse immediately responded. "That's it." Troy allowed the horse to nudge him, a velvet-soft muzzle nibbling as the animal checked the stranger out. The horse raised its head and lightly shook its mane but didn't retreat. Troy took this as the animal's consent to be touched and stroked the flat expanse of fur between the horse's eyes. Long lashes blinked, taking him in without concern. Warm feelings spread throughout Troy's chest. Man, but this one was a fine specimen of horse. Did they get him from Mr. Foster? He didn't remember this fella and Troy remembered every horse. Maybe they had more than one supplier for the hotel.

"Troy."

Startled by the cut of her voice, he whirled, grasping a cold metal bar as he said, "Miss Delaney."

"Long time no see."

Standing there in jeans and tank top, her long blonde hair pulled back into a ponytail, Delaney Wilkins looped thumbs from her front pockets. Four inches shorter than him, she stood rigid, as though on the defensive. She didn't smile, didn't move. She simply stared with those dark brown eyes of hers. Black brows and butter yellow hair made for a striking combination. Troy always found her to be an attractive older woman, one who didn't take crap. He considered the gun he knew to be kept in her boot and gulped. A stern tone wasn't the kind of reception he'd been counting on. "I hope you don't mind me walking in uninvited, Miss Delaney, but Mr. Foster said I might be able to find you here."

"You're looking for me?"

"Yes, ma'am." Troy removed his hat and advanced toward her. "He told me you were in charge of the stables."

"I am."

"I was interested in getting work. He told me to talk to you."

"Work?" Curiosity sparked her black gaze. "What kind of work?"

"With the horses," Troy replied. "I can train them, clean them, pick up after them. Whatever you need, I can do it for you."

She cocked her head and crossed her arms. "Why are you looking for a job, Troy? Felicity told me you were working a ranch in Kentucky."

"I was..." He dropped his gaze. "But I quit."

"Quit?"

"Yes, ma'am," he replied, hating the suspicion swirling in her gaze.

"Why?"

"I wanted to come back home." At this, her features softened a hair, giving him the first hint of the woman he knew growing up, the one who treated Travis and him like her own. "But I need work, Miss Delaney, and horses are what I know. I'd make you a great ranch hand. Ask Mr. Foster—he can vouch for me."

"Are you drinking?"

Nerves fired at the blunt question. "No, ma'am. No way. Not a drop."

Delaney expelled a sigh and approached him. Her eyes darted back and forth across his as though she were looking for something, something hidden deep inside him. "Have you talked to Casey?"

"Yes, ma'am."

"And?"

Strands of resentment grew taut in his chest. "And she dumped me," he wanted to spit. She moved on with that loser, Jimmy Sweeney. The thought scraped at his heart, made him bleed fresh and raw. Of all people, why did Casey have to pick him? The skinny dude was half-girl the way he always hung around, quiet, not saying two words most of the time.

*My girlfriend.* Two words Troy could have gone his whole life without hearing come from Jimmy's mouth. "I saw her at the diner today."

"And?"

"And..." he tightened his grip on his hat, "she was with Jimmy Sweeney."

"So?" Delaney pressed.

"So?" Troy grew angry but held himself in check. Did she need to drill it into him? Did she need to rub his face in it? What the heck—*had everybody turned against him*?

"Troy, stop playing games. Did you talk with her?"

"Dad gum, Miss Delaney, I saw her at the diner with Jimmy. They were sittin' in a booth together. They're datin' now, I got the message. What else do you want me to say?"

Delaney stared at him mouth agape, like she didn't understand English or something. What part didn't she understand? He got it. Casey and Jimmy were dating. Did she expect him to be okay with it?

Because he wasn't. He wasn't okay with it and he wasn't giving up. It wasn't like Casey was married. Jimmy said *girlfriend*. That's all the hope Troy needed.

But first, he needed a job. "Miss Delaney? Can I get a job or not?"

With a dumbstruck glance, she waved him to follow. "C'mon. Let me show you around." Relief washed over him, the knots of doubt releasing as he did so. "I'm not saying you have a job," she clarified over her shoulder, "but I'll show you around just the same. I need to discuss it with Mr. Foster first."

"Yes, ma'am," he replied, wondering why. The man said it was her decision but Troy wasn't about to argue. A chance was a chance and he'd take every one he could get.

After a tour of the stables, Delaney showed him around the barn, the paddocks. There were tractors and wash racks, a feed room and another office. The second one in the barn belonged to the groundskeeper while hers was in the main building. Passing by a pen on their way back, Troy noted the dirt was raked clean. It reminded him of the horse he'd trained for Mr. Foster, the one they said went sour. Did they ever find a home for the animal? He hoped they finished the job of training and hooked the horse up with the right owners. He was a sweet animal. Nothing wrong that a little TLC and rebuilding of trust wouldn't fix. The black foal instantly came to mind. "How's that little foal working out for you?"

"Excuse me?"

"The one you got from Mr. Foster. Vegas. Did you take him and his momma?"

She nodded, realization lighting up her eyes. "They're here." She pointed back toward the stables. "Fourth one down on the left."

"Mind if I take a look at him?"

"Actually, Troy, I do." Surprise cut him in half. Slowing, she stopped. Turning her back to the low rising sun, she cupped a hand over her eyes and said, "I think it's best if we don't get your hopes up."

"My hopes?" he asked, his heart sinking into his boots.

"I need to think about it, discuss it with Mr. Foster."

Because she didn't fully trust him. Because he didn't have a great track record of staying put. Either by his own will or his own stupidity, Troy couldn't manage to keep a job for more than a few months. "I understand."

"Do you?" she asked pointedly, the razored-edge of her question catching him off guard.

"Yes, ma'am. I've made some mistakes, but I'm here to fix them."

"Fix them?" she looked at him queerly. "How so?"

"I know Casey's with Jimmy Sweeney now, but I'm going to show her that I'm worth a second chance. I can be the man she needs me to be." Casey had to see. Troy had to prove it to her. She didn't like that guy. She'd been on the rebound from him and Jimmy took advantage. It was an advantage Troy was gonna wipe clean. "If you'll give me the chance, I'll prove it to you, too."

Delaney ran a palm over her head and blew out a heavy breath. "I believe you will. Unfortunately, I'm not the one who matters."

Chapter Four

Pulling up to Ashley Fulmer's house for the annual Memorial Day party, a swarm of adrenaline pummeled Troy's chest. One of the first ones here, he was practically able to drive onto her front porch. The party started at one and it was one o'clock on the dot. He'd never made it this early before, but he'd been so damn anxious for the party to begin he couldn't wait. Now that he was here, fear battered like a jackhammer. Why was he so nervous? What did he have to fear? If he couldn't win Casey back from a guy like Jimmy then he had no business trying to get her in the first place. Jimmy was nothing. He was skinny, stupid and totally not her type. Travis said the two were taking college courses together, but that didn't mean anything. Travis was only trying to stir up trouble, rubbing it in that *he* wasn't in college. So what. Troy parked and jumped out of his truck, slamming the door closed. Casey understood his desire to work with horses. She didn't think he needed to go to college to do what he loved.

Hiking the short distance to Ashley's house, Troy settled his gaze on the front porch. The house was painted barn red, flower pots spilling over with color, a pink hydrangea bush off to the side. There was an old wagon wheel propped up on one end of the home and a line of rockers set out across the front porch. Last year he and Casey had sat right there, in those very rockers, talking about his plans to skip college. She agreed with him. She told him he was the best horseman she knew. Said he could do things with a horse nobody could. Pride mingled with doubt. Did she still think so?

She'd wanted him back then. They were friends, but then they were lovers. Vivid images of their last night together overwhelmed him. Her body, her willingness. She hadn't been the least bit reserved. She'd forgiven him, heart body and soul. *Could she want him again?*

Troy dodged the front door and headed for the back. He'd learn soon enough.

Casey sat in the backseat of her stepfather's truck, currently parked in the yard of Ashley Fulmer. Hands shaking, she tucked them in the wedge beneath her belly. Looking out over the sea of cars and trucks parked on the front lawn, dread rose like floodwaters in her chest. The three of them were here for Ashley's annual Memorial Day picnic, but Casey couldn't bring herself to open the truck door. "I'm not going in."

Her mother, Annie Owens, sat in the front passenger seat, exchanging another one of those looks with her husband Cal, the ones that shouted, *She's fragile, she doesn't know what she's doing.* "You can't hide from him forever."

"I'm not hiding."

Oceans of blue submersed her with one look—the look of a parent who knew better and was about to say "I told you so." "What do you call refusing to show yourself in public for the last forty-eight hours?"

Casey glanced away, her gaze inescapably pulled to Ashley's house. Beyond the roof line, smoke billowed up into a blue sky from charcoal grills manned by her husband Booker. Every year he cranked out ribs and burgers and dogs that were to die for. Through rolled-up windows, Casey could faintly hear the sound of music. The party was in full swing—a party where everyone and anyone would be, including Troy. Nerves skirted through her pulse. She knew she couldn't avoid him forever. She knew it was inevitable he find out about the baby.

But she wasn't ready to have that discussion. There were too many unanswered questions and feelings tumbling through her. "I'm tired," she lied.

"Casey."

At the stern tone, she looked at her mother. "I'm not ready," she insisted, suddenly overtaken by a wave of tears. They swamped her lower lids, drowned her eyes. She blinked and the tears fell hot onto her cheeks. "I'm not ready—can't you understand that?"

Cal placed a hand to Annie. "Maybe we should let her come up when she's ready."

*Yes*! she wanted to shout. *Listen to him*! Her mother wavered and Casey held her breath. *Please. Give me time. I need more time*!

Acceptance slowly seeped into her gaze. "Do you promise you'll come?"

"Yes." The reply was automatic. "Yes, I'll be in later." Later, after she had time to make a plan, devise a way to avoid Troy, the hurt she'd caused him during their last encounter. He'd be here, she was sure of it. The Parkers never missed one of Ashley Fulmer's parties. Ever.

"Okay." Annie Owens reached a hand back and clasped one of Casey's. With a gentle squeeze, she said, "Promise me you won't take too long."

"I won't."

"Okay. You can do this."

Casey nodded.

With a ragged sigh, her mother looked to Cal. He pushed out his door, the metal closing with a thud. As he circled the hood to open her mother's door, she said, "You can't hide from him forever. At some point, you have to tell him."

"I know," Casey replied, her body fatigued by the mere thought.

Cal opened her mother's door and held out a hand. "I'm here if you need me," Annie added.

A fresh round of tears pushed into Casey's eyes. "I know."

For a moment, Casey thought her mother might stay put, but after a quick nod of her head, her mom smiled, her blue eyes brimming with love, the depths of which Casey was only beginning to understand. "Okay. See you in a few," she said, her voice no more than a whisper.

Casey watched them go, the couple twin-dressed in their blue jeans and red shirts as they head in for the party. Regretting the need to sit alone in a car but knowing she couldn't arrive unprepared, Casey had to get her mind right. She had to make a plan. Panic lodged in her throat. What would he say? What would she say?

*I made you a promise when I left here and I aim to keep it.*

What did he mean by that? Didn't he already break it when he abandoned her for Kentucky? Didn't he already break his word when he said they'd be together forever? Casey didn't call leaving her home while he took off for Kentucky "being together." Old anger threaded through her heart. Troy ditched her. Made love to her, made her believe in him and then ditched her. Ugly thoughts of Jillian Devane and Loretta Flynn entered through a side door of her mind, scraping and clawing and revealing their bodies to her like they most probably did to him. Casey slammed the door of her imagination closed. Her stomach tightened in one long spasm that stretched clear over the mound of her belly. Troy was nothing but a cheat. On a good day he was a dreamer. On a regular day he was a cheat.

Catching sight of the tall, lanky Jimmy Sweeney, Casey swiped the tears from her cheeks. She yanked at the door handle and pushed it open. "Jimmy!" Confused to hear his name, he turned. With another jab to dry her tears, she waved frantically. "Over here!"

His angular features softened in recognition. Brushing long hair from his eyes, he changed direction and headed toward her. "Hey, Casey!"

Easing down from the vehicle, she tugged at her dress hem and tidied her hair. "Let's walk in together," she said as casually as she could.

"Sure." He stood by as she closed the door and came up to his side. Looking into the cab of the truck, he asked, "Where's your mom and Cal?"

"They're already inside."

Disapproval pushed into his gaze. "And left you out here alone?"

"I wasn't feeling well, but I'm better now."

"Oh." His expression tripped. "Are you sure?"

Irritated by the switch to mother hen mode, she said, "I'm fine." Casey took off for the house, assuming Jimmy would kick into step with her.

He did. His long jean-legged strides closed the distance in seconds. "You're looking nice today."

Dressed in a bright red tent dress and black boots, her outfit hardly qualified as "nice," but Jimmy insisted on complimenting her every time he saw her. It was as though he'd been reading from some pregnant mother manual. *Pregnant women are insecure about their appearance so reassure them on a regular basis.* Casey scoffed at the idea. Being pregnant didn't bother her a bit—except for the change in her diet. She missed cheeseburgers and French fries. She missed drinking coke like it was water. She did like the way pregnancy felt, knowing she was carrying a baby around, one she could feel and talk to, one she was already experiencing incredible emotion toward. It was surreal in a way. Her body felt normal yet looked anything but.

As they rounded the last row of cars, Casey spotted Troy's truck. Her heart stopped—then galloped out of control. *He was here.* Her limbs became hay sticks, her thoughts a jumble of emotion. The band was rocking loud and clear and by the number of cars parked out front, the dance floor would be full. Brushing shaky fingers through her hair, she organized it as best she could, then ran them over her brows to make sure they were in place, no hairs sticking up in odd positions. She cleared her throat, calmed her breathing and followed Jimmy to the back yard.

Turning the corner, Casey slowed, the smoky scent of grilled barbecue filling her nose. Her stomach grumbled in response. Tables were laden with food, a band belted out a rowdy tune. Another one of Ashley's parties was in full swing. Running hands over her belly, Casey edged behind Jimmy as they neared the throng of party-goers, people she knew well, people she knew vaguely, everyone carrying on, laughing and smiling but not her. She searched for sight of Troy.

"Are you thirsty?" Jimmy asked as they weaved between clusters of guests, raising his voice in competition with a lively CCR tune blasting from speakers across the lawn.

"No," she clipped. Angling for a better view, she searched between bodies but didn't see him. She saw Travis, Felicity, Delaney, Nick, Lacy, Malcolm, but no Troy.

"Are you hungry?" Jimmy asked.

"No," she muttered, distraught by the possibility he might see her and she might not see him. She didn't want him to have the upper hand. She wanted to see the look in his eyes when he discovered she was pregnant.

Jimmy stopped and she bumped right into him. "Jimmy!"

"You're gonna hurt yourself cranin' your neck like that."

"I'm not doing anything of the sort!"

Taller than most, Jimmy scanned the crowd, able to see much more than she could. "He's over there, by the band."

"He is?" Casey rose up on tiptoe and struggled for sight of him. Using Jimmy as a balance, she studied faces but there were too many bodies between them, dancing, talking, eating, drinking—she couldn't make his out!

"He's coming over," Jimmy said plainly.

Alarm fired through her veins. "He is?"

"Yep."

*Ohmigod, ohmigod.* What was she going to do? What was she going to say? Hello again. *Yes, I'm pregnant with your child, the one you ran off and left me to handle alone.*

Fear tingled across her skin. What would he think? What would he do?

As he came into her line of vision, Casey ducked behind Jimmy, pretending she was looking in the opposite direction. Heartbeats thundered in her chest. *Ohmigod, ohmigod.*

"Jimmy." Troy spoke the name evenly.

"Troy," came Jimmy's steady return.

"Casey?"

At the sound of her name on his lips, her heart exploded. His voice was soft, supple, the same way he spoke to her that night, the night he promised he'd change and they'd be together forever. Casey turned, unable to hide her body a second longer. Guilt feathered through her body, petered through her limbs. "Troy."

It was barely a squeak but no more was necessary. His gaze dropped to her mid-section and he blanched. Barely controlled civility became total shock. Troy smacked her with a direct gaze. "You're *pregnant*?"

## Chapter Five

"Yes," Casey stammered. "Isn't it obvious?"

The party dissolved into a sea of nothingness. The smell of food disappeared from his senses, the music extinguished. Troy couldn't breathe. He couldn't move. He searched Casey's face for explanation. She seemed so angry, so mad. "Is it mine?" he asked before he could stop himself.

"No"—she thwacked Jimmy on the arm—"it's his."

Troy's gaze sprang to Jimmy. The guy looked like a deer catching whiff of a trigger pull.

Jimmy swallowed, his boy Adam's apple bobbing up and down. "Yep. That's right." He slanted a gaze down to Casey and slid an arm around her shoulders. "The baby's mine."

*Son of a bitch.* Troy wanted to scratch his face off, wanted to pound him into the ground, kick him in his teeth. He glanced to Casey, stunned by the pathetic look of fear on her face. What the hell was *she* afraid of? He's the one standing in the middle of the picnic like a fool!

The party came back to life around him, people carrying on like nothing ever happened. But it did. Everything happened. Troy whirled and headed for his truck, bombarded by shock and anger. He finally understood why everyone had been acting so strange. They knew. They knew his girlfriend was pregnant with another man's child.

Hurt fired through his veins, punctured him to the core. There was no chance for them now. There was no way she'd come back to him with Jimmy's baby. There would never be a Troy and Casey again.

He didn't want her back. He didn't want any part of her. Jerking the door to his truck open, he tore the hat from his head and threw it inside. Jumping in, he slammed the door closed. He clutched his head, emotions imploding inside him. How could she? How could she have done it so quick and with him? By the size of her belly she hadn't wasted any time—like Troy had been *nothing* to her. Tears filled his eyes, blurred his vision. Images punctured his soul.

Casey slept with Jimmy. She was having his baby. Troy tried to shut out thoughts of them, but festivities surrounded him, penetrated his vehicle. It was a mistake to have come here. Casey was pregnant. He couldn't ignore the facts. Casey had moved on and slept with Jimmy Sweeney. Troy slammed a fist to the console sending car keys rattling to the floor. Despair closed in around him. Heartache wound deep. He whacked a hand to the dashboard.

Everything he believed to be true was a lie—a dad gum *lie*! Wrapping his throbbing palm around the steering wheel, Troy dropped his forehead and closed his eyes. All those months in Kentucky spent pining for her had been a waste. A stupid, idiotic waste. Casey had been with Jimmy. She had moved on and left him behind. What a fool he had been.

Casey watched in horror as Troy stalked off. What had she done telling him the baby was Jimmy's? Was she insane?

"Oh, brother," Jimmy muttered beside her, dropping his arm.

Casey began to tremble. She didn't dare look at Jimmy. She couldn't look him in the eye after what she'd done. Her mother appeared by her side in seconds. With an arm to her back Annie asked gingerly, "Casey, are you okay? What happened with Troy?"

Glancing in the direction of parked cars, she murmured, "He left."

Annie followed her gaze. "Is everything okay? He didn't look too happy."

"Casey told him the baby was mine," Jimmy informed her.

"*What*?"

Casey closed her eyes. She hugged her arms to her body. *Way to go, Jimmy.* Bring my mom into it. Great way to make everything worse.

Annie began to unravel. "I thought we discussed this, I thought we agreed it was best to tell him sooner rather than later! Telling him a lie is only going to make it worse when he learns the truth. It's not fair to let him believe something like that, not to Jimmy either."

Casey opened her eyes, "Ask him why he told Troy he was my boyfriend."

Jimmy remained mute, avoided her mother's questioning gaze.

Ashley Fulmer strolled up, a rhinestone flag emblem on her T-shirt glittering in the sunlight, competing with dangling firecracker earrings. "Darlin'?" she asked, turning to Casey's mom as though the answers could be found with her. "Everything all right?"

"She told Troy the baby was Jimmy's."

"Do you think that was wise?" Ashley peered at Casey, blue eyes echoing the sentiment of her mother. Obviously they didn't approve. Looking between the women, Casey gave herself a quick shot of self-preservation, ejecting their concern.

*What was she supposed to do?* Tell him it was his so he could ditch her again? This was *her* decision. She decided when and if he knew the truth. "Troy doesn't need to know," Casey insisted. "He'll just leave again so it's better he doesn't know in the first place."

Annie and Ashley stilled. They exchanged a look, then glanced to Jimmy, to her, then back to one another. Neither said a word, probably afraid she might do something stupid, like take drugs because she couldn't handle a difficult situation. Casey glanced in the direction of Troy's departure. But she wouldn't. Longing filled her as she recalled the tortured look in his eyes. This had hurt him. More than believing she and Jimmy were dating, this had been the final blow. It was a bad situation but they were wrong about one thing. Casey would never harm her child. *Their* child. This baby meant more than anything in the world.

Retreating to the solitude of the front porch, Casey deposited herself into a rocking chair. Staring out over the lawn, she located the spot where she'd seen Troy's truck earlier and parked her gaze there. No one had claimed the empty space. Probably because no one expected anyone to leave this early. No one in their right mind left Ashley's party before sundown. Then again, Troy wasn't in his right mind. He was in a poor state of mind, a false state of mind. Encircling her pregnant belly, Casey cursed herself for telling him the lie. It was stupid. Her mother and Miss Ashley were right. It was dumb, the dumbest thing she ever did. Of course he would find out the baby was his. It was a small town. Small towns talked. Some folks might think it was Jimmy's, seeing as how the two of them spent so much time together, but not anyone who knew her personally. Anyone who *knew* her knew the truth.

Pushing a toe to the porch floor, she rocked the chair back and forth, back and forth, running idle hands up and over her stomach. Was she wrong? If she told Troy the truth and he left her, what would that do to her baby? Wouldn't it make her feel like a loser knowing her daddy had abandoned her? Casey grew up without a father and even though her mom said it was a mutual decision, she always sensed it wasn't. She always harbored a feeling of abandonment. Turned out she was right. Worse, turned out her father should have stayed gone. Then she wouldn't have had to learn what a loser he really was, up close and personal. Narrowing her gaze on the vacant spot of grass, she tried to wall her mind from the party sounds, from thoughts of Jeremiah Ladd's face. His ugly face. His mean face. But she could see it as clear as if the man were standing before her.

She remembered the day he came over to the table where she and Troy had been sitting together at Fran's, his face beaten and bruised. He was looking for his girlfriend, wanted to know where she was. Fresh resentment swathed Casey's heart. He was asking Troy, because Troy had been flirting with her, something he claimed to be doing on *her* behalf. Visions of the sleazy blonde woman and Troy pushed in but Casey shoved them aside. Then there was the brown-skinned developer woman who tried to cozy up to Troy at Whiskey Joe's. The same woman who tried to buy Casey's half of Ladd Springs so she could destroy it. Casey's eyes glazed over on the patch of green. There was no room for memories of other women.

Mired in thoughts of the past, of her father, of how Jeremiah and Troy had sparred, two macho egos fighting for control, Casey recalled how her father left without saying a word to her. No "How are you?" "Are you supposed to be my kid?" Not so much as a hello. Jeremiah Ladd totally ignored her—other than staring at her like she was some kind of science experiment turned mutation. He'd totally dissed her.

Suddenly realizing she was clenching her dress, Casey let go Jeremiah Ladd. He wasn't worth her time or thought. Hauling her eyes away from the vacated parking spot she looked in the opposite direction. Trees in the distance, the layered green mountain range, were so familiar, tears filled her lids. But hatred coiled around her heart, her legs, squeezed her arms her shoulders, threatened to choke the very life from her. Casey hated that man. Hated Jeremiah Ladd with every cell in her body.

"Casey?"

The gentle voice cut like a knife. Casey turned to see Felicity Wilkins standing three feet away. Like everyone else at the party, her attire consisted of red, white and blue. In her case it was a red and white striped sleeveless top and blue denim skirt. Strawberry blonde hair was braided in twin ponytails and hung past her shoulders. Green eyes were soaked in pity. *How long had she been there?*

Shifting in her seat, Casey acknowledged her. "Hey."

"Want company?"

Not really, but to say no would only make Felicity run tell the others what a sad state of affairs her cousin was in and then *everyone* would be out here. "Sure."

Felicity walked around her outstretched legs and took a seat in the opposite rocker. She crossed booted legs and settled in.

Casey pushed back and forth, like she was just hanging out, relaxing. "Too noisy out back," she replied.

Felicity nodded but Casey knew she didn't believe a word of it. "How'd it go with Troy?"

Right to the point. Did she expect any less? Casey heaved a sigh, the moisture of her breath warm against the skin at her breast. Even sitting in the shade and wearing a flimsy cotton dress the day was still hot. "Not good."

"I hear you told him the baby is Jimmy's."

"I did."

"How come?"

No complaint, no blame, no disapproval, Felicity merely asked the question. Casey appreciated the lack of criticism. It was nice to have someone simply let things be for a change. "I don't want him to think it's his because he's only going to leave again and then what?"

Felicity nodded. "I hear ya." No attempt to persuade or defend, she simply let it go.

Casey was glad for Felicity's friendship. Over the last six months, the two had grown closer and it made the pregnancy easier to deal with, knowing she could share it with someone who cared about both parties. Delaney had encouraged their relationship, actually insisted they were family and family should be close. It wasn't like they didn't know each other from school, but now that paternity had been proven and she owned half of Ladd Springs, Casey felt a whole new appreciation for Felicity. After the initial awkwardness, the two had come to talk like friends, discussing whatever was on their minds without worrying what the other would think. Felicity never mentioned Troy, didn't harp on college like she had over Thanksgiving. She seemed content to let Casey be who she was.

Maybe it had something to do with the fact that Casey was taking a few classes at the community college, but she believed it was due to changes in Felicity. She wasn't nearly as innocent and naïve as she used to be but instead felt more open, objective. It was like her professors had peeled back the layers of home, exposing Felicity to the real world. Casey's mom said Felicity was maturing, expanding her horizons, coming into her own. Maybe. Sliding her hands in a wide arc over her belly, Casey thought it ran deeper, as if her cousin was taking a new look at her life now that she'd seen it from afar.

"Are you ever going to tell him?"

There was no reproach in her voice, only sincere interest. "Do you think I should?" Casey asked.

Felicity shrugged. "I don't know. I hear what you're saying about him leaving."

"He's done if before, why wouldn't he do it again, right?"

"Right. I mean, Troy's a great guy and I love him to death but he's made mistakes."

"Yes," Casey agreed, staring at Felicity, struck by the sadness in her voice.

"Good guys make mistakes but can they recover?" Felicity asked. "That's the question."

Casey nodded, a funny sensation slipping in.

"Maybe Troy would stay and do right by you if he knew how important it was to you and the baby."

"Maybe."

"But the fact is"—Felicity turned away—"some dads don't."

Gripped by an urgent curiosity, Casey asked, "Did you miss your daddy when you were growing up?" Startled by the question spurting from her lips, she was suddenly intrigued to hear the answer. Had Felicity ever thought of her father? Did she care that he didn't call, wasn't present? Casey had met him once. She was sitting at Fran's Diner with Delaney and he showed up, asking questions about Felicity. He seemed normal enough, came from a decent family. Technically he was her uncle, now that her mom was married to Cal Foster. What did Felicity think of him?

Glancing sideways, Felicity's eyes became fluid with emotion, as though her entire childhood was swimming in her vision. "Yes. I did. A lot at first but then I got over it."

It was a simple answer to a complicated situation. Delaney's mom divorced him and never looked back. According to her mom, the two never should have gotten married. Jack Foster was wild and crazy and Delaney was not. She was brazen and tough but not rowdy the way Jack had always been. After the divorce, Felicity's dad moved to Nashville. For years he was gone until he showed up recently over Thanksgiving. It must have been strange for Felicity. Casting her gaze back out over the mass of cars and trucks, Casey wondered which was worse—knowing and having contact with a father who was a jerk or living with the knowledge he might be an okay guy who didn't want you?

Lowering her gaze to the stretch of fabric over her stomach, Casey realized it was a question she was going to have to ask on behalf of her own daughter.

## Chapter Six

Seated at the lunch counter at Fran's Diner, elbows propped on the counter, Felicity read from a paperback novel. Three thirty, there was hardly anyone around, the bulk of the lunch crowd cleared out and the early bird diners not expected until four. It suited her fine. Fran Jones welcomed her to hang out, served up a plate of burger and fries too. Dining alone gave Felicity quiet time to read while she waited for Travis to finish with his dad. They were fixing the screen around the patio of their home, a job she wasn't invited to help with nor did she care. She was content to read.

Her current book was a book about a family in crisis. The father was an over-achiever, the mother an alcoholic; a young son lived in their shadow with his own set of problems at school. Written in three points of view, it was one of those stories that wrenched your heart from the inside out. It made Felicity feel like no one was right, no one was wrong, but everyone was lost in a confusing mess. Slapping the open-faced book down, she reached for her coke and sucked in a mouthful of sweet carbonated soda. It was ridiculous the dysfunction that went on in a family. Why couldn't people work together? Help each other out like a team?

"Looks like some pretty heavy reading."

"Oh!" Felicity spit liquid onto her hand. Turning, she wiped the soda away as she came face-to-face with her father, Jack Foster. His dark gaze shot to her book and a smile crossed his lips. She flashed a glance to the obvious title. *When Families Hurt.* "I'm reading it for school," she blurted. "It's a psychology class."

"They make you read over summer break?"

"Yeah." She tried to shrug it off. "Go figure." Flipping the book closed with one hand, she set it cover-side down. "I guess professors don't believe in taking breaks."

He laughed, the sound easy and warm and nothing like the selfish man her mother described. "I remember those days well," he said. "Their whole life was about drilling work into their students." Friendly eyes crinkled within his sun-tanned skin, the white of his shirt contrasting sharply and somehow making him look younger than his forty-plus years. Up close, his brown eyes danced as though he didn't have a care in the world. Squared jaw, strong nose, her father's complexion was shades darker than her own. Felicity found it odd that she didn't resemble him. Granted his skin was browned from his time spent outdoors, but even in the dead of winter she could tell his skin would be shades darker than her own. Her mom was blonde with a medium complexion. Maybe it was true what her mother always said. She claimed Felicity favored the Ladd side of the family, red-tinged hair and freckles to boot. But still, she mused, peering at the stranger who was her father. It was weird how different he could look from her.

"I hear you're doing amazing things with your flute."

Lifting her shoulders, she replied, "I don't know about *amazing*. I play..." Felicity pressed her side against the counter, wondering who would have told him about her flute. No one knew anything about her music who would have said the first word to Jack Foster.

"Don't sell yourself short, kid. It's a tough world out there with far too many people ready and willing to take you down." She nodded, imagining him as a young man enjoying his college days, replaced by more recent thoughts of him telling her to pay her own way through school, build some character. He gestured like he was going to tap her arm, but didn't and said, "Stand up for yourself. You deserve it."

Felicity caught sight of Fran Jone's net-covered red-head of hair through the kitchen service window and groaned inwardly. *Great*. She'd be hearing about this encounter later on.

As though sensing her distress, Jack turned around and looked in the same direction. Fran stared him down, but then disappeared into the recesses of her kitchen like a groundhog popping back into its hole. His dark eyes cooled a degree. "Don't let old Fran get to you. She's always been a nosy one."

"She's only looking out for me," Felicity defended.

About to object, he seemed to think better of it, nodding instead. Returning focus to her plate, she picked up a French fry, dropping it three fries over. It was awkward to be alone with him. Well, not alone-alone but without sight of her mother. Felicity didn't remember the last time it happened.

"So how about dinner?"

She glanced up. "Huh?"

"Dinner with your old man, catch up on old times?" The breath caught in her throat and he chuckled. "You can't avoid me forever. I have a right to visit my own daughter, don't I?"

A million responses flew through her brain, a million reasons no, a million reasons yes, but none of them made it to her lips.

"Your grandparents would like to see you."

"Grandparents? As in the Fosters?"

He nodded. Setting a hand to the counter he leaned his weight into it. With a fleeting glance toward the kitchen he said, "They've invited you to dinner at the house."

"Why?"

He laughed. "Because you're their granddaughter? They care about you and want to know how you're doing." He dipped his head near. "Is that so strange a concept?"

The man spoke with an intimacy he hadn't earned. He hadn't been in her life all these years, hadn't cared what she was doing, cared to help her in any way. He never called, hardly wrote. Why now? "They never asked my mom to see me before."

"Probably because they were afraid to ask." Jack glanced askance and then, as though sharing a secret, said, "She's kind of thorny, if you know what I mean."

"She is not—she's protective."

His brow rose, lines forming across his forehead. "Well, that's a nicer way to say it but the point remains. She hasn't thrown down the welcome mat for my folks, and because they're nice people, they haven't pushed."

But he was. Felicity stared at him, mesmerized by the ease with which he spoke to her. It was like he'd forgotten the past between them, preferring to resume his role as wonderful and loving father. Felicity never fully understood why her parents split. Her mom said it was because they didn't see eye-to-eye on things. Her dad once commented it was because her mom was uncompromising. Several years back, Felicity had heard someone say it was because of his drinking. When she asked her mom about it, she acknowledged that he drank and that was part of the problem, but lots of people drank. Didn't mean they ended up in divorce.

Whatever the truth, Felicity knew her mom could be difficult. She was demanding and a bit on the controlling side, but it was only because she was looking out for her daughter. Whether it was forcing Ernie to stand by his promise regarding the property rights to Ladd Springs or waiting at the cabin every day when she arrived home from school, her mom didn't cut any slack.

It was possible she didn't invite the Fosters to spend time with her because it would bring up too many painful memories. Felicity could imagine the same would be true if it were her and Travis were in the same situation. Once you loved someone, that love never went away. It changed or dulled, but Felicity couldn't imagine ever hating Travis. It would always hurt to be apart from him, whatever the cause. Take Casey and Troy. If Felicity were carrying Travis' child and he left her?

It would kill her.

"So what do you say? Dinner tomorrow night?"

Glancing away, she pushed at her coke. "I don't know."

"What's to know? You need to eat, right?"

She allowed herself to look at him. No horns were popping out of his head. She detected no demonic glaze in his pupils. "Yes."

"You don't have anything against my parents, do you?"

Her neck and cheeks flushed warm. "No, of course not!"

"Well, then. What's holding you back?"

What always held her back. "I have to ask my mom."

"What?" He dropped his head back and laughed. "You're eighteen, the owner of hundreds of acres of land, the proud landlord to the fanciest hotel property in Tennessee—you don't need your mother's permission to do anything anymore. You're your own woman."

Felicity cast her gaze to the plate of fries, her discarded novel. Distant thoughts wondered if Fran's eyeballs were focused on her at the moment. Contemplating her father's statement, Felicity disagreed. She might be her own woman in theory, but in reality her mom still called the shots. "She won't be happy if I go without telling her."

Jack dipped his head and peered up into her eyes. "See what I mean?" He winked. "Thorny."

"Sweetheart, there's nothing to worry about." Annie patted her daughter's thigh as they sat in a brightly lit patient room, waiting for the doctor to appear.

Casey sat on the raised bed, idly swinging booted legs to and fro, careful not to hit her mother who stood beside her. The room smelled of alcohol. A small corner sink counter was covered with exam supplies—a clear jar filled with cotton balls, a box of latex gloves along with some instruments she couldn't identify. An instruction sheet was taped to an upper cabinet. On the wall were posters depicting the female body, one showing a baby inside, the other without. Casey thought it weird how babies were tucked inside the womb, squashed in the cramped confines of a woman's womb. She looked around the stark white office, a bit unsettled. This wasn't her favorite part of pregnancy.

"Your weight is on the light side," her mother continued, "but it's not out of range. Your blood pressure is a little high, but that could be stress. You're taking your vitamins, right?"

"Yes," she replied glumly.

"Okay, then there's nothing to worry about."

Except the funny feeling she had. Insistent, gnawing, she felt like something wasn't right. Not like she'd ever been pregnant before, but she was starting to sense things before she thought them. Know them before they happened. It was weird. She was beginning to feel like she had a sixth sense. Did all pregnant women feel this way?

"You're anxious. It's normal. This is your first pregnancy. It happens to a lot of new mothers. I was anxious when carrying you."

Casey looked into her mother's face, searching for what she wasn't saying. Did she know something? Was she keeping something from her?

The door opened and the doctor walked in. Older, his hair receding, his midsection rounded from lack of exercise, the man reminded her of a grandfather type. A good thing. Casey wasn't sure if she'd feel comfortable with the new guy in town. What if he didn't know what he was doing yet?

With a manila file folder in his hand, he greeted, "Good morning, Casey. Mrs. Foster."

"Hello," her mother replied. Casey remained mute.

"How's momma feeling?"

"Good." Shifting position, the stiff paper bed cover crinkled beneath her.

Nodding, he flipped through pages in his folder, made short grunting sounds. He didn't say anything, only uttered his noises as he thumbed through his notes. Casey and her mother exchanged a look. Were they supposed to ask questions right now? Wait? Casey fidgeted with the hem of her dress. It was a simple white cotton shirt dress with a bright floral pattern, a mix of blues and yellow. It wasn't bad, but none of the maternity clothes appealed to her. They were frumpy, dowdy. Then again, she didn't expect them to be fashionable or trendy. Comfortable. That's what she needed from her maternity clothes. Large tent dresses—as she had come to call them—weren't attractive but they suited her needs.

Peering at her over black-rimmed reading glasses, he asked, "Do you have a history of high blood pressure?"

Casey looked to her mother. "No," Annie responded for her. "Mine is normal. So is my sister, Lacy's. I don't recall any trouble with my parents."

Centering on her mom, the doctor asked, "What about on the father's side?"

"I don't know," came the automatic reply.

The doctor raised a brow. When her mom didn't elaborate, he looked to Casey. "Is there a way we can find out?"

"Is there a problem?" Annie asked, her posture stiff.

"Casey's pressure is on the high side. It's not unusual, considering the added stress on her body, but with her lack of weight gain and elevated heart rate, I'd like to rule out anything more serious."

Annie sent a sketchy gaze to her daughter. Casey swallowed. Neither of them knew anything about her father's family history, other than Ernie had been a grumpy old man. He died of cancer. His brother Albert was still alive, living in a small cabin Nick Harris had built for him in a private wooded section of the property, just beyond and out of sight from the hotel. Albert was a loner, his two sons long since gone from Ladd Springs. Casey's throat constricted. Were they even alive?

She didn't have a clue.

"I can get the information," Annie said quickly. "I'll talk to her aunt. She'll know."

Her mother was going to ask Delaney? Would she know any details about Jeremiah's health?

"Are you looking for anything specific?" Annie inquired.

Setting his file aside, he removed his glasses and massaged the red dent of skin at the bridge of his nose. Taking her mother in with gray eyes a shade bloodshot, he said, "I'd ask about any known history of high blood pressure, heart disease, diabetes. Find out if there were any issues with low birth weight, premature delivery."

Her mother snatched the phone from her purse and began to type furiously into the keypad. Watching her, Casey felt glued to the patient bed. Casey's bad feeling returned. Jeremiah Ladd was cursing her baby's existence before the child was even born. As the doctor went on to describe any one of a hundred reasons she could be having these issues, Casey only heard trouble. There was trouble with her pregnancy.


"I'm going to call Delaney," Annie declared as they walked to the car. "She'll be able to answer all these questions."

Casey experienced a blast of heartbeat, a brief sensation of dizziness followed by a swooning rush. Perspiration gathered beneath her dress, inside her boots. Her feet were sweating. Her chest was sweating. The sun was hot. She was hot. *Nervous.* What made her mother so sure Delaney would know anything? If Casey recalled, Delaney and her uncle weren't on the best of terms. The old man hated her guts and according to her mom, Ernie's wife left him and never looked back. How were they going to find out a family history from a family that was history?

Unlocking the car doors, she went on, "Between her mother's history, Ernie's and Albert's, we should be able to get something definitive."

Casey paused at the passenger door. Staring over the car at her mother, she saw blue eyes that held none of the confidence her lips were describing. It was like her mother had detached from reality. She was saying things as if it would make them so.

What about Troy's history? Did any of that matter when it came to the baby she was carrying?

She didn't dare ask. The doctor would probably tell her to get all the information she could and discussing the well-being of her baby would mean revealing the truth. Opening the car door, Casey lowered onto the seat with a thud. *What a mess.*

Her mother gunned the engine to life and Casey pressed back into her seat. She pulled her seatbelt into place, adjusting the straps around her belly and buckled it secure. Troy was going to find out. Between Delaney hiring him and giving the rundown on Jeremiah's health history, Troy was going to find out. What was she going to say?

*I lied. It's not Jimmy's—it's yours.*

Troy would have a fit. Nerves swarmed her stomach. Would he leave town the second she told him? Would he try to marry her?

*I made you a promise when I left here and I aim to keep it.*

Troy told her he loved her and they were going to have a future together. He was going to prove he was worth the faith she'd put into him. Her pulse scattered, hammered against her ribcage. But that was before she got pregnant. It was before the added responsibility of a baby. Pregnancy changed everything. It ruined everything. Changed everything. Made everything different and new and exciting. Gazing out the window as her mom backed up, she wondered, *How could she feel all these things at once*?

## Chapter Seven

Delaney swung into the diner, stepping aside as a couple entered behind her. The dinner hour was upon them, the air saturated with the rich scent of fried chicken and steak coupled with the sweet aroma of freshly baked biscuits. Most tables were occupied, the senior crowd reliable as clockwork. 'Course, when Fran offered half-priced meals from four to six, who wouldn't take the deal? She sighed. Those who had a job. Searching for sight of Fran, Delaney wondered what she wanted. She'd called an hour ago and said to come quick. She had stables to run and dropping everything to come see Fran took some doing. Extending her search to the kitchen, Delaney was surprised to see Fran hustling out so fast she nearly knocked over a waitress in her haste. What could possibly be so interesting that warranted such a hurry?

Fran grasped her arm and corralled her to an empty space near the pie case. Decked out in her customary starched white uniform, red apron tied at her waist, Fran checked for the nearest set of ears, then ducked her head close and whispered, "Sugar, we need to talk."

"So you said when you called. What's got you so wound up?"

"Jack was here. Jack was here and he was talking to Felicity."

Alarm bells sounded in her skull. "What? What was he doing with Felicity?"

"I don't know. It was after the lunch rush, but you know that man is meaner than a flea-bitten hound dog. I don't know what he was saying 'cause I didn't want to venture too close, you know what I mean? But I know it couldn't have been good."

"Did Felicity look upset?"

"No, no, she didn't look upset, but he looked mighty happy when he left so you can see why I'm concerned."

"I hear you." A happy Jack Foster meant a miserable someone else—usually her. Delaney dumped her gaze to the racks laden with perfectly baked pies, mostly peach. Peach pies were Fran's specialty and Felicity's favorite.

Fran cupped a hand over her hair net, brown eyes sharper than a hawk on the hunt. She was all too familiar with the Ladd-Foster history and liked Jack Foster least of all. If she could, she would have banned the lot of them but there were rules against such things. not to mention it wasn't good for business. Looking at Delaney intently, Fran said, "Now you know I don't want to be upsetting you with your new marriage and all but, Lord a'mercy, I don't like him poking around Felicity."

Delaney placed a hand to Fran's shoulder. "I know you don't. I know you're looking out for her and I appreciate it."

Somewhat mollified by the comment, Fran gave a small smile. "You know I love that girl like she's my own flesh and blood."

"I know you do. I'll talk to her."

"You do that but keep it close to your heart, will you?"

"Because she fussed about it the last time?" Delaney asked.

Felicity had made a point of objecting to the last time Fran "told" on her, stating she was old enough to make her own decisions and didn't need her mother or Fran spying on her every move. But Jack talking to Felicity could only spell trouble—the kind of trouble Felicity couldn't understand.

"Well, yes but..." Fran hedged, acting a bit too dodgy for Delaney's comfort. It wasn't like Fran to dance around a point. She was like an archer with a bow.

"When I asked Felicity about the meeting with Jack after he left, she said it was nothing, really, something about the Fosters wantin' to see her."

"Jack's parents?"

Fran nodded. "You see what I mean? He ain't playin' fair if he's willing to use his folks to get to Felicity."

Delaney stroked a hand over top of her head, wrapped her hand around her ponytail and wanted to pull her hair out. "You can say that again!"

"I don't blame Felicity. It's only natural for her to be curious, you know what I mean?"

"I hear you. Felicity shouldn't be a pawn in this game."

Fran's eyes leapt to the front door. At the clang of bells, Delaney turned. Her heart lurched. Casey walked in, alone, looking like she'd lost her best friend.

"Oh, that poor child!" Fran cried under her breath. "She's nothin' but a bag of bones, I tell you. Wait until I get a hold of that mother of hers—she isn't eating a morsel of that food I'm sending home with her."

Delaney had to admit Casey looked thin. The cotton dress hung stick-straight from her body, her stomach no more than a bump beneath the floral material. Could be those skinny white legs of hers, disappearing into a pair of black boots. The combination made her legs look all the thinner. Casey's lack of weight gain rivaled that of Lacy's, but at least Lacy looked healthy during her pregnancy. Casey looked drawn, stressed, and Delaney had a feeling she knew why. "I need to talk to her," she murmured to Fran.

"You do that, sugar. And get her to eat while you're at it, will you? I'll bring you anything you want."

Delaney smiled. "I'll try." But she had a feeling food was the last thing on Casey's mind. Undoubtedly Troy would be front and center and probably sole occupant.

Approaching Casey slowly, Delaney winced at the purplish tint beneath her eyes. Her skin was so fair, tiny blood vessels were literally visible through the translucent flesh. It couldn't be good for the baby. "Hey, Casey."

"Hi, Miss Delaney."

"Are you meeting your mother for dinner?"

"No."

"I could use some company. Are you hungry?"

She wavered, shooting a quick eye to locate Fran and mumbled, "I'm here to pick up some food for home."

"Mind if I wait with you?"

Casey shrugged. "Sure." With a protective hand over her stomach, she walked over to the food counter and Fran appeared within seconds.

Wiping her hands with a white dishcloth, she called out brightly, "Hey, sugar!"

"Did my mom call you?" Casey asked.

Elderly brown eyes muddied in confusion. "No, why. Something wrong?"

"She was going to call to order dinner. I'm here to pick it up."

Fran's expression burst with pleasure. "I'll get right on it! Little fried chicken and biscuits? Some boiled peanuts for Cal?"

"I don't know. You might want to call her."

"I'll get right on it."

"Thanks."

"Can I get you a coke while you wait?"

"No, thanks."

"Water?"

Casey didn't appear to want anything at the moment, but reluctantly agreed. "Sure." If only to end her great aunt's ceaseless questions, Delaney mused, watching in amusement as Fran hurried back to the kitchen on a mission of love. Casey lowered to a stool and Delaney mirrored her movements. "So how're you holding up?"

"You mean the pregnancy?"

Delaney cocked her head. "Sure."

"Fine," she replied, a hesitance sliding into her blue-eyed gaze. "The baby has been moving more these days."

The mention pulled warm memories of Delaney's pregnancy with Felicity. She had enjoyed being pregnant. It had been such an exciting time in her life—from the joy of anticipation, the nervous excitement, the fuss from everyone to sharing the entire experience with her mother. Susannah Ladd

Wilkins had been with her every step of the way. She had gone with her to the doctor, helped her pick out clothes, bottles. She'd even been in tow for the delivery. Jack couldn't stand hospitals, content to allow his wife to bear his child alone. Delaney's insides cringed. She should have known then and there what she was in for, but he was the father of her baby, the man of her world, and she'd been too young to pick up on the signs.

Peering at Casey, Delaney was struck by the faraway look in her eyes. She'd be willing to bet the girl was thinking of Troy. He was in town and Casey was probably consumed with him—as she should be. For better or worse, he would forever be a part of her life, marriage or no marriage. Lying to him about the pregnancy had been a mistake. It was only going to agitate the situation when the truth came out. "Troy came by to see me," Delaney said, watching closely for Casey's reaction.

"He did?"

Struck by the naked desire staring back at her, Delaney felt the hit. Despite her actions, Casey was clearly interested in the boy. Delaney nodded. "He was looking for a job."

"Oh." Crestfallen, a shade of embarrassment colored her pale cheeks. "That's because he quit his last one."

"So he said." Did Casey know why? Had Troy told Casey what he told her? "Says he's back in town for good."

"Do you believe him?" Casey asked.

The sheer vulnerability in her voice cut Delaney's heart in two. "Not sure." Casey glanced away. It was clear she wanted to believe him. "Do I take it you don't?"

"Troy gets fired or quits everything he starts," she mumbled, drawing circles on the counter with a finger. "I don't see any reason to think that's going to change."

A pretty harsh condemnation coming from the woman who loved him. Had she written him off completely? Had she lost her capacity to encourage and support him through the tough times? "You don't think people can change?"

"Do you?"

Visions of Jack came to mind. No, not Jack. But Troy? Maybe. It was possible. When Casey didn't respond, Delaney said, "I called his employer in Kentucky. They seemed real pleased with him." Casey turned to her. "Mr. Foster had good things to say about him as well."

"But they fired him."

"He made a mistake."

"A pretty big one, don't you think?"

"I think we're all fallible. I don't think any man or woman is immune to a fall from grace. I think it's more important to know whether or not they're interested in picking themselves up and moving on."

Casey pivoted on her stool. "What are you saying? You're going to give him a job?"

"I sure could use a stable hand who knows his way around a horse. The hotel is booked clear through Christmas and I'm going to need hands to accommodate all the guests who will want to ride." Thoughts of the next six months warmed her heart. Delaney couldn't wait to share her horses with people from all over the world. The first batch of guests had been thrilled with their trail rides. Word would spread like wildfire, and she predicted her stables were going to be the hottest spot on the property!

"He's the best rancher there ever was," Casey said. "Nobody knows horses better than Troy."

Delaney slipped into a smile. "Are you endorsing the hire?"

Casey retreated just as quickly as she had advanced. "No, not really, but—"

"But you think he'd be a good fit."

She nodded.

"I agree. I've known Troy since he was a boy. He's a good egg."

"You're not worried about him drinking or quitting?"

"I'm willing to give him the opportunity to prove otherwise."

Casey stilled. A light switch had been turned on, its dimmer slowly increasing the luminescent of her blue eyes. "You are?"

"I am," she said, deciding on the spot.

Casey fidgeted on her stool, glanced into the kitchen as a new energy swirled about her. Visibly curbing her enthusiasm, she remained silent, as though she feared jinxing it.

Placing a palm to the counter, Delaney relaxed into her decision. "I guess I do think people can change, at least grow and mature and find their way." She'd done it herself over the last year. No reason why Troy couldn't do so.

"Thank you, Miss Delaney. I know he'll be happy to hear it."

"Are you?" The blunt question sideswiped Casey, knocking the cheer from her expression. Nibbling a nail, she rubbed a hand over the high mound of her belly. In the space of an instant, Casey looked young, vulnerable. Delaney could smell the insecurity and her heart went out to her. "You need to tell him about the baby." Casey dodged her gaze, seeking the activity in the kitchen. Delaney followed her line of vision, catching glimpse of an elusive Fran. Instinctively intuiting the conversation, she was giving them time. It was time Delaney appreciated. Moving a hand closer to Casey, she added softly, "He needs to know."

"I don't know."

"What are you afraid of? Him leaving?"

She nodded.

"What if he stays? What if once he knows you're carrying his child, it gives him the motivation he needs to stay? Have you thought about that?"

Tears pushed into her eyes. "I don't want him to stay because of the baby."

Comprehension zipped Delaney tight as a drum. *She wanted him to stay because of her.*

Not out of duty or obligation but because he wanted her. Of course she did. Struck by the simplicity of Casey's desire, Delaney was surprised she had missed it.

DIANNE VENETTA

## Chapter Eight

Delaney leaned over and pulled the pistol from her boot, tucked it into her rear waistband, then tugged her boots off. Setting them alongside those of Nick and Felicity, she pushed through the front door of her cabin, a torrent of emotion rumbling through her. She'd hired Troy today, his first day set for tomorrow. While she felt good about the quality of the hire, she remained torn about the consequences, predominantly for Casey. If he quit, she could hire someone else. If he abandoned Casey again, it would kill her. Then there was Jack and Felicity. She'd have to talk to her, tell her she knew about Jack's offer and counsel against it.

Met by the glum faces of Nick and Felicity seated at the kitchen island, Delaney went on instant guard, their erect body language signaling a less than friendly reception. Closing the door behind her, she advanced with caution, trying to read Nick's gaze for clues. "What's going on?"

"I'm going to have dinner at the Fosters," Felicity announced. "Don't try and talk me out of it either." She flicked an accusatory glance toward Nick. "I've made up my mind. I'm going."

Nick's restrained look registered the enormity of his displeasure.

Delaney ventured closer uncertainly. "Don't you think we should discuss it, first?"

"No. You'll only try and talk me out of it."

"Do you know why that would be?"

Taking her mother head on, green eyes fierce and determined, Felicity replied, "You don't like my father and you don't care for his family."

The weight of past decisions crashed onto Delaney's shoulders. Felicity had no idea about the physical abuse, the history of Jack's drinking, the vehement defense from his mother, Victoria Foster. The woman looked Delaney straight in the eye and accused her of lying, trying to ruin the Foster's reputation because of quarrels from the past, ancient history regarding Delaney's mother and Victoria's husband, Gerald Foster. Delaney had been too stunned at the time to fight back and instead retreated. If Victoria didn't want to have a relationship with her granddaughter because of past grievances, that had nothing to do with the child then so be it. And shame on her. Avoiding Nick's "I told you so" gaze, Delaney focused on her daughter. Why Victoria was interested now seemed the more important question. "It's a little more complicated than that, honey."

"How so?"

Nick eased back on his stool. Seemed he wanted to hear the answer to that one, too.

Angling her shoulder to him, she decided, fine. She'd been right in not telling her daughter about the abuse, and she was standing by the decision. There'd been no need to taint the child's heart with the ugly details of her father—unless of course, it would have prevented her from heading into the monster's lair all these years later. Flashing her gaze to Nick, she briefly second-guessed herself. Would telling her years ago have avoided this very scene?

Maybe. Possibly. But it was too late. Delaney kicked into step and circled around to the opposite side of the island. The butcher-block surface was littered with grease-stained paper napkins and yellow crumbs, remnants of a half-eaten pan of cornbread. She eyed Nick. Someone must have been hungry when he came home and raided the goods. Pushing thoughts of dinner aside—and the lack of a side to accompany it—Delaney zeroed in on her daughter. At the moment, food was irrelevant. "Why do you want to go over there? Hasn't your father proven himself over the years? Hasn't he demonstrated his penchant for leaving, for ignoring your needs? His family never tried to see you before. Why now?" Delaney hated the picture of abandonment she was painting. It didn't exactly foster self-esteem. But it was the truth. It was ugly, but it was the reality of her daughter's life. Why prolong the misery by allowing the man to set fresh hooks?

"He seems different to me." Glancing to Nick, currently leaning over the counter on his elbows, she added, "He's been here since Thanksgiving. He hasn't left. Doesn't that suggest he might actually plan to stay?"

"And if he does?"

"Well, he's my father. Shouldn't I give him a second chance?"

Delaney's heart twisted at the yearning staring back at her. Fine strands of strawberry-blonde hair framed her daughter's heart-shaped face, curls that had escaped her French braid. The creamy soft T-shirt she wore underscored the delicacy of Felicity's state of mind. Her words were tough but her eyes spoke volumes. She wanted her father to be different. She wanted him to be the father she'd never had. It broke Delaney's heart to think about the pain that lay ahead for her.

Nick came to life and turned to his side. "It's like I said...not everyone deserves a second chance, Felicity."

"Why not?"

Because some things are unforgiveable, Delaney rebutted silently. Because some people never change. Ignoring Nick's reproachful gaze, she crossed her arms. Rehashing *their* prior conversations wasn't going to help. "What if he hurts you?"

"Hurts me how? It's not like my having dinner with his parents is dangerous. They're nice people."

"It's not his parents that concern us," Nick pitched in.

*Speak for yourself*, Delaney scoffed privately.

"It's not like I'm going to be alone with him. I'll drive over myself, have dinner and be done with it." She glanced between the two. "I'm an adult now. I've completed a year of college away from home, and it's time you started treating me like one."

"Yes, but college is different," Delaney said, stumbling over the idiocy of her own words. Of course her daughter was an adult. Of course she could face a dinner with her grandparents on her own. It wasn't the capability that concerned Delaney. It was the emotional consequences.

"Next year I'll be living in an apartment off campus. Two years after I'll be completely on my own."

Translation: *You have to let go at some point.*

"There's no harm in having dinner with my grandparents," Felicity stated, as though it were settled.

Yes, no, there were so many things Delaney wanted to say, but the staunch conviction scoring her daughter's tone indicated this was a hill the girl was prepared to die on. Delaney sought Nick for help. He merely arched a brow. *Your move, dear.* "When are you planning on going?" she asked, bracing herself for Felicity's answer.

"Tomorrow night."

The reply gutted Delaney. Unwinding her arms she objected, "So soon? Don't you want to give yourself some time to think about it?"

"Do you see any reason to wait?"

Reason to wait? Delaney saw no reason to go in the first place.

Annie dialed Delaney's number. After the doctor's appointment this morning, the day had been swallowed up by a packed salon, a pile of paperwork and a constant stream of worry over Casey's pregnancy. She'd been mentally unprepared for the challenge, though to the staff's credit, guests were accommodated beautifully. It was a heady experience dealing with foreigners, wealthy women draped in fine clothes and jewelry, exotic accents and exquisite good looks. They were nothing like the awful Jillian Devane woman, the she-devil who almost prevented this salon opportunity from becoming a reality, yet they were exactly like her. Exacting, demanding. Annie had gained an entirely different perspective dealing with the clientele of Serenity Springs versus women from a community she'd lived with and known all her life. It required more energy, more focus. Despite doing nails for almost twenty years, this salon felt new and fresh every day, requiring her to be as alert and focused as a newbie.

The process was exhausting. Invigorating, rewarding, but exhausting—especially today. Talk about unprepared—Annie couldn't answer the first question regarding the Ladd health history, Jeremiah's mother or father, his grandparents. None of it!

Delaney would know. She'd have to know more than Annie.

Settling into a leather chair in her fancy new office, the walls painted a soothing cream and illuminated with recess lighting for a calming effect, Annie waited for Delaney to answer. With the salon closed and Cal working the front desk, she'd have all the privacy she needed. She hated to bother Delaney at this hour but she couldn't wait another second. Notepad and pen in hand, she was ready to take notes.

"Hello?"

"Delaney, its Annie."

"I know. What's up?"

"Do you have a minute? I have some questions I need to ask you."

"Yes." There was a pause. "Shoot."

Mildly put off by the detached tone, Annie asked, "Do you know anything about Jeremiah's health history?"

"His health history? As in, what, was he sickly?"

"As in, does his family have a history of heart disease, diabetes, high blood pressure?"

"What's this about?"

Annie heaved a sigh. Couldn't Delaney simply answer the question? Did she always have to answer a question with a question? "Casey's doctor wants to know."

"Is she all right?"

Encouraged by the switch in tone, Annie replied, "We think so. Her blood pressure is running a bit on the high side so the doctor wants to be rule out anything more serious. My family doesn't have any issues with blood pressure, but I have no idea about Jeremiah's. Do you?"

"Casey didn't mention anything about health problems to me this afternoon. What's going on?"

Annie wasn't surprised. Ever since they left the doctor's office, Casey had detached herself from the subject, immersing herself in denial. She continually claimed she was fine and the doctor was overreacting. Truth be known, Annie understood her bigger concern was the need to involve Troy. "Casey's downplaying the doctor's request but I'm not. He asked and I want to give him as much information as I can."

"Understood," Delaney clipped. "Unfortunately, I'm not sure how much help I can be. You already know that Ernie died of lung cancer."

"Yes, but his smoking probably contributed to that, don't you think?"

"Probably. Albert never smoked or chewed and he's still kicking about. My mother died of breast cancer."

Okay. It was established that cancer existed in Delaney's line. But Annie was interested in Casey's at the moment. "What about Jeremiah's mother? Do you know anything about her?"

"Well, she left when he was a teenager, so I don't know if she's alive or dead. I do remember stories about her losing a baby or two."

Annie shot forward in her chair, clutching the collar of her blouse. "What?"

"During pregnancy. They weren't born yet. She had trouble with miscarriages."

"Oh," Annie gripped the edge of the desk, stricken by relief. "Casey doesn't have that problem. She's well into her third trimester."

"Good. Other than that, I don't know a whole lot about Ernie's side of the family. As you recall, we weren't real close."

"No," she murmured, more to herself than Delaney. "Is there anything about your grandfather that stands out?"

"Not really. I think Grandpa Ladd died from a moon-shine overdose."

"And your grandmother?"

"Not sure, really. She was a mouse of a woman from what I remember. Died early but I can't say from what. A blessing in disguise, if you ask me."

Annie understood. Old man Ladd was a bear of a man, his reputation for violence scorched the earth around him. She'd heard stories about him whipping the boys, even the occasional whisper about him taking his belt to his daughter, Susannah. Annie didn't remember much about Mrs. Ladd, only that her husband was a man to steer clear of. "Okay. If you think of anything else, let me know will you?"

"Is there something the doctor is worried about in particular?"

"Not that he said, other than a complete history would help in diagnosing any problems before they became significant."

Delaney scoffed. "That sounds reassuring."

Annie thought it vague as well, but without the first scrap of medical knowledge she was in no position to question the man. "Like I said, if anything comes to you, give me a call."

"Will do."

Ending the call, Annie pushed up from her desk, staring at the blank notepad in dismay. She didn't know any more now than when she'd initiated the call. Thoughts of Casey barreled into her mind. She'd been upset when they left the office, more concerned than she let on, and it worried Annie. Of course it had to do with Troy. She asked the doctor if the baby's father mattered when it came to his health history questions and his muted response of "perhaps" had thrown Casey into a tailspin. Clearly, she didn't want to tell Troy the truth, and she certainly didn't want there to be a *reason* to tell him. Turning out the light, Annie felt her own tailspin of emotion coming on. Watching her daughter bottle up emotional stress during her pregnancy was taking its toll. From what she read in the baby magazines, stress could be a killer. Physical, emotional, mental stress could take a toll on a woman's body and wreak havoc on her unborn child, yet Annie was powerless to do anything about it. Casey had to be the one to calm her fears. Casey had to be the one to settle her heart. Could she?

That was the question.

Lying in bed, Delaney trained her eyes through the black of night, locating a knotty patch of log above. Roughhewn, the construction of her mother's hideaway cabin was as rustic as it came, the bare minimum in construction and shelter. But then again, considering the entire cabin was built by her mother's brothers, Ernie and Albert Ladd, the feat took on a whole new value. Amazing really what they were able to accomplish, and as teenagers no less.

Motivated by love and a fierce sense of devotion, the boys would have moved mountains for their sister, Susannah. They would have done anything to protect her from the brutal hand of their father. Delaney closed her eyes, warding off visions of an abusive Grandpa Ladd against his helpless daughter. Delaney remembered bits and pieces of his rage from her own childhood, but it was the tales Uncle Albert told that set her heart on fire. Not only was Grandpa Ladd's heart hard as rock, but his hand was swift with a belt, whipping the boys on a regular basis. Knowing them as she did now, Delaney could understand they might have deserved some of it, at least on occasion. But her mother?

The bastard even took the leather strap to her. Thinking back, Delaney couldn't imagine her mom enduring anything so brutal, yet she never once mentioned it, never once spoke a cross word against her father. Granted her mom didn't speak many kind words either, but from what Delaney had learned, the man deserved a tongue lashing and then some. Delaney likened Ernie's and Albert's efforts on her mother's behalf to what she was trying to do for Felicity, only it wasn't physical abuse she feared for her daughter. It was emotional.

Next to her, Nick caressed the fine hairs around her forehead. He was a gentle and loving man. It felt good to have him close, felt good to have him in her life. She could hear his soft rhythmic breathing, sense the mutiny of words brimming at his lips. He was a strong man, a good man. The idea of striking a woman was as reprehensible to him as it was to her, yet he didn't agree with her choice to withhold the truth from Felicity. He believed she should have been told. It would have helped her to understand the divorce, understand the grit of her mother's love.

It was a decision Delaney was beginning to regret herself. If she'd been honest with Felicity years ago, she wouldn't be facing the current predicament. Felicity would understand why a relationship with her father was toxic. But Felicity didn't understand. She didn't understand the first hint of the reality that awaited her, disguised behind the walls of an elegant home and beautiful people because Delaney had withheld the information.

"Should I tell her?"

Nick's hand stilled. "Now?"

"Better late than never," she said, pathetic words fading into the darkness.

"Do you want her to have a relationship with her grandparents?"

"They've never been interested in one before."

"Why not?"

A host of reasons, not the least of which was embarrassment. Mrs. Foster was a society type. Her son's behavior was a stain on her reputation, one she couldn't remove, no matter how hard she tried, and she'd claw her way past any truth to prevent a town full of gossip. Then there was her animosity for Susannah, borne from a jealousy she couldn't get past. Jack's father didn't help. Gerald Foster understood his sons were hellions, accepted the fact. They were his blood and he wasn't going to forsake them. He might try to round them up and tie them to nearby post on occasion, but he wasn't about to abandon them.

Susannah Ladd's granddaughter was a different story. The spitting image of her grandmother, Felicity could only remind Gerald of the one woman he loved and lost. It was a love story of epic proportions in the local rumor mill. To this day, almost fifty years later, the town whispered about Gerald Foster and Susannah Ladd, at least those who knew them back then. But Susannah married Harry Wilkins, forever scarring Gerald's heart. A reality Victoria had to live with every day. A reality that bit deep.

"Jack's mother has never invited Felicity over because it's a cap of crickets she doesn't want to open."

"Huh?"

Delaney rolled her head toward Nick. "Jack's father used to have it bad for my mother. He wanted to marry her, but Ernie hated him with a passion and did everything in his power to split the two apart. Since Ernie was her older brother, my mom listened to him. She wouldn't go against him." After all, she owed her safety and well-being to him, as well as this cabin. She ended up falling in love and marrying my father."

Nick rose up onto an elbow. Resting his hand on her abdomen, a sharp interest cut into his voice. "You don't say?"

"I do. It was a big to do back in the day. Some of the ears in town still burn with the story of Gerald and Susannah."

"What's that got to do with Felicity and Gerald's wife?"

"Felicity is the spitting image of my mother."

Nick let out his breath in a heavy sigh. "Enough said. And Victoria knows?"

"I don't know how much she knows about the relationship between Gerald and my mother. She's originally from Chattanooga, and I doubt anyone around here would have filled in the blanks for her. But Gerald knows. I'll guarantee you it's why he hasn't pushed the subject."

"My, my, you mountain folks never cease to entertain."

Delaney jabbed him with an elbow.

"Ouch!" Grabbing hold of her improvised missile he said, "I meant that as a compliment."

"Sure you did."

Nick chuckled, sliding her arm over her midsection to keep it securely intact with his hand. She could see every line in his face, every ounce of his smile, the glimmer in his eyes. Even in the dark Delaney could envision her husband as clear as if he were standing in a valley of sunshine. He leaned close and whispered into the side of her head, sending a shaft of tingles across her chest. "I was referring to the level of passion. You country gals can really lasso a man into knots."

The image amused her. "So take notes."

He laughed. "I am, sweetheart. I am."

"Anyway..." Delaney sighed, thrusting a stream of tension from her lungs. "Felicity is walking into a hornet's nest over there and I don't know what to do about it."

"Do you think they're going to rehash the past for her benefit?"

"No. I'm afraid they're going to be tense and edgy, and she's going to think they don't like her."

"Don't sell your daughter short. Felicity is made of strong fiber. A few stiff old folks aren't going to injure her soul."

"Rejection is a pretty strong weapon. It's something you wouldn't understand."

"Because I come from a picture-perfect family?"

"Don't you?" At Nick's hesitation, Delaney grunted. "At least you can't lie," she said. Nick interlaced his fingers with hers and Delaney was glad for the connection. The weight of their hands together felt firm, solid. Like him. It wasn't his fault he was raised by two loving parents. Nor was it hers that she came from a family of dysfunction. "I don't want her to get hurt. You can understand that, can't you?"

"Life is full of hurt. She's a young woman with a good head on her shoulders. She's smart and strong and she has you to thank for that." Nick lightly squeezed her hands. "She'll be fine."

Delaney appreciated the vote of confidence but didn't share his conviction. When loved ones let you down, it hurt like a knife through the heart. A stake through the soul. It was a hurt that never left you.

"Speaking of hurt, are you sure about your decision to hire Troy? Talk about hornet's nest. That young man has a knack for smacking things."

Taking in the shape of his head and face, Delaney imagined his eyes as deep and dark as endless pools, pools that could swallow her whole. "Honestly?" She closed her eyes. "I'm not sure of anything at the moment.

## Chapter Nine

Troy's body gently swayed side-to-side as his truck rolled over the gravelly road that led to Hotel Ladd's staff parking lot. At six-thirty in the morning, he was challenging the sun in both vigor and timing. He was pumped to start his first day on the job. Delaney had called him last night and told him to show up first thing in the morning. No questions, no threats, no conditions. *You start tomorrow at seven.* He couldn't believe his luck, but he was going to make dang sure she didn't regret it. He was gonna be the best stable hand she ever saw this side of the Appalachian Mountains. Clear across to the Rockies, for that matter. She'd given him a chance because she believed in him.

It was a trust he wasn't going to break.

Delaney told him the staff parking area was hidden from hotel view by a pack of trees, the center of which was cut by a stretch of trail connecting hotel and stables. He found it easy enough and pulled into the space closest to the trees. Grabbing his hat, he climbed down and tossed the door closed, headed in. It was a quiet time of day when only the birds were awake, swooping overhead in the trees, their high-pitched whistles distinct, penetrating the misty mountain morning. At this hour the air was marked by a chill, the damp smell of earth pronounced as he followed the path through the trees. Used to be he never saw this hour, let alone looked forward to it. He used to sleep in every chance he got, including school days if his parents would have allowed. He'd rather stay up late and wake up late. But his life had changed. It had to change. He couldn't go on hurting the people closest to him by slacking.

Looking ahead through the trees, Troy immersed himself in the sensation of boots and ground, the fragrant pine and laurel and the fresh scent of land. Branches floated overhead, roots jutted up from an uneven path of clay dirt. Gray rocks of all sizes lined the way, most covered by patches of white fungus. Inhaling deeply, he thought this was pure Tennessee. Pure mountain living. There was no place he'd rather be than right here, headed for a day with his horses. They weren't technically his, but when Troy worked with horses, they became a part of him, like his very own. He bonded with each and every animal, forging a connection that allowed him to speak their language, train them for a purpose that suited them both. Horses were work animals, social animals. They liked to serve, liked to be part of a group. The only thing that would make the day better was knowing he'd be going home to Casey afterward where he could share his day. His heart squeezed. But that wasn't gonna happen for a while. If ever, his heart whispered, though he refused to listen. He couldn't give up on her. Not now, not ever. A flash of black caught his eye. He stilled. Was that a bear?

Examining the distant foliage for signs of movement, Troy held his breath. His pulse quickened. Sure enough, a black patch of body was negotiating its way through the wooded space. Slow, leisurely, the animal picked its way through the brush, emerging onto the trail ahead of him. Troy edged off the trail a hair, careful not to draw attention to himself. The bear was a good size, too, easily capable of causing harm if he wanted. The bulky animal swung its head around, a tan tapered snout lifting in his direction. Troy tensed. Curious but unfazed by his presence, the animal returned to its business, lumbering in the direction of the stables. The bear didn't seem to care one whit about him, sniffing and poking into bushes. Troy instantly wondered at guest encounters with the animals. Was Mr. Foster worried about such a thing?

They claimed the hotel was at one with nature. Did visitors from other countries really understand what that meant in these parts? Troy chuckled to himself. He sure hoped so or they'd be in for one heck of a surprise! Allowing the animal to put some distance and privacy between them, Troy continued but at a slower pace. While they were at it, he mused, folks better keep their eyes peeled for snakes too. They were plenty of them along the riverbanks and creeks, openly sunning themselves on rocks and logs. Deadly ones, to boot.

As the trail widened, Troy's thoughts shifted toward the horses. He wondered what Miss Delaney had in store for him. Would she let him work with the horses or assign him clean-up duty? He was willing to do anything, though he'd prefer one-on-one contact with the animals. It'd be nice to see Vegas and his momma. Delaney had taken both of them which made Troy feel good. That mare sure was a beauty and good breeding stock from what he'd seen. Delaney would be fortunate to have more like Vegas.

Troy stopped suddenly, struck by a strange sound. Turning his head, he listened. It sounded like someone was whistling. A body came into view where the trail converged into the main one leading out from the hotel. Troy straightened. It was Cal Foster. What was he doing here at this hour?

Kicking into step, Troy approached, the whistle tune becoming clear. *I wish I was in the land of cotton, old times there are not forgotten—look away! Look away! Look away, Dixie Land!* Troy grinned. It was a song he knew by heart. As he waited for Mr. Foster to notice him, Troy silently chimed in. *In Dixie Land I'll take my stand, to live and die in Dixie!*

Recognition was quick as Mr. Foster realized he had company. "Troy!"

"Good morning, Mr. Foster."

"I didn't expect to find anyone out this early. Where are you headed?"

"The stables," Troy informed him proudly. "Miss Delaney called me last night to say I had a job."

Cal laughed. "Well, you're an early one, aren't you?"

"Yes, sir." He gave an eager nod. "Early bird catches the worm."

"Congratulations."

"Thank you, sir." Coming to within feet of each other, Troy was glad the man was happy to see him, happy to hear he'd been hired on.

"It's a beautiful morning, isn't it?"

"Yes, sir."

"Early morning hikes remind me of why I love living in Tennessee."

"Agreed. Kentucky was pretty but didn't have near the appeal."

Cal pressed his lips together in contemplation. "Same with Arizona. You can take the boy out of the mountains but you can't take the mountains out of the boy. They live inside in you."

"Agreed."

"I always do my best thinking at this hour of the day."

Troy couldn't agree on that count. The majority of his thinking was done at night, when he was lying in bed alone. One of the reasons it especially hurt to be away from Casey for so many months. When they were living together in Murfreesboro, his thinking had been easy and free. He could speak openly about what he thought, listen to her opinion on how she saw things. Longing pulled at him. Casey was smart. She could see things he couldn't, hear things he didn't know he was saying. Shaking the emotion, he said, "Saw a black bear back a while ago."

"Did you?"

"Sure did. A real fine sized one out for an early morning stroll like you."

Cal smiled. "Guess I'm not the only one out poking around at this hour." He fixed his gaze on Troy, familiar brown eyes warming. "How are you doing?"

"Fine, sir. Just fine."

"That's good to hear." Troy sensed Mr. Foster wanted to say more, something important, and waited in the thick of the quiet. It was unsettling to feel like you knew a man on the surface, a man who was damn near family yet didn't feel like you had the first clue as to what lay beneath the surface. "Why did you leave, Troy?"

Startled by the abrupt question, he stepped back. "Sir?"

"Tennessee. Why did you leave Tennessee for Kentucky?"

Clearing his throat, he said, "I wanted to prove myself to Casey."

"By leaving her?"

"I didn't *leave* her. Why does everyone keep actin' like I deserted her? I tried to call her but she didn't answer. I called you and told you to watch out for her until I got back."

Cal returned a stern gaze. "It wasn't my responsibility to convince a young woman that her man hasn't run off and left her. I believe I told you as much at the time. She was pretty torn up."

Irritation pitched and heaved in his heart. How could Casey think he would have done such a thing? Because he didn't call her every single day? That was the part that didn't make sense. Sure, she might have been unhappy with the separation, same as him, but how could she think he was never coming back?

"She has her pride, Troy."

Troy dumped his gaze to the trail. "Dad gum," he said, frustration boiling over. "It was a miscommunication. I told her I had to get a job and make something of myself so everyone around here would understand I wasn't a loser!"

Cal's accusatory gaze softened. "No one thinks you're a loser."

Troy nearly tore the hat from his head at the lie but instead turned away with a grunt. Casey's mother was number one on that list, but he wasn't about to insult Mr. Foster's wife by speaking the same. Shoot, his family was a close second. "After what happened, it wasn't like I could've gotten a job around here. I had to start fresh. Kentucky was the only place I had any contacts."

Cal nodded, as though he understood. Troy hoped that he did. He could use some allies right about now, especially if he were going to convince Casey's momma he was worthy of a second chance. Or third. *But who's counting*?

"Have you seen Vegas?" Cal asked, moving to completely different terrain.

"Not yet," he replied, grateful for the shift, "but I was hoping to today."

"He's a strong one. A real fighter, just like you predicted. Six months old and he's already challenging the ranch hands!"

Pride swallowed Troy whole. "He's spirited, is all. Just needs a firm hand an encouragin' word. I bet he'll grow into one of your finest stallions."

Cal winked. "I believe you're right and I bet you're the man to do it."

Troy's cheeks warmed at the compliment. "Thank you, sir. I'd sure like the chance to work with him."

Cal glanced up the trail. "Speaking of work, I'd suggest you get a move on it. Delaney's an early riser too and not the woman you want waiting on you."

"No, sir." Troy tipped his hat. "I'm on my way."

Cal's expression quieted, an understanding simmering in his brown gaze. "Glad to have you on the team, Troy."

No more than he was to be a part of it.


Entering the stables, Troy cruised down the center corridor, searching for sight of Delaney as he skimmed horses in passing. The smell of hay and horse surrounded him, filling him with a pleasure and comfort he'd missed. Hooked by the shake of a small black-maned head through a metal grill, his heart bucked. Was that Vegas?

Troy hurried over to check out the foal. His spirit soared at the distinct white star stamped in the inky black space between his eyes. Black ears perked and big eyes honed in on him. Excitement bounded as he took in the animal. "You're a big one, ain't ya? Just like I thought you'd be." He was strong, sturdy, not spindly like some foals, fully proportioned, only smaller than a full-grown animal. The horse angled its head as Troy reached between the bars for a stroke of the solid-muscled neck, the super-sleek black coat. One ear went forward, the other drifting back as the horse raised his snout. Troy grinned. "You remember me, don't ya?" he asked, more statement than question. "You remember I helped bring you into this world."

The animal gave a soft snort, clearly enjoying the attention. Troy laughed, warm pleasure spreading through him. "They treatin' you all right around here?" He examined the animal from head to toe, noting the shiny hair, the intelligent black eyes. Vegas was relaxed but alert. Troy definitely thought he had a mark of intelligence about him. "You sure do look good. You're gonna grow up to be a big one. Real strong," he said softly. "Fast too, by the looks of those legs of yours."

"I see you've met our star attraction."

Troy whirled, yanking his hand from between the bars. "Hey, Miss Delaney."

She was dressed as usual in ratty low-waisted jeans and tank top, her boots muddied by her active lifestyle, her blonde hair long and loose down her back. A few strands framed her sun-tanned face, her brown eyes gazing at him with a fondness he remembered well. "Vegas seems to have taken a liking to you."

Slightly embarrassed at being caught loving on the animal, Troy replied, "This here's the one I was telling you about. The one I helped deliver over at the Foster ranch."

She nodded. "Looks like he remembers you."

Gratification swept through him. "Maybe." Casting a glance over his shoulder he said, "He's a smart one. Gonna make you a real fine stallion one day."

"All he needs is the perfect trainer."

Hope bounded. "I sure could teach him a thing or two."

"I'll bet you can."

The sentiment was more observation than encouragement and gave him pause. Troy focused on Delaney's eyes, searching for the reassurance he so desperately yearned for yet finding a reticence instead. "Everything all right?" he asked as casually as he could. "You seem a little down."

A faint smile crossed her lips. "You've known me a long time, haven't you?"

"Yes, ma'am," he replied, grateful to realize this might not be about him but about her.

"It's Felicity."

Concern jabbed at him. "She okay?"

"Yes. She's going to the Fosters to meet the family."

Foreboding erased all question. She didn't have to say another word. Troy knew the history. Felicity didn't have a relationship with her grandparents on her daddy's side. They were kin, lived in the same town, but as remote as family could get. Growing up, Felicity never talked about them much. Maybe she said more to Travis than him, but it was understood by the three of them to be a taboo subject. Jack Foster and his family weren't on the list of conversation. Not until Casey's momma began dating Cal did they even dare mention the family. When Miss Delaney began puttin' Casey and Felicity together, Troy understood it was only a matter of time before the Fosters could no longer be ignored. But Felicity was harboring thoughts of getting to know them better? "What for?"

Delaney's mouth tipped up at one corner. She must have been wondering the same thing. "They invited her."

Pulling his hat slightly forward, Troy scratched behind an ear. "That seems odd. Real odd. Anything I can do to help?"

"Talk her out of it?"

"Seriously?" Delaney's quick half-laugh assured him she was kidding. Troy tried to laugh with her but came up short. "I mean, I would if you wanted me to..."

"But it wouldn't do any good," she finished his thought. Delaney stared at Troy, her dark gaze hot, intense, like she was trying to see clear through him. He'd always known her as a sharp-edged woman, but he'd never been on the wrong end of her blade. It was a bit unsettling. Planting her hands to her hips she said, "Can I ask you a question?"

"Sure."

"Has Felicity ever mentioned the Fosters?"

"Mentioned them how?"

"You know, has she ever indicated that she wanted to see them? That she missed out on being with them through the years?"

"No." He shook his head. "Never did." It was the honest truth.

"What about her father? Did she ever mention wanting to get to know him?"

"No, ma'am. Felicity didn't ever mention wantin' to be close to the man." Strange, but where Troy thought she'd be happy to hear the words, Delaney seemed depressed by them.

"A girl needs her father, Troy." He returned a blank stare. Was he supposed to have a comment on that? "A girl needs a strong man in her life." A point he couldn't argue. "I told Casey I was going to give you a job."

Troy lost balance at the blunt statement. "Was she mad?"

Delaney shook her head. "Actually, she was pleased. Said you were the best horse man around."

Pleasure swamped him like a tidal wave, forcing him to take a step back. "I know my business, Miss Delaney. I'll do right by you, you can count on it."

"I know you will."

Her reply was soft as a drifting cloud, yet it was her gaze that punched him in the chest. She believed in him. There was no doubt in her eyes. There was no question, only a vague something hovering behind the deep brown of her gaze. It wasn't doubt, it was...it was...

Troy didn't know.

In the blink of an eye, whatever had been hiding behind her eyes disappeared. Delaney straightened, shook her hair and returned to business mode. "C'mon. I'll check you in at the office then introduce you around to the staff. We have guests signed up for trail rides at nine and running all day, with a carriage ride at sunset."

Troy fell into step beside her as she strode toward the office, unsettled by a twinge of uncertainty. Why had Delaney brought up Casey? Did she think there was a chance for the two of them? Was Casey really happy to hear he was working for the hotel?

## Chapter Ten

Felicity sat in her car outside the Foster estate, her heart riddled with nerves. Her stomach was a mess, her insides churning up a storm. The Foster home was so big it looked like a hotel. Two-storied and completely built from brick, it had a porch that stretched from one end to the other, wrapping around both sides. A huge lantern hung from the second floor ceiling by a thick chain and centered over two massive front doors. Windows lined upstairs and downstairs, causing her to wonder how many rooms were inside. The tiny cabin she shared with her mother had one bedroom, one living area and a kitchen tucked into a corner. Her bedroom wasn't enclosed, rather a loft overhead with a makeshift bathroom. She'd always loved her home. It was like living in a tree fort, a secret hideaway in the woods. She gulped. She'd never been inside a home as big as the Fosters. Even the Parker home wasn't as big as this one. Shoot, this wasn't a home—it was a mansion! Would there be servant's quarters? Maids and butlers running around asking what they wanted, if they were okay?

She was going to stand out like a dope on a highway. She didn't know how to act around wealthy people. Were their plates made of gold? Their glasses made from expensive crystal? The front door opened and her heart stopped. A dark-headed man stepped outside and relief swept through her. *It was her father*. Words she was still getting used to. Dressed casually in jeans and a button-down plaid, Jack Foster was a man she hardly knew—in and out of her life for as long as she could remember—yet here she was about to have dinner with him and his parents. He spotted her and a quick smile formed on his lips. He waved for her to come on, a gesture so casual, so normal, it felt strange.

Pushing from her car, Felicity gathered her purse and instantly assessed her attire in comparison. Had she overdone it by choosing an ankle length skirt and heels? Her blouse was a silk floral that could go either way but... She raised her head to face him. Her father looked like he was hanging out at the stables. She looked like she was going to some ladies' luncheon. When she didn't move from her car, he began to walk toward her. Shoving the car door closed, she hurried to him.

When she neared, his smile grew into one of genuine appreciation. "Well, don't you look beautiful this evening."

"Thank you," she replied quickly, privately cursing her reaction. Her fair skin freckles would light up like a sheet of red bulbs and surely expose her for the simpleton she was! She inhaled as deep and full as she could to calm the flutter of pulse.

"My parents are anxious to meet you."

"Me, too," she replied and followed him inside the enormous wood-paneled front door.

Weird. She had grandparents who lived in the same town but who had never officially met their granddaughter. Felicity had seen them around town, of course. But usually flanked by her mother or the Parker boys, and it never seemed like a good time to say hello. Then again, how did one say hello to family members she barely knew? *Hiya, I'm your granddaughter, the one your son abandoned.* Or did her mother leave *him*? Felicity was fuzzy on the details. All she knew was her parents divorced and the relations were sour as buttermilk.

As she entered, the interior took her breath away. In the foyer sat the largest bouquet of flowers she'd ever seen perched on a pedestal table beneath a huge chandelier. It was glittery and glassy and light sparkled through it like diamonds floating in the air. Inclining her head forward, she noted a huge stone fireplace across the room, empty of flame at the moment, topped by a wood beam mantle. It looked more like a heavy log than an actual mantle. On it were a bunch of framed portraits. She couldn't make out any of the faces from here but assumed they included the extended family. A fleeting thought occurred to her. Was she up there? Did they display a picture of her even though she wasn't actively part of their life? Allowing her gaze to drift over Oriental rugs sprawled across shiny wood floors, she gazed upon sofas of soft brown leather, their seams lined by rounded metal bolts. Fat, interior wood posts reached from floor to ceiling, supporting equally large beams overhead, their wood surfaces sanded to a polished shine. The smell of evergreen potpourri infused her senses.

"What do you think?" Jack asked.

"It's gorgeous," she murmured. Ambling further inside, she realized the extended family was in attendance. She flung her gaze to him. He didn't mention all these people would be here!

Mrs. Foster rose from a wing chair. Gliding across the floor in almost fairy-like movement, she reminded Felicity of the dance majors at college. As a flutist, she often spent time in the Theater Department watching waiflike actresses dance and sing. Some were amazing, mesmerizing her with their ability to sweep across a stage in weightless fashion. Jack's mother could have been one of them. Extending a hand, the woman introduced herself. "I'm Victoria Foster. Your grandmother."

Anxiety streamed through Felicity's limbs as she accepted the slender hand. Mrs. Foster's skin was so delicate, it felt paper-fine in her grasp. "I'm Felicity Wilk—" Realizing her error, her cheeks burned hot.

Mrs. Foster simply smiled, overlooking it as nothing more than a minor misstep. The senior Mr. Foster shadowed her, staring at Felicity with a strange look on his face as his wife said, "We're so glad you decided to join us."

"Thanks for having me."

Mrs. Foster turned, and introduced the rest of the family. "Boys, come say hello to your niece. Two strapping men stepped from behind the sofa. Two women she assumed to be their wives remained seated until their prospective men escorted them forward. "Clint, Beau, I'd like you to meet Felicity."

Mrs. Foster spoke as if they hadn't been standing there the entire time, witnessing the previous exchange. The tallest one of the group stuck out a hand to greet her. Warm and firm, his grip matched the strong lines of his face, his skin tanned and weathered from a life outdoors. He looked a lot like her father, only bigger. "Beau Foster. About time my lazy brother brought you around to meet the family."

She smiled, accepting the insult as a compliment to her. "Nice to meet you."

"I'd like you to meet my wife, Becky Lynn."

Felicity greeted the attractive brunette by his side. Trim and fit, she could have been a model in her form-fitting denim skirt and high-heeled boots. Her white blouse was adorned with a row of frilly lace down the center, her teeth perfect and gleaming white.

The second Foster brother did likewise. "I'm Clint. This here's my wife, Tara." Felicity shook hands with the woman. A bit more subdued than the first yet equally as good-looking, she wore a simple cotton skirt and matching top, the sandy color a near match to her long straight hair. "You sure are a pretty thing," she said.

"Thank you," Felicity replied, annoyed by the repeated flare in her cheeks. It undermined any savvy she attempted to exude.

"I told you she was a looker," Jack said. "Looks nothing like her mother."

"Hush your mouth," Mrs. Foster admonished with a sharp glance.

Felicity wasn't surprised by her father's comment. After living with the animosity for all these years, his feelings popped out naturally. Her mom's did the same. "It's okay," Felicity assured. "I know what he means."

"You look exactly like your grandmother."

Startled by the fragile quality of his voice, Felicity looked to Jack's father. His plaid flannel shirt and pressed jeans suggested a strong outdoorsman—tall, in pretty good shape for his age, complete with a full head of brown hair. She would have expected him to be more outgoing, yet his first words—practically a whisper—were powerful enough to strike the room silent. *How did he know her grandmother*?

No one said a word as he approached her, muttering, "It's uncanny, the resemblance."

And eerie, the way he was staring at her. He looked as though he were under some kind of spell. Mrs. Foster must have noticed it, too, because her expression had changed from friendly to stunned. Felicity took a step backward, closer to her father. Suddenly, the man she hardly knew felt like a security blanket.

"Dad, you're staring." His blunt observation cut his father's stupor. It was like an eraser had been swiped over a whiteboard. Collecting himself in a complete sweep of transformation, he boomed with a large, affable smile, "Excuse my manners. Gerald Foster." He reached for her hand and shook gently. "We're happy to have you in our home, Felicity."

Felicity peered at the solemn expressions surrounding him and thought, *Turn around. You might discover you're alone in that sentiment.*

The air of discomfort was cleared quickly as Mrs. Foster regained control of the situation and re-directed everyone back into party mode. She unleashed a litany of questions, beginning with how did Felicity enjoy college, what courses was she taking, what was her major, her future plans, what did she think of the new hotel... It was an exhausting dialogue, punctuated by the occasional question from other family members. Everyone took part except Mr. Foster. He took a back seat to most of the conversation, though he was clearly dialed in, staring at her in the oddest way.

As they sat down to dinner, her father lit the line of tapered candles, elegant symbols of family unity coming to life one by one, pulling a subtle gleam from the silver lighter he used. Rimmed in gold, it seemed pretty fancy for a lighter, more like an heirloom or valuable collectible. After the senior Mr. Foster led them in blessing, talk slowed, grew comfortable, and Felicity found she was actually beginning to enjoy herself. Her father was nowhere near the monster her mother described. He seemed intelligent, witty, good-natured. No one at the table seemed to have a problem with him. Sure, he was family and family tended to overlook the blemishes, but she'd seen strained family relations and these weren't it. They were downright friendly people and Felicity was glad she accepted the invitation. Wait until her mother heard.

The two wives stood and began clearing plates. Plucking the cloth napkin from her lap, Felicity rose to do likewise, but her father's hand stopped her. "Sit. Relax. You're a guest this evening."

She looked to him in objection. "But—"

Mrs. Foster reinforced the fact with a tip of her head. "The girls will see to the dishes. Thelma's in there to help them. I'd like to hear more about your flute. I'm fascinated. Do you play as part of an orchestra?"

Slowly Felicity dropped back into her chair, a river of mixed emotion tumbling through her. Her mother would not be happy to know she sat during cleanup. It was her job as the youngest female in the group to clear dishes and clean pots. On the other hand, Mrs. Foster was the matriarch and she dictated which women did what. Besides, she sounded genuinely interested in her music. Glancing aside to her father, his wink reinforced the request to sit and discuss her music. "Well, sometimes." Settling onto the plush seat cushion, she readjusted to being in the spotlight. "Mostly I play solo. Eventually I'll take part in a symphony performance, but for the time being, I'm concentrating on improving my skills."

"You must be so dedicated, dear. Playing a musical instrument requires a due diligence none of my boys seemed to master."

Beau and Clint sat neutral while her father shrugged it off. "Music isn't for everyone," he said.

"As I recall, you were too busy for music lessons," Beau said.

Jack laughed. "That I was and having a heck of a good time!"

Both Mr. and Mrs. Foster ignored the commentary, she interjecting, "Music will take you far, Felicity. There are so many ways it will benefit you in the long run, you have no idea."

"She's right," Mr. Foster chimed in, drawing her attention to him. Seated at the head of the table, his wife at his side, he definitely felt like the head of the household despite his tendency toward quiet observation. His presence was imposing, commanding. He felt every bit the wealthy, successful man she'd always heard him to be. One of the Foster wives removed his plate and he immediately filled the space with the spread of his elbows. "As a musician, you'll broaden your horizons, travel in good circles, meet good people. I have several friends back in Chattanooga that might be able to help you should you pursue a career as a flutist."

"Oh, I'm definitely going to be a flutist," Felicity replied. She was unequivocal about her career choice. Travis was going to law school and she was going to pursue her music to the Masters level and beyond.

Gerald Foster smiled, a bit patronizing but affably so. "I believe you will. But life has a way of changing hearts. What we start out wanting isn't always what we end up having."

A distinct chill entered his wife's eyes. Oblivious to the change, Mr. Foster continued, "Ask any one of my boys. They'll tell you. Your job is to keep moving forward, upward until you find your way. My advice is to try and enjoy the ride."

"Yes, sir." Felicity lowered her gaze, uncomfortable with a new agitation creeping into the dining room, beginning and ending with her grandmother. Suddenly Felicity felt like an intruder. "If you'll excuse me, I'd like to freshen up."

Mr. Foster arched a brow as Mrs. Foster replied, "Certainly, dear. Bathroom is down the hall past the kitchen."

"Thank you."

She stood, the men mirroring her movements, then hurried from the table in as controlled a manner as she could. Once clear of the room, she could hear the muted whispers commence in her absence. Something was eating at them—something they didn't want her to know. Passing the kitchen, Felicity glimpsed the wives setting plates in the dishwasher, the housekeeper moving in and around them. Second-guessing her obligation to help, Felicity forced herself forward, reminding herself she was a guest here. She didn't know these people. Maybe this was the way they preferred it.

Safely inside the bathroom, Felicity marveled at the stone vanity, the intricately carved cabinets. Elaborate sconce lighting glowed from either side of a wood-framed mirror, its finish glazed gold. The ceramic toilet gleamed, appearing untouched by a human hand. Turning from it, she wasn't about to be the first. She'd only come in here as escape. Drawing the length of her French braid forward, she peered at her reflection, wondering if anyone else noticed. Every time Mr. Foster spoke up, he punctured the mood with innocent commentary. His words seemed harmless yet the reaction they incited was anything but. *Did no one care for the man? Were husband and wife at odds?* Her mom never mentioned any problems between them. Then again, she never mentioned them, period.

Felicity wasn't naïve. She knew there were people who put forth a pretty face for the community while they clawed each other's eyes out behind the scenes. Were the Fosters that way? Was this entire evening a charade for her benefit? Why waste the effort? She hadn't seen or talked with them for the last ten years, why start now?

Because her father insisted. Because her father wanted to re-establish their connection. Jack Foster had moved back home. He was rebuilding his life, he claimed, and wanted it to include her. Just because her mother didn't like him didn't mean *she* had to dislike him. She'd learned a lot about relationships during a psychology course at college. People were complicated, unpredictable and weird. They had issues and usually communicated their feelings poorly. That was her take away message. Her family was only proof positive. Seemed maybe the Fosters were, too.

Felicity inhaled deep and full, calming the last flitter of doubt. This wasn't her issue. Whatever their problems were, they weren't hers. She was here because her father asked her to be, nothing more and nothing less. If this dinner led to a deeper relationship in the future, then so be it. Like he said, she was her own woman. If her mother didn't like it, tough. She'd have to live with it. A smile erupted from Felicity. Part of her liked challenging her mom. It made her feel strong, independent. Tossing her braid, she thrust her shoulders back and emerged from the bathroom. Giving a tug to her blouse, she felt good.

There had been no harm in this dinner. None. Nearing the open doorway to the kitchen, Felicity overheard, "I'm surprised Jack invited her over in the first place."

"Me, too. Between him and his father, the two should be ashamed of themselves."

Felicity paused, her pulse lodged squarely in her throat.

"Gerald is making a complete fool of himself over the girl."

"It's embarrassing. I feel so sorry for Victoria."

"Do you think she knows about the beating?"

Felicity clamped a hand over her mouth and stepped back against the wall. *Beating*?

"I doubt it. Gerald does, I know that for a fact. Abby Sue told me that her daddy confronted him directly on the issue. Asked him point blank if his son was guilty."

"He *didn't*!"

"Yes, ma'am he did and Gerald confirmed it."

"I would think he'd deny it to his grave."

"Apparently not. And why should he? The whole town knows."

The other woman hummed in agreement—an agreement to what, Felicity had no clue. Was her father guilty of a beating? Had he been in a bar brawl? Arrested?

"I'm only surprised Delaney didn't stop her from coming."

"I am, too. Especially with that new husband of hers."

"You'd think he'd mind his new daughter going to the home of her mother's abuser."

"Even if it is family."

Dread iced Felicity's bones.

"Jack always was a cold-hearted one."

"Even Beau agrees."

"Clint, too. You know he supported Delaney when she moved out. Offered to help her find a place."

"He's so sweet."

"Jack isn't. I tell you, I don't know why we even had to be here. Hitting a woman casts a black mark on the entire family and now I feel dirty. Guilty by association. You know what I mean?"

"Uh-hm, I do."

Felicity shrank away from the doorway, melted into the wall. She couldn't listen to another word. Her father an abuser? Against her mother?

## Chapter Eleven

"Calm down, Felicity. You're not making any sense! What beating? Who are we talking about?"

Felicity clenched the phone in hand, nerves peeling the skin from her body. Travis wasn't getting it. He wasn't getting it! "My father! My father is an abuser!"

"What? Did he hit you?"

"No, not me!"

"Then who?"

"My mother!"

"What?"

Felicity couldn't respond anymore. Her vocal cords had been stripped taut, her eyes swollen with tears. Listening to those women gossip about her parents had been the most horrible moment of her life. She'd been humiliated, reduced to hiding in a bathroom until her father came looking for her. *Felicity, are you all right in there*?

She pretended to be sick. She pretended to be vomiting. She ran the faucet, flushed the toilet, refused to talk to him. Her father had abused her mother. Her mom left him because he hit her. *Why had she never said anything*?

"You're not making any sense," came Travis' rational voice through the phone—rational to the point of madness. "Start from the beginning and tell me what happened."

When was the beginning? The day her father beat her mother? The day they were married? How often had it happened? How long did it go on? Why?

There were so many questions, none of which made sense. Felicity couldn't imagine any man hitting her mother and living to tell about it. Her mother was a bull. She was tough and strong and while sometimes it got on Felicity's nerves, it certainly would have served her well if a man came at her with his fists. Why didn't she shoot him?

She carried a gun. Without fail she carried a pistol tucked in her boot. Where was that when all this was happening? It didn't make sense. None of it made sense.

"Where are you?" Travis asked, his tone placating, cautious, as though he didn't want to spook her. "I'll come and get you."

Felicity looked around her. Where was she?

After splashing her face to mimic a sick person the best she could, she'd made her excuses and drove away from the home, drove as far and as fast as she could. "I'm in a parking lot at the Piggly Wiggly."

"Which one?"

She glanced around the premises, but nothing looked familiar. There was a liquor store, a gas station, several lamp posts casting the parking lot in dingy yellow. "I don't know."

"Are you near a road? Can you check?"

The impatience in his voice grated on her. "I don't know where I am, Travis. I left as fast as I could." She couldn't stand to be in that house with those people another second! Didn't he get that?

"Okay, okay, I'm sorry. I'll check the Piggly Wiggly locations and find you. Don't move."

Done. She couldn't move if she had to, her body limp from fear, nerves, shock—all of the above. Jack Foster had hit her mother. It was unforgivable. Unfathomable. What hurt worse than knowing her father was a creep was the fact that her mother knowingly allowed her to go into his home unescorted. Let her waltz in there thinking everything was okay, these people were normal, they could kiss and make up. It cut Felicity in half, split her heart in two like nothing ever had. What happened to the overprotective mother, the one she grew up with, tolerated? Didn't she care about her well-being? Didn't she care what happened to her daughter?

Gnawing on her lip, Felicity double-checked the locks on her doors. Phone clutched in lap, she watched for signs of trouble. But with few people walking around at this hour she felt okay. She was temporarily okay. Her thoughts reverted back to the Fosters. Those women talked about father *and* son. What did Gerald have to do with any of it? Had he covered for his son? Gone against her and her mom somehow? Horrible images of him hitting Victoria Foster crossed her mind. Was he an abuser too?

It might explain his odd behavior tonight. He hardly said a word and when he did, it seemed to be the wrong one. The whole deal was wrong. She should never have gone. *Would* never have gone if she knew the truth. Tears swam into her eyes. Why didn't her mother prevent this from happening in the first place? And Nick. The women mentioned Nick. Did he know? Was that why he tried to talk her out of coming? But he had to. They said the whole town knew. Everyone knew. Everyone knew but her!

Delaney paced the living room. Nick remained on the couch, calm, quiet. He didn't try to stop her. He didn't say a word. He sat and he waited. Regarding him with a wary heart, she asked, "Where could she be? It's eleven o'clock?"

"Maybe they're having a good time."

"I doubt it."

"It's possible."

"Doubtful."

"The Fosters seem like nice people."

"Jack isn't."

"But she's not with Jack alone, is she?"

"No."

Nick outstretched an arm along the back of the couch and cocked a brow. "Well, then?"

Delaney grunted. Felicity was not having a good time. She couldn't be. Not when Jack was involved. Felicity was a smart girl. She'd see through the Fosters and her father's charade in no time.

Time. That's what Delaney had given her. Time and space to learn the truth on her own. The truth. Well, not the *whole* truth but enough of the truth to trim her curiosity. Jack was playing games with Felicity and while Delaney didn't know his end game, she did know it was a game. Jack didn't care about anyone but himself. She'd missed it as a teenager but it was clear as the blue sky to the adult in her. Jack was self-indulgent, self-centered and insensitive. He might convince himself he was the good guy here, but he wasn't. In time Felicity would discover the same for herself. And it would hurt.

Delaney stopped, glanced over at Nick. As though sensing her need, he rose and came to her. Sliding her arms around his solid torso, she sank into the hard line of his body, inhaled the warm subtle traces of his cologne. He was her strength, her support. Whatever happened, Nick would help. "I'm worried about her."

He stroked her head, the hair down her back. "I know you are."

"She's going to get hurt."

"We've discussed this. It might be a reality she has to face, come to terms with."

"But she's not prepared."

"She'll deal with it. She's a strong young woman. She'll cope with whatever comes her way."

Delaney gazed up at him. Soothed by the steel underlay in his dark eyes, she knew. If the sky fell into the valley, Nick would pick it back up and stuff it back into place. No matter what happened, he'd make everything right. He did it with Jillian. Sent her packing after she tried to steal their land. He'd do so with Jack. There were no words for the gratitude and love Delaney felt for Nick. No words to describe the support she knew she could count on from this man. Nick was her rock. "Thank you."

"You're welcome. Now come over here and warm me up some cornbread. I'm starving."

"Starving?" She gaped at him, glad for the reprieve into normalcy. "You ate half the pan of bread with your chicken—the second pan!"

"And I'm still hungry. Now go on and make your man some food, woman." He kissed the top of her head with a simultaneous pat to her rear. "It's in the contract."

Delaney remained in his embrace, smiling up at him. "I signed no such contract."

"Well, you should have. I'll never be the same without your cooking."

"You mean my cornbread." Nick ate the stuff like it was candy.

"Cornbread, chicken, grits, it's all good. And speaking of good, when are you going to make me some of that sweet potato casserole?"

"Sweet potato casserole?"

"Yes, you know, the stuff Ashley served us for Thanksgiving. How many times do I have to beg before you give in and make it?"

Delaney laughed. "It's not sweet potato season."

"It isn't?"

"No."

"Well, how long do I have to wait?"

Delaney released and shook her head. "You sure do have a one track mind."

He grinned. "That's what makes me successful in life. Now when?"

"I'll talk to Ashley and find out when she's pulling them up."

"Good. My mother didn't grow sweet potatoes when I was growing up. I think they're my new favorite."

"What happened to my cornbread?"

He pecked her nose. "Right after your cornbread."

Plodding off to the kitchen, she plucked the cornbread pan from the counter and toted it to the oven for a re-heat. At least cooking gave her something to do other than worry.

In the dark of night, Delaney heard the metal click. She bolted upright, rousing a sleeping Nick who muffled into the sheets by her side, "What's up?"

"I think Felicity's home. I heard the front door."

"Good. Now go back to sleep."

"Good? I can't sleep—I need to know how it went."

"Can't it wait until morning?"

She whipped the blanket from her body, swung her bare feet to the floor and said, "No, it can't wait." It was all she could do to let Nick convince her to go to bed and wait. Now that her daughter was home, she was finished waiting. Tying her hair into a loose knot behind her head, Delaney padded to her bedroom door. Peeking out through the crack of opening, her heart caught. Felicity looked horrible. Distraught. Had she been crying?

Delaney burst out of the room and rushed to her side. "Felicity? What happened? Are you all right?"

Her daughter turned, trapping Delaney within the hot confines of an angry gaze. Up close, Felicity's fair skin was blotchy, mascara and shadow wiped from green eyes. No longer soft as heather green suede, her eyes were hard, jaded. "Why didn't you tell me?"

Fear razored through Delaney's lungs. "Tell you what?" she asked, but she knew—with deadly precision—she knew what Felicity meant.

"Why didn't you tell me my father beat you and it's the real reason you left him?"

Delaney felt like someone punched her. Someone told her? Someone told Felicity the truth? But who—who would have done such a thing? Victoria? Jack? Images of each and every Foster filed through her brain, churned her heart with disgust. What vile person would have delivered such news during a friendly dinner?

"It's true, isn't it? He beat you up and you left him."

Delaney didn't want to relive the past. She wanted to erase it. But with Felicity staring her down like a criminal, she felt defenseless. "He hit me, yes."

"Why wouldn't you tell me something like that? Why would you let me go over to that house not knowing what he was capable of?"

"I didn't want you to go, Felicity. I tried to talk you out of it."

"Without giving me any details!" she shrieked, whipping up a stiff finger between them. "In one sentence you could have stopped me. You could have stopped me in my tracks. Why didn't you?"

Because you were hell bent on going? Because I was afraid to hurt you? Regret poured into Delaney's soul like salt on an open wound. Because I didn't tell you when I should have and telling you now would have only resulted in this same scene.

"I can't believe you!" Felicity screeched, the intensity startling Delaney. She sounded like a dying animal. "You let me believe a monster could be a loving father! That his family could actually take me in with loving arms... How could you do that to me? Where was the overprotective mother when I needed her?"

Delaney stood as though naked and vulnerable, each accusation lodging deeper than the last. Her final words hurt the worst. *Because they were true.* Delancy had spent Felicity's entire childhood watching over her like a mother bear, scraping the flesh from anyone who dared hurt her daughter, even look at her wrong. Visions of Clem Sweeney and his threats rose sharp and raw in her mind. Delaney remembered the emotions thrashing through her at the time. If that skunk had laid a hand on Felicity Delaney would have killed him. Her guttural reaction would have been instinctual, automatic. Yet she had allowed Felicity to go in private with Jack. She had allowed the man to sink his claws into her daughter, and as expected, the man drew blood. Standing exposed in the headlights of her daughter's wrath, Delaney shriveled to nothing. She had no response. None that would suffice.

"You make me sick," Felicity hurled nastily. "You're as big a monster as he is." Felicity's gaze shot to the door behind Delaney, then speared her mother with one last withering look. "I don't think I can ever forgive you for this."

Delaney thrust out a shaky hand. "Felicity—"

But her daughter was gone. Footsteps pounded the stairs as she fled up to the loft, each one a hammer to her chest. Delaney hugged arms to her body, suddenly cold. Large masculine arms encircled her in a soft embrace. "Let her go. She needs time to cool down."

Standing rigid against the warm body of her husband, her life crumbled around her. "She hates me," Delaney whimpered, her throat nearly closed. Tears filled her eyes. "My daughter hates me."

Nick dropped his face to rest on her head. Hot breath mumbled into her hair, "No she doesn't. She's angry. She'll get over it."

Delaney's eyes shot to the ceiling, the loft, her daughter's safe haven—a safe haven unnervingly similar to one her mother Susannah had sought all those years ago. Abuse, violence. Callous disregard for others. It seemed inescapable. "That family stole her security, her peace of mind."

"You don't know what happened. Let's reserve judgment until we get all the facts."

"I don't need any more facts." A well of fury gurgled from deep within. "Jack did this to her."

"Life did this to her."

Delaney's heart hardened. "Jack will rue the day he ever tried to lure her back in the Foster fold."

"She's a big girl. She'll deal with him."

With ramrod determination, Delaney said, "Right after I deal with him first."

## Chapter Twelve

Delaney was up and out of the house before sunrise. No sense wasting time in bed. She couldn't sleep, might as well do something useful. Besides, when stressed, there was no better place for her than the stables, spending time with her Palomino, Sadie. Standing in her stall, Delaney brushed the blonde coat of her horse, the movements releasing the earthy musty fragrance of her animal. Mixed with the sweet scent rising from the hay-covered floor, the combination provoked a visceral reaction, a deeply-rooted pleasure. Delaney had been around horses all her life, practically riding before she'd walked.

It had been her mother's doing. Susannah Ladd loved the animals and like her, only rode bareback. Walk or run, river or trail, it was a passion they shared, a pastime they spent hours enjoying as mother and daughter. As Delaney brushed, Sadie stood idle, her ears flicking forward and back as though she were bored. Delaney grunted. Nice life, standing around and getting stroked to her heart's content while her owner ruminated over what to do about the mess her ex-husband had made.

Felicity was upset, angrier than Delaney had ever seen her. She lost her temper so seldom Delaney couldn't remember the last time. Felicity was the calm one. She was sensible, quiet. Of the two of them, she was the level-headed one. Seeing Felicity riled up to the point of losing control—shouting, crying—Delaney had been shocked. Not only by the words her daughter had spoken but the intensity with which she'd said them. Stroking a hand over the enormous belly, Delaney shook her head. Maybe the girl was more like her than she thought!

"God love the smell of horses."

Delaney flinched at the sound of Nick's deep voice. She hadn't heard him approach, though half-expected as much. When he was in town, the two shared a cup of coffee amidst the horses in the quiet of morning. It was a ritual she had come to love. After last night's episode, he'd know she'd need company. "It's glorious, isn't it? Nice and stinky."

He chuckled. "I need to get you out of here and soon. You're losing your sense for the finer fragrances in life."

Her hand stopped mid-motion and she turned. It was a razz he'd begun soon after he met her, continuously commenting on her affinity for her horse as though Sadie were human, and more important to Delaney than him. Far as Delaney was concerned, it was a close call. "What? Don't you like the smell of a good stinky horse?" Sadie shook her mane, rolling her head back to face him.

Leaning against a post, Nick screwed his expression. "Unfortunately, I have to admit that I do. Better when combined with the rich scent of expensive leather. Which reminds me, I bought you a new pair of chaps."

Delaney rolled her eyes and went back to her brushing. She followed the brush with her free hand, soothed by the solid muscular feel of the animal beneath her touch. "I'm not in the mood."

"Well, you should be. A good roll in the hay might relax you."

She grunted in response.

Pushing free, Nick strode over to her. "C'mon. You've got to calm down and think straight. You had a fight with your daughter. It happens."

Gliding her palm over the round of Sadie's rear end, she said, "Not to us, it doesn't."

"Happens to everyone eventually. It's nothing that can't be fixed."

Pausing, Delaney looked up at him, glad for the quiet strength emanating from his dark eyes. Combined with his dark hair and tanned skin, his six-foot four stature, his were eyes that exuded calm and wisdom. Eyes that could also blaze with fire and temper. Right now, she needed the former. "You heard her, she hates me."

"She doesn't hate you. That girl doesn't have a hateful bone in her body."

"She does now."

"She doesn't." Nick grabbed hold of Delaney's hand, pulling it from Sadie. Turning her within his arms, he brushed the hair from her face, curved a finger under her chin. Gaze darting back and forth across hers, he said, "She loves you. She'll come around when she's ready. Give her time."

Delaney wanted to believe him. She wanted it with all her heart. Last night had been miserable. Felicity was her whole world. To hear her spit venom and spite was painful. Her accusations were white-hot daggers through the chest, especially because they were true. This was partly her fault. Mostly Jack's, but partly hers. If she had been honest with her daughter, none of this would have happened.

"Listen, I have to go out of town."

She started. "What?"

Nick took hold of her shoulders, her body narrow and small within his grasp. "Come with me. It'll give you time to think, give Felicity space."

Sadie kicked a restless hoof to the ground. "I can't go anywhere—I have stables to run, a hotel full of guests. How can *you* get away?"

"I got a call from Lanny. Seems we have some legal trouble with our property in St. Kitts."

"What kind of legal trouble?"

"One of our vendors is suing over a contract dispute. It's nothing serious, but I can't ask Malcolm to go with a newborn on his hands. Besides, it will give you and me a chance for a honeymoon." He winked. "You want one, don't you?"

"Well, sure, but..." Delaney glanced to her horse, the Palomino lazily bumping against her. Delaney placed a light hand to Sadie's back. "There's too much going on here, you said so yourself. It's why we didn't take a honeymoon in the first place."

"I know, but business happens."

"When are you leaving?"

He frowned. "You, as in not we?"

Delaney sighed. "I can't. Not with Troy newly signed on. I want to be sure he gets a good foothold."

"Because he can't handle himself without you?"

"Because I feel responsible for the hire."

Nick smiled, a dash of merriment livening his gaze. "Hate to inform you, Mrs. Harris, but as owner and stable manager, you're responsible for all the hires."

She furrowed her brow. "You know what I mean. Troy is on rocky ground. I think I might be able to get him and Casey back together, but he can't mess up this time."

"You're a matchmaker now?"

"Add it to the list," she said, unexpectedly overwhelmed by a slew of emotional turmoil. Casey and Jimmy were playing games, Jack was leading Felicity astray, the Fosters were stirring the pot and Felicity wasn't speaking to her. It felt like people were going mad around her, tossing her between them like a rag doll. Delaney prided herself on being made from some tough fiber, but she could only take so much! Settling on Nick, she longed for his support, not his absence. "When will you be back?"

"Few days. Shouldn't take too long to nail this one down. In the meantime I don't want you confronting Jack about Felicity. Let it lay until I get back."

"Why? I'm not worried about Jack."

Nick pulled her to him and looked at her directly. His smile was gone, replaced by a seriousness she thought excessive. "I am. The man has already proven he's willing to stir up trouble. Don't antagonize him until I return, okay?"

Delaney suppressed a smile. "I can handle Jack, Nick."

"I'm sure you can, but I'd feel better knowing you don't have to handle him alone." She hesitated and he pressed. "Promise me.

"Fine."

Nick peered over her shoulder. "There aren't any crossed fingers I have to worry about, are there?"

"Not my style."

"Good." He kissed her forehead. "That's one of the reasons I married you."

"What were the others?" she asked, trying to lighten the weight of his leaving.

He grinned. "Tell you when I get back." Nick leaned down and kissed her. Long and deep, filled with an unexpected urgency. A swell of desire surged low in her abdomen. Maybe a roll in the hay wasn't such a bad idea after all.

Felicity checked her watch. She was meeting Travis for breakfast at Fran's Diner, though she lacked the first ounce of appetite. She couldn't eat, couldn't sleep. She could only think—how everything she thought she knew wasn't true. How her mother lied to her, allowed her to believe in a man who was no man at all but a monster. An abuser.

Last night when she confronted her mother, she didn't have anything to say. She stood there, the truth rearing between them like a two-headed monster. That's what her father was—a man with two heads, two personas. Like the people she read about in her novel, *When Families Hurt*. The father in that story was leading a double life. He was Mr. Wonderful and Professional at work but when he came home he was mean, criticizing everything his wife and son did as inadequate. The mother in the story was weak, turning to alcohol for escape. The boy had anger issues—issues Felicity suddenly understood. How could he not when presented with two adults making bad choices? Overcome by a fresh swell of her own anger, Felicity deemed the son's role was the only one that made sense to her!

Bells clanged at the front door, snapping her attention. Casey Owens stood behind an elderly couple waiting to be seated. A glance around the restaurant showed, the place was packed, standing room only. Shooting up from her seat, Felicity waved to her cousin. "Casey!" She turned at the sound of her name. "Over here!" Felicity gestured her to her table.

Casey reacted, accepting the invitation to join her. "Guess I should have come earlier."

"You can sit with me," Felicity said. "I'm waiting for Travis."

A shadow flitted behind Casey's blue eyes. "Oh, well," she said, brushing fallen black strands of hair behind an ear. "I don't want to intrude."

"Don't be silly. It's no intrusion at all."

Reluctantly, it seemed, Casey sat. As was becoming her habit, she caressed her growing belly in what Felicity thought a protective manner. Casey was going to be a good mom. "How's the baby?"

Casey's smile was quick and bright. "Good. She's an active one."

"Really? Watch out. That means she's gonna keep you on your toes."

Casey looked down as she paused, a hand over her stomach. "I'm looking forward to it."

"Travis told me Troy is working for Delaney." Casey nodded. "Are you happy about it?"

"Why wouldn't I be?"

"I don't know. You haven't told him about the baby. I assumed you didn't want him around."

Casey paused. Uncertainty pulled a veil over her gaze. "It's not that I don't want him around..."

"You want him to *stay* around."

Her expression slackened. "Well, yes."

Felicity nodded. "I understand."

"You do?"

"Sure. If a guy's gonna commit, you want him to mean it, to follow through. There's nothing complicated there."

"Right." Casey relaxed. "That's the way it should be."

"I think so."

Casey smiled and for a moment, the two young women sat alone with their thoughts. Felicity knew Casey was going through a hard time with Troy, given the unpredictability of his behavior. One minute he was here, doing a great job, the next minute he was gone. She couldn't blame Casey for having mixed feelings. Having a baby changed things. A child needed stability, commitment. It wasn't a game. Casey couldn't up and leave to follow Troy when the whim struck—or his bad luck. She couldn't uproot a child, separating them from everything they knew and loved. She had to stay and commit. Something a lot of parents seemed to have trouble doing.

"Can I ask you something?"

"Sure."

"Do you blame your mom for being with Jeremiah Ladd?"

Confusion tangled in her eyes. "Blame her?"

"Yeah, you know, like, are you mad that she slept with him and made him your dad?"

Easily readable, thoughts rose and fell as Casey considered the question, actively examining what she thought, how she felt. Seconds passed before her gaze filed to a fine point. "No. Not really."

"Even though she picked a man like him?"

"*Like him*?" Casey parroted warily.

Felicity immediately walked the statement back. "Like him, I mean, you know, a man who has proven not to be such a great guy."

Casey stiffened. "Why are you asking?"

Felicity dropped her gaze to her lap then faced Casey fully. It was time to spill. "I went to the Fosters for dinner last night. I found out my dad isn't a great guy."

"Was that a surprise to you?"

Casey was genuinely astonished. Felicity felt foolish. Was she the *only* one who didn't know? "Do you know why my mother left him?"

"They didn't get along?" Casey offered.

"He hit her." *Spit it out*, Felicity told herself. *Say the words aloud and remove the stigma of secrecy. It's what*

*Travis told her to do. Don't let this man hurt her any more than he already had.* She needed to hold her head high, not hide from the truth. "He beat her and she left."

At Casey's mouth agape, a strange relief swept through Felicity. *She didn't know.* At least Casey hadn't been part of the rumor mill around town like all the others.

"I'm sorry."

Felicity nodded and fought back a rush of tears. She didn't want people to be sorry for her. She wanted a normal life. The one she thought she had before last night. When she left the Foster's home, she believed those people knew the reason why. She could see it in the eyes of the wives. Mrs. Foster clearly didn't believe her impromptu illness. Jack questioned her all the way to the car as he walked her out. He'd called several times this morning but she hadn't answered. She wasn't going to. She never planned to speak to the man again.

The wisp of Casey's voice cut through her fog, reached deep into her heart. "No, I don't blame my mother. She was young and in love." Gripped by the intensity with which Casey spoke, Felicity hung in expectation. "She wasn't thinking about anything but the present moment, her own desires. It's not like she purposefully gave me a rotten father. It happened, is all." Moisture collected in her lids and Felicity thought Casey was about to cry. Crossing arms over her mid-section, she added, "It wasn't what she wanted. It wasn't what she planned but she raised me, did it on her own."

Staring at a napkin roll of silverware, Casey continued, "I think she did the best she could. Given the circumstances, the difficulty." She paused, gathering Felicity in her gaze. "I think in the end she did her best. Can we ask for anything more? Can we make someone give more than they are?" Casey glanced away. "I think life is hard. It's harder than any of us expect, and some people handle the challenge better than others. Doesn't mean they're better people. Just means they handled that situation better."

Struck by the wisdom, the forgiveness in her voice, Felicity fell back. From what she understood, Jeremiah Ladd
was not a nice man. He was a lowlife, a bad guy. He wasn't
always that way, but her mom said that when he came back
home after living in Atlanta, he'd changed. Had there been a
challenge in the big city he couldn't handle?

What about her mother? Had she done the best she
could? Felicity had always believed she had. She'd always
believed her mom was amazing. She was strong and smart
and took care of Felicity all these years on her own. Like Casey's mom did with her. But Casey's mom didn't lie to her
about her father. Her mom never hid the truth from her, good
or bad. But hers did. "My mom never told me."

Casey gaped at her. "Would you have wanted her to?"

"Yes," she replied, but the minute the word left her lips,
Felicity wondered about its validity. "I think so."

"Not me." Casey shook her head. "I wished I didn't
know anything about my father."

"You wouldn't have wanted to know the truth, one way
or another?"

"What good did it do me? My father's in jail. He's a loser. How does that help?"

"But, he's your—"

"Sperm donor. That's all he is to me. A sperm donor."

Felicity closed her mouth, bit back her objection. Casey
had turned cold. Completely shut down. Could she really
view her father in those terms? Was she really okay with the
loss? After years of spotty contact with her dad, Felicity had
always harbored a secret wish for things to change. One day,
when their paths crossed, maybe they could find each other,
work through the past and form a new relationship. It was
possible. She'd heard stories of people who had done the
same.

It was her mother who had been standing in the way. Felicity had decided she was the obstacle. Her father had vali-
dated the same when he invited her to dinner, claiming it was
her mom who had stood in the way of a relationship with her

grandparents. Looking back, Felicity couldn't deny her excitement. She'd been nervous but looking forward to opening a new chapter in her life. Her heart closed. Unfortunately, it turned out to be the beginning of a horror story.

Living a common nightmare, she felt allied with Casey. "So that's why you're okay with not telling Troy about the baby."

The comment caught Casey on the chin. "What do you mean?'

"He's a sperm donor. He's not going to be in her life, so why tell her about him?"

"Well, not exactly. I don't want him to stay *because* of the baby." Her face changed. The grim lines slipped away, exposing the vulnerability of her true motivation. "I want him to stay because of me."

"Ah... And you don't think he would?"

Casey averted her direct gaze. "I don't know."

"You have to tell him," Felicity said, on-the-spot adamant it was the right thing to do. "He's a good guy. I've known him my whole life, and no matter how misguided he can be at times, he's a good person." When Casey didn't argue the point, Felicity wasn't sure if she was agreeing or resisting. "You have to give him the chance to make that decision. It's his right to know. Just because our dads aren't good fathers doesn't mean Troy won't be." Tears filled Casey's eyes but she remained mute. Fueled by outrage over her own loss of choice, a decision made for her and not with her, Felicity urged Casey not to do the same to Troy. It wasn't fair. It wasn't right. "It's his baby too, Casey. Let him decide what he wants to do about it."

Chapter Thirteen

Stowed away in the privacy of her bedroom, dressed comfortably in T-shirt and baggy shorts, Casey mulled over the conversation with Felicity. Alone in the apartment, the one she now shared with both her mother and Cal until their house was built, Casey sat on her bed, surrounded by frilly girl-aged pillows, a collection she'd built over the years. Her ivory-painted furniture was the same set she'd had since middle school, the culmination of months of saving and pleading with her mother that if she bought this set Casey would never ask for another thing again. Photos of her and her mom on her dresser instilled a sense of warmth, comfort. This was her home. No longer a place she loathed to be, but a place of love, connection. Family.

She wanted to tell Troy about the baby. She wanted him to know, to be excited, to care enough to want to become a family. It would be a dream come true. They'd talked about a future together. The night before he left, they talked about him working his way to owning a ranch one day while she continued classes at the local college. Casey told him she wanted to study stars. When he didn't laugh, she confessed it was her passion. There were so many intricacies in the sky, hundreds of thousands of constellations. Millions, really. The sky was unlimited, a concept that appealed to her. When he asked what she'd do with a degree in star-gazing, she couldn't say. She wasn't quite sure herself but she'd do something with it. Kids entered the conversation but they were a distant desire. Some day. One day. Neither expected that day to be today.

Casey thought back to that night and what Troy said about "forever." He claimed she was his best friend and he couldn't live a life without her. If that was true, how could he have walked away from her? He didn't tell her where he was going—he told Travis. She had to hear about it from a third party. When he finally called a week later, she'd told him where to go. He couldn't walk out on her without a word and expect her to be okay with it. She had her pride, didn't she? He didn't get to make the call on how things went, what she was supposed to be happy about.

Pulling a pillow onto her lap, she settled her chin on top of it and gazed at her outstretched legs. Her red toe polish was chipped, a sign of her neglect of her appearance. But looks weren't a priority, especially when she wore boots everywhere. Not like there was anyone around to see it, she bemoaned. Images of Troy and other women coursed through her. After what he did with that Loretta woman and the Devane woman, he should have considered himself lucky she was even speaking to him. He'd said as much that night, hadn't he? He had begged her forgiveness—something she nearly didn't give him—sworn he was going to change his ways. Then he turned around and deserted her? Casey clutched a pillow tightly to her chest, heartache gushing anew. He should have been on his knees pleading for her approval for his decision to move. He should have been afraid she might not want to go with him. But he wasn't. Troy didn't even ask her to go with him. There was no "pack your bag, we're going to Kentucky." No "what do you think about living in Kentucky?" Nothing. Troy had up and left without a kiss goodbye.

*I'm back. For good.*

A spasm squirmed high in her belly. Casey slid a hand beneath her T-shirt and cupped her stomach holding it close. Her bare skin was warm, taut. A long spasm writhed beneath her fingertips. Casey smiled. "Are you trying to tell me something, baby girl?" The rolling sensation continued, clear down to her hip bone. "You're getting big. You're running out of room in there, you know."

In another two months, she'd be out, with all the room she needed. A flutter of nerves erupted at her breast. Childbirth scared Casey. She'd read books, watched reality television. The women screamed in agony the likes of which she'd never heard. Casey liked being pregnant. She liked feeling her baby close, liked thinking about their future together. She was sure she'd like it once she could hold her in her arms. Casey swallowed. It was the getting her out part that scared her.

Would she go through it alone? Would it be her mom who held her hand, whispered soothing words as her patient gown filled with sweat. Casey shuddered. Women on television looked as if they'd run a marathon by the time they were finished. Sweaty, exhausted, they looked relived when it was all over. And happy. When they held their baby in their arms their faces were awash in joy.

Maybe Felicity was right. Maybe she should give Troy the opportunity to be with his baby, the mother of his child. A niggle of doubt scraped at her. He'd come back for her, didn't he? Isn't that what he said at the diner? *I came by to tell you I'm back. For good.*

Maybe he meant it. Maybe he realized his mistake of leaving and meant what he said.

*I made you a promise when I left here and I aim to keep it.*

Was it possible he spoke the truth? After all, she and Jimmy never gave him a chance to explain. Jimmy blurted out the lie about her being his girlfriend and Troy left. Then at the picnic, she told him the baby was Jimmy's. Casey closed her eyes and pressed her face into her pillow. She never gave him the chance to do anything *but* be mad! How could she know what he was really thinking? How could she know anything—the two hadn't spoken the first word about it!

A torrent of misgiving flooded her. She knew lying about the baby was the wrong thing to do, but leaving her without a word or a plan had been wrong too. If Troy really loved her, he should have called her before he left. He should have called and said "I'm going to Kentucky. *Come with me.*"

He was the guilty party here, not her. Recalling the pain in Troy's eyes at Ashley's picnic, she struggled with the assignment of blame. He'd been devastated to hear the baby belonged to Jimmy. Shattered to learn she'd slept with Jimmy after being with him. Shame wound through her. Pulling the pillow from her face, Casey glanced around her bedroom. Cluttered with clothes and books, a few stuffed animals leftover from her younger days, her room was that of a girl's. Walls were painted yellow, the furniture adorned with flowers. A poster of a movie star heartthrob hung above her bed. She couldn't remember his name, only that she'd been gaga over him in seventh grade. She turned away. Silliness. Youthful silliness. She was a woman now. A woman with a child growing inside her. Closing her eyes, Casey knew what she had to do. Troy should know the truth. Whether it would make a difference for the two of them didn't matter. He should know that the baby belonged to him. From the crevices of her soul came the echo, *her heart belonged to him as well.*

Scooting from her bed, Casey pulled the shirt from her body and tossed it to the bed. Removing the stretch shorts she wore around the house, she chucked them next to her shirt and walked over to her closet ignoring her egg-shaped reflection in the mirror. She pulled a dress from a hanger and slipped it on over her head. She was going to the stables and tell him the truth. Whether he liked it or not, Troy was going to know exactly what he left behind when he moved to Kentucky. Let him decide what to do from there.

Walking the long trail up to the stables, Casey dammed a tide of nerves. She didn't tell anyone that she was making this trip. She didn't ask for a ride or assistance. She was perfectly capable of walking the hill and delivering the news in person. Up close and personal. This way she'd know in an instant what he thought. She'd be able to see it in his eyes. If he wasn't happy, she'd know it.

And, she'd decided, so be it. If Troy didn't want this baby, she'd raise it on her own. Her mother and Cal had offered her a place to live, offered to help her with the baby while she earned her degree. They offered to do everything within their power to make her road as smooth and easy as possible. It was more than she could have hoped for, more than she would have asked for, but then again her mother was proving to be so much more than she ever gave her credit for.

Nearing the stables, she spotted a black-headed cowboy walking from the stables to the paddocks. Her heart skipped. It wasn't Troy. She could tell by his movements. From a mile away she could spot his swagger, his angular, muscular build. Thoughts of their night together drifted through her mind like a movie reel. She had memorized his every curve, his every muscle. No freckles, no markings, other than the nick of a scar on his cheek, Troy's body was incredible. Strong. He was perfect.

Tamping down the spurt of thrill, Casey wanted to jog the rest of the way but, fearing it would jostle her baby, instead held her stomach firmly and kicked up her pace. It was an easy hike, especially now the land had been grazed by bulldozers, rocks and dirt leveled for a smooth carriage ride. That's how some of the hotel guests made it to the stables. Not her. She was walking with her own two feet.

Nodding to a passing couple, she smiled politely. Cal said guests roamed the property on and off marked trails, a practice he and Malcolm encouraged. Folks were supposed to feel like they were in the wilderness, like they were explorers or something. Casey didn't care. So long as they didn't trespass around their home once it was built. The last thing she needed was to be worried about people peeking in through her windows. Shaking the disturbing image, she entered the stables, the shade a welcome relief. Perspiration coated her neck, breasts and back. Her forehead and cheeks felt flushed, but that was to be expected after the uphill hike in the heat.

There were clouds out there but it was hot. Too hot. Fanning herself, she strolled through wide corridors where the air was cool and drenched with the smell of hay and horses. She could see several animals through metal bars that lined their stalls. Why weren't they in use?

Several stable boys walked by, one carrying a bucket, another toting a bale of straw. Across the way was the Delaney's office. Her pulse accelerated. Would she be upset to see her? Would she be mad Casey was interfering with an employee while on the job? As if on cue, the blonde-headed stable owner strode out of the office and stopped short at sight of her. Casey gulped. Guess she'd find out soon enough.

"Casey!" Sporting her usual ripped up jeans and tank top, Delaney hastened over. Casey wondered why she didn't buy better clothes. She was the owner now. Didn't she care what guests would think when they saw her?

Coming to stop within feet of her, Delaney asked, "What brings you around?" She looked from side to side, as though searching for someone. "No one told me you were coming."

"They didn't know. I just decided to visit."

"Visit?" Sharp brown eyes turned appraising. "Who exactly are we visiting?"

Casey's voice evaporated as she croaked, "Troy."

Delaney smiled, wide and full. Setting hands to her hips, she asked, "Have you decided to tell him, then?"

Casey nodded, rendered mute. She stole a quick glance around the vicinity. Was he here?

Delaney hitched a thumb over her shoulder. "He's out in the barn working a horse for me. Should I get him for you?"

She shook her head. "No. I'll go find him."

Approval glinted in dark brown eyes, the eyes of a woman Casey had come to lean on for solid advice and support. Delaney had counseled her early on to give Troy a chance, to let him find his way. But after he left town without her, it was the last thing she wanted. Her mom said enough was enough. It was time Casey built her own life without grazing about waiting on Troy to figure out what he wanted from his. At the time Casey believed her mother was right. At the moment, she realized it might have been Delaney's word she should have heeded.

"Take all the time you need," Delaney said. "Tell him to take a break, if you need it."

Joy flushed out Casey's angst. "Thank you."

Delaney stepped aside. Drawing her buttery yellow lengths of hair aside, she waved Casey forward. "Now go on. Don't keep the boy waiting. You remember where the barn is, right?"

"I do." She took a few steps in that direction and stopped. "Thanks." Casey meant for everything—for giving Troy a job, for believing in him, for encouraging her to be with him. Delaney had turned out to be a real ally, and Casey appreciated her more than she could say.

"I'm here anytime you need me."

Passing through the stables, Casey emerged, instantly warmed by the open sky. In the distance she could see the barn. The barn. Where Troy was working. A huge building, she knew it housed equipment, feed rooms, wash stations. Nerves battered her heart but she shook them away. Would he be happy to see her? Mad?

Whatever. Come what may, she had a message to deliver!

Casey neared the building and reservations inundated her. Slowing, she edged around the open doorway and froze. There in the center of the spacious high-ceilinged barn was Troy and a gorgeous dark brown horse, free of gear except for a bridle with a lead rope attached. The sight took her breath away. Standing before the massive animal, dressed in his black hat and T-shirt, Troy was in his element. Casey flattened her body against the wall. He was perfect. Beautiful.

Man and horse were seamless in their focus.

"Good boy," Troy cooed to the horse he was working, gently placing pressure against his neck. "That's right, Spirit. We're friends." With his other hand, Troy tossed the lead rope over the horse's body. The animal was alert, but calm. Not jumpy. "Good job," Troy said, giving a gentle stroke to the horse's snout.

Spirit was a real beauty, a chocolate brown Quarter Horse that reminded him of his own stallion kept at his parents' place. Both were tall and strong. Strong-bodied and strong-willed. Troy moved to Spirit's opposite side and repeated the gentle toss of rope over his body. The horse didn't flinch. "That's a boy," he rewarded softly, maintaining contact with the animal, mindful of the ears which were twitching. One went back and forth, stiffened. "Nothing going on here," Troy told him, lightly patting the horse on the neck. The animal pushed into Troy but Troy held firm. "It's okay. I hear you but I'm not doing anythin' to hurt you," he said, following up with a stroke along the animal's body. "I just want you to feel it. Just want you to get used to it, that's all."

Delaney had asked him to train the animal for riders. She'd received the horse from a friend of hers in Georgia, but it came with a warning. The animal wasn't suitable for trail riding. Didn't matter. Delaney fell in love with the horse at first sight and bought him on the spot—something Troy totally understood. This boy was special. You could see it in his eyes. Animal and man were equally tuned in to what the other was doing. So far, Spirit was proving an easy train.

With measured movements Troy wrapped the rope around the animal's front hoof and lifted. The animal resisted, stepping forward. "It's okay, buddy." Troy leaned down and brought the hoof up again, repeating his rope wrap. Spirit eyed him but allowed him to hold it steady in the air for several seconds. "That's right," Troy said with a smile. "Didn't hurt a bit, did it?" He proceeded to repeat the move with the other hoof. "Good job, Spirit."

Yesterday the animal refused to let him loop and lift. Troy gave a vigorous stroke down the length of the animal's snout. Today was an improvement. "Excellent."

But next came the most risky move. Dialing in, Troy watched the animal's head as he moved the rope and lightly brushed it over and around the flanks. The horse turned his head and stepped away from Troy. "That's it, boy. All done. Nothin' but a simple brush," Troy said, stepping with him. The rear was a sensitive area. If the horse became uncomfortable with the feel of the rope, he might kick. But Troy needed the animal to understand that if he let his defenses down around people, no one was going to hurt him. He was safe. It was the key to training an animal for use around people.

Troy tried again—keeping his pressure light and tender, reassuring. This time the animal moved in a circular fashion with him, allowing Troy to maintain his rope contact. Troy pulled the rope from his body and that's when he saw her. His heart stopped—bucked out of control. Casey was hovering by the entrance to the barn. The horse circled him, momentarily blocking his view.

*What was she doing here*? Gently moving the horse from his line of vision, Troy was stunned to see her approach. Instinctively, his gaze dropped to her stomach. With the sun at her back, he could see the outlines of her belly through the sheer material, the sticks that were her legs disappearing into black boots. Next to him the horse tugged at the rope but Troy held firm. He was busy right now.

As Casey neared, he tried to read the expression on her face, the strange look in her eyes. She seemed uncertain about him, like she didn't know him the way she did but was advancing anyway. Like a stranger. Recalling their night together, the fact that she'd been with Jimmy, he resented her for making him feel like the bad guy. Drawing Spirit close, Troy shook it off. Why was she here? What did she want?

"Troy."

"Casey," he replied coolly, avoiding the impulse to stare at her stomach, the immensity of what it meant to him. "What are you doing here?"

"I came to talk to you." She glanced up at the horse, shuttering her gaze in a timid sort of way.

"About what?" he asked. And what did she have to be timid about? She was the one holding the gun. She was the one who'd fired first. Impatience got the better of him. "I have work to do," he said, leading Spirit to a wood railing. From the corner of his eye, he saw her follow him. Desire and longing tore at him, mingling with anger and hurt. Why was she here? Hadn't she said enough already? The horse snorted, jerking its head up as Troy tied him to the top board. He turned. "What did you want to talk to me about?"

Blue eyes quieted. "I came to tell you the baby..." she began, but her voice fell away.

*The baby.* Disgust roiled through him. Jimmy's baby. Troy stepped away from her, adjusted his hat forward. The way she was looking at him—her gaze filled with longing, want—it was too close to the way she looked at him the night before he left.

"The baby is yours."

"*What?*"

Troy dropped his gaze to her stomach as she took a step toward him. "The baby," she murmured, cradling her belly with both hands, exposing the size and dimension of her stomach clear as day. "It's not Jimmy's. It's yours."

"What are you talking about?" Troy stepped back, grappling for reason. What did she mean the baby was his? It didn't make sense. She and Jimmy were dating. She'd said it was his. Why was she telling him this now? "I don't believe you," he snapped.

"It's true."

"You said it was Jimmy's."

Sadness punctured her gaze. "I lied to you at Ashley's."

Troy walked away from her, a tide of emotion choking his thoughts. "I don't understand," he said over his shoulder, unable to look at her. Part of him wanted it to be true. Part of him feared it was a lie. "Jimmy said you two were dating."

"We aren't."

Troy whirled on her. "Why would he say it then if it ain't true?"

"He was trying to protect me."

"Protect you—from what? Me?" Troy spit. He turned from her, tired of feeling the bad guy, someone to be afraid of. He wasn't, yet that's how she was making him feel.

"From myself."

The fragile quality of her reply shattered his anger. When he returned to face her, the beaten look of defeat that met him split Troy in two. What was going on? First she was mad, now she was sad. "Dad gum, Casey. You're not making any sense."

"I know. I'm sorry." She brushed strands of silky black hair behind an ear, stepped closer. The stallion he'd been training was watching them, its ears forward, dark eyes glancing at them as he angled away from them.

The baby was his? Was she for real?

"I just... When you left..." Casey narrowed in on him with a pop of emotion, "I was so hurt and angry. You didn't ask me to come with you. You didn't tell me where you were going. I had to find it out from Felicity, because you didn't have the decency to tell me yourself!"

Surprised by the hit, Troy knew she was right. He should have been the one to tell her, but he didn't know where he'd end up when he left, and dragging her around the country while he looked for a job wasn't gonna happen. She deserved better than that. They'd talked about this!

"Then I found out I was pregnant"—she continued through his silence—"and I was scared. I was really scared. Jimmy was there for me but as my friend. We were never more than friends, I swear."

Old resentments flared. "Not cause he didn't wanna be more."

Casey shook her head. "Jimmy is my friend, Troy. He's been good to me. I don't want you to hold that against him."

Troy cursed under his breath, hating the void he'd left for Jimmy to fill. It was *his* fault the guy ever had the first chance with Casey.

"Then all of a sudden you showed up, and I didn't know what to do. I, I..." She fumbled, fiddled with a tie on her dress. "I didn't want you to know." Tears moistened her eyes. "I didn't want you to know because I didn't want you to leave me again."

"Leave you?" Troy rushed to her, searching for reason. Grabbing hold of her arms, he forced her to look him in the eye. "But I never left you, Casey. Don't you get that? I never left you."

"You moved to Kentucky!" she shrieked, unsettling the horse.

Troy calmed his voice. "I told you I'd be back. I went there to prove myself, to show you I could be a better man. I thought you understood." Her gaze darted back and forth across his. "It was *you* who turned away from me. I told you I'd be back and I am. Only I came back earlier than I planned to," he said, the admission a stain on his heart. "Because I quit."

"Why?"

The doubt in her eyes hurt him. There was still a part of her that believed he was a loser who couldn't hold down a job. Well, he might be a loser when it came to quitting but not when it came to working with horses. He was good at what he did. Horses were part of him. They were in his blood. He could beat any challenge thrown his way when it came to training, but his heart?

That was a different story. He thought he could handle the challenge of being away, but he couldn't. "Being away from you was too hard. I told myself it was for the best. I told myself it was the only way to prove to you that I could do a good job. When you didn't return my calls, I figured you were mad, that your momma was probably turning you against me. I figured you needed time, and once I got settled in with the new ranch, I'd call and you'd move to Kentucky."

Casey slackened within his grasp. "I'm sorry about that."

"Mr. Foster said you were okay so I figured it couldn't be that bad."

"You called him?"

Troy nodded.

"He never told me."

Troy stilled. "He probably didn't believe me."

"Oh, Troy..."

Her pity only made it worse. Mr. Foster was right not to believe him. Troy hadn't shown him anything different. Why believe he'd changed? Troy shrugged it off. "It don't matter. I couldn't do it. I had to come back. I love you, Casey." Then it hit him. The baby was *his*.

He was going to be a father.

A thousand thoughts ripped through him at once. He was going to have a baby. He was a stable hand, making minimum wage. He didn't have a place to live. He had a wife and child to support. A baby. He honed in on Casey. *Would she marry him*?

"What's the matter, Troy? Are you upset now that you know?"

Realizing she was misreading him, he said, "No, Casey. I'm not upset."

"You're not?"

"You're not really dating Jimmy, right?"

She shook her head. Looking her directly in the eye, he asked, "You never slept with him?"

"Never."

Troy swung an arm under her legs and swept her from her feet. "How could I be upset? I'm going to be a daddy!" he exclaimed, mindful of her swell of body between them.

Casey clung to his neck. "You're happy?"

"On my honor." Troy beamed, euphoria pouring into him. Casey wasn't with Jimmy. She was carrying *his* child. "I'm happy as man ever could be." He kissed her without thinking, and the feel of her mouth caught him unprepared. Desire surged. Holding her slender body in his arms, taking in the light scent of her hair, her skin, brought so many memories and feelings rushing to the surface that his head swam. How many times had he thought about this moment? Holding her again, kissing her, touching her? Hunger and need coursed through him. Too long. It had been too long. She tasted so good...

Casey pulled away. Eyes wide, lips swollen, she held him in her gaze. "Troy, we can't do this here."

A sudden hilarity jolted through him. "Dad gum, Casey. I'm not trying to make love to you—I'm kissing you!"

A tinge colored her cheeks. "I know, but—" She glanced around. A few men stood near the barn entrance, watching with heightened amusement. Spirit whinnied in protest of being neglected.

Troy set her down to her feet. He straightened her dress, careful to avoid contact with her stomach. He didn't want to hurt her. "I'll leave you be." Flecks of alarm filtered into her gaze. "For now." He pecked her nose. "But later—"

It occurred to him there might not be a later. She was pregnant. She couldn't do anything while she was pregnant. He peered at her. *Could she?*

"What?" she asked.

"Nothing." Troy laughed at himself, warmth spreading through his chest, filling him with a happiness he hadn't known in too long. He was gonna have to learn about pregnant women, having babies, the works! He was going to be a father. *A daddy.* It was a thrill he never expected to affect him quite this hard and strong. Brushing the hair from her eyes, he traced her brow. "You know you have to marry me now."

She giggled. "What?"

"You heard me. You have to marry me." Casey glanced away, seemingly uncertain as what to do next. "I have to buy you a ring first. I don't have a lot of money, but I have saved up some from my last job."

"Troy, you don't have to spend your money on a ring for me."

"Yes, I do." Offended she would even suggest such a thing, he added, "I'm going to buy you a diamond and you're going to wear it when we get married. You can help pick it out, if you want." She giggled again and this time the sound reached straight into his heart. "Dad gum, Casey. You're not supposed to laugh when a man proposes."

"Is that what you're doing?" she asked coyly, a bright smile embedded on her face.

Troy dropped to one knee. An outbreak of nerves wracked him as he took her hand. "Yes, ma'am, I am." His pulse ricocheted like a pellet in a tin can as he asked, "Casey Melody Owens, will you marry me?"

Her eyes glistened. Placing her free hand over theirs together, she whispered, "Yes, Troy. Yes."

Chapter Fourteen

Casey swung in through the front door of Fran's Diner, flying higher than she had in months. Troy was excited. Happy. He wanted to get married. A swarm of butterflies took wing in her chest. *Married*!

Heading straight for the kitchen, she had to tell Jimmy. She had to explain to him why she told Troy, that it was the right thing to do. She knew Jimmy wasn't fond of Troy, didn't care for him because he believed Troy was a selfish hothead. At the same time, Jimmy understood her desire for them get back together. He knew she still loved Troy but felt taking him back was the wrong thing to do. Troy would only end up hurting her. Well, he was wrong. After clearing the air between them, Casey finally understood Troy had never left her. He might have gone about relocating in a way she disliked, but in his heart he never left her. He simply crossed state lines for better opportunity.

Coming to a stop at the food counter, Casey searched for sight of Jimmy. Through the service window, she glimpsed his mismatched head of hair on the opposite side of the kitchen, next to the sinks. His turned and their eyes locked. She smiled, he smiled, and for a second they were the same old friends they had been for the last six months. Then a realization deepened his features. Casey's heart caught in her throat. *He knew*.

Jimmy combed a hand through his hair, looked around his immediate vicinity and then retreated from sight. And he wasn't happy.

"Casey."

Startled by the voice, she turned to find Felicity standing by her side. "Are you here for dinner?"

"Um..." She glanced back to the kitchen, "I don't know."

Felicity turned her mouth down in a mock frown. "You don't know?"

Seeing no more sign of Jimmy, lead poured into her chest. Jimmy wasn't happy. She'd chosen Troy, but couldn't they still be friends? Glancing back toward the kitchen, Casey glimpsed a busboy depositing a load of dishes into the sink where Jimmy had been standing. She slumped with a sigh. "I was here to talk to Jimmy but it looks like he's busy."

"Is everything okay?"

"Actually," Casey replied, inhaling deeply, "I told Troy the baby was his."

Felicity grabbed hold of her shoulders. "You did?"

She nodded, encouraged by the excitement in Felicity's voice. "I did."

"And?" she asked, brimming with eager anticipation.

Casey broke into a grin. "He wants to get married."

Felicity enfolded Casey in a hug and squeezed. "I'm so happy for you!"

"Thanks," she replied. "Me, too."

Pulling away, Felicity asked, "What made you change your mind?"

Casey shrugged. "I thought about what you said. What-ever happens, the choice should be his. It's his child, too."

Felicity flung a glance toward the kitchen then back to Casey. "You did the right thing. I know it was hard, but you still did it. And now look. You're getting married!" she squealed.

Part of Casey cringed. She didn't want Jimmy to hear the news this way, like she hadn't come to him first. Struck by a thought, Casey lingered on the notion. Jimmy had asked her to marry him. It was a pity proposal, but he'd done it with a sincere heart and a genuine desire to help. Casting a limp gaze toward the kitchen, Casey was saddened by his re-sponse. Jimmy was one of the good ones.

"Felicity!"

Both turned. Travis waved her over to a booth. "Food's here."

"In a minute," she called back to him.

Casey wondered at the mild grunt that accompanied the reply. Was she mad at Travis?

"Come join us," Felicity invited.

"Oh, I don't think so." Casey gave a dismissive wave. "I'm not really hungry."

"You're here, aren't you?"

"Yes, but I was here for a different reason..." Unwilling to explain how she managed to ruin Jimmy's day, she let go of further explanation. Maybe she could still talk to Jimmy. Once his shock wore off.

"C'mon, Travis won't bite. Besides, you and he are going to be family!" Felicity squealed again, more excited than Casey would have believed possible. Casting a wary gaze toward Travis, she groaned inwardly. *Oh, brother*—literally. Though not interested in sharing her good news with Travis, Casey followed Felicity over to their table.

Travis didn't think much of her. Despite Felicity's protests to the contrary, Casey accepted that he didn't like her, believed she was "beneath" him because she wasn't going to college. Evidently, a few classes here and there didn't count as going to college. Travis didn't approve of Troy's choices either. But Travis was an over-achiever. He aced everything he did. A guy like him didn't understand doubts, insecurities. He didn't understand when people strayed off course. Felicity said to give him time, he'd come around. Casey disagreed. Travis had no interest in straying off course—not from his life plan and not from his opinion.

Felicity sat next to him and said, "Travis, guess what?"

His gaze trailed Casey as she sat across from them, filled with mild alarm. He was probably wondering why Felicity had invited her to join them. Warily, he asked, "What?"

"Troy and Casey are getting married! Isn't that great?" His gaze hardened, a reaction that said it all, and one he quickly tried to cover as she continued, "She told him about the baby and he proposed." Felicity lightly punched his shoulder. "I *told* you he'd do the right thing."

"About time," Travis replied.

Casey shifted her gaze to the back as Jimmy emerged from the kitchen, arms loaded with plates of food. Totally ignoring her, he walked to a table on the other side of the diner. He didn't make eye contact, didn't smile. He was grim. Gloomy. Shafts of remorse stabbed through her. She should never have dragged him into this mess in the first place. She and Jimmy were friends, but when Troy left, Casey had leaned on him all the harder. She'd needed him—someone— and Jimmy was it. Troy's unexpected departure had hurt. She'd been sure he had dumped her. Why else would he have skipped the state without telling her?

Casey's heart wrenched. Tracking Jimmy to the kitchen, she knew she'd hurt him. A part of her had always known that he wanted more than she'd been offering. Even when Troy was here and the two were together. At work, after their shift, Jimmy always stayed late to help her finish closing out—because she was slow, taking her sweet little time to get things done.

They'd talked and laughed, but she'd never been interested in more than being friends. Not in her darkest days had she wanted to be with anyone but Troy. Pulling her gaze away from Jimmy, as their friendship pulled away from her, Casey stared at the plates of food before her—crispy drumsticks, steaming mashed potatoes soaked with a melting patch of butter in the middle—and felt the full brunt of his pain and disappointment. Jimmy was a good guy. He deserved someone to love him. That someone just couldn't be her.

The sunset ride long since returned, the horses cleaned and put away, Delaney closed the books for the day and pushed back in her seat. Slants of afternoon sun cut across the stalls, painting the white wood in creamy gold. It was her first week on the job in full swing, and she was still getting a fix on how she wanted to run things. She needed to establish a flow, a rhythm. She needed her employees to work as a team, be in sync with her expectations and those of the guests. Kicking her boots up onto the desk, she laid her head back and laced hands together across her stomach. So far she was pleased. The men she hired were strong and reliable, the female riders equally as capable. Especially Troy. Only a few days on the job, but already he was proving himself a standout, staying late, volunteering for extra jobs. She'd been delighted by Casey's surprise. It appeared the two were working through their differences. A good thing. Troy clearly loved the girl and she loved him.

Exhaling a sigh, she ran a mental review of the entire staff. Most of the employees had come to her on strong recommendations from area ranches, one of them a man from the Foster's ranch. Misgiving spiked her gut. Gerald's call to apologize for the evening-gone-wrong with Felicity came to mind. Seems he understood something more happened to her daughter than a case of sick belly. He was right, though he didn't seem to understand the extent of it.

Which didn't prevent Delaney from appreciating the gesture. Gerald was a good man, a generous man. He might not have ended up with the woman of his dreams, but he stood by the woman of his choice and his family as a loyal and devoted husband should. It was a respectable trait in a man. Unfortunately it wasn't a trait he passed on to his son, Jack.

Visions of Jack acting the good son, entertaining his lovely daughter in his lovely home soured in her belly. At least it was a charade that didn't last. Felicity finally understood what Delaney had been dealing with all these years. Unfortunately, she learned it the hard way. It must have been painful for her to flee that house like a scared mouse. Jack had called, demanding what she had said to Felicity, as if Delaney were the cause of his troubles. Reeling in her legs, she placed hands to the arms of her chair and pushed up from her desk in one fluid motion. *Try again.* She wasn't the troublemaker. Ruining lives was Jack's job.

Turning out the office light, Delaney went to say good-night to Sadie. It was a ritual she'd begun since her mare's first night in the new stables. Delaney wanted Sadie to know she hadn't been abandoned, only moved to a new home, a home they would continue to share. She smiled inwardly. Sadie had exhibited a case of the jitters when a dozen new horses entered the stables the next day, taking up residence alongside her. Delaney shook her head. Like she would forsake her precious baby for some other horse. She chuckled. Guess animals were like humans that way. They needed reassurance they were loved.

Rounding the corner to Sadie's stall, she clicked her mouth. The horse turned and shook her white-blonde mane with a soft nicker. "Going home, baby girl," Delaney said, reaching through the metal bars to stroke the flat space between her eyes. Big brown eyes blinked as the horse pushed up her nose. Delaney rubbed a hand beneath the velvety muzzle, the whiskers tickling her fingers as she scratched along the horse's jaw line. "We're going to have fun tomorrow. You and I are taking a group out on a trail ride." Cupping the rounded jaw bone, Delaney moved her hand back and forth then scratched behind the horse's ear. "You up for it? Promise I won't bring that rowdy Brandy with us."

Brandy was an Arabian they'd acquired from a ranch in Nashville. Sadie didn't care for her at all, surprising Delaney one day with an uncustomary nip to the horse's side.

Sadie's ears pricked forward. "What's up, girl?" Delaney laughed softly. "Afraid old Brandy is listening?" Stiff ears began to twitch. Brown eyes grew alarmed. Delaney's antennae shot up.

"Talking to your horse?"

Hairs rose on Delaney's neck at the sound of Jack's voice.

"Careful," he said, "or people are going to think you're crazy."

Delaney recognized the thick edge in his voice. He'd been drinking. Slowly, she turned from her horse. Ten feet away, Jack stood like a sheriff ready for a pistol fight. Legs slightly parted—probably for balance's sake—his hands hung by his side. As expected, his eyes were glazed red from a day at the bar. "What do you want, Jack."

He snickered. "Stopped by to pay my old lady a visit."

"Go home."

"Now what kind of reception is that?" He swayed ever so slightly. "You treat all your guests this way?"

Ignoring the barb, she repeated, "Go home."

"I don't want to go home. I want to discuss our daughter." He took a step toward her and Delaney went on high alert. "What poison have you filled her with this time? She's not returning any of my calls."

Disgust overrode any and all caution as she said, "You're the poison, not me." Behind her, Delaney heard Sadie snort.

"I invited her to dinner. She had a wonderful time. She went home and now she won't speak to me. Fill in the blank."

"Someone told her the reason I left you. That you're an abuser."

"What?"

Jack seemed genuinely surprised but Delaney didn't care. The dinner was the reason her daughter wasn't speaking to her either. "Yes. It was a fact I left out and your family filled in."

Anger stormed his dark features. "You're a liar. No one told her a thing. I was with her the whole time and no one said a word."

"I'm telling you the truth. She came home and told me."

"You're lying. Same as you've always done." The change in his demeanor sent shivers across her skin, causing Delaney to instantly assess the accessibility of her gun. "You're jealous she accepted my invitation to dinner and decided to fill her head with ugly lies." Jack closed the distance before Delaney could step clear. He trapped her against Sadie's stall and hissed, "Nothing's changed. You're a lying bitch but this time you've gone too far."

"Jack." She pushed back, his breath putrid in her face. "Stop it!"

"Why should I?" he growled, hands pinning her shoulders. "You didn't see fit to stop with your lies about me." He rammed her against the gate, the metal grill gouging into her shoulder blade. Jamming one arm sideways across her chest, his other hand went to her stomach, digging under her shirt.

Panic stabbed at Delaney. "Stop! What are you doing?" she shrieked. Sadie whinnied in fright. Several nearby horses began to follow suit.

Delaney struggled against Jack, fear warring with disbelief. He was heavy, strong, his fingers clawing at her skin as she shoved at them.

"I'm gonna teach you a lesson once and for all," he ground out, his alcohol-soured breath filling her nostrils. "I'm gonna teach you not to mess with me."

"Jack, you're drunk—you're hurting me!"

He laughed as she tried to push him off, his size working against her. He tore at her shirt. She brought a knee up between his legs. Slipping on the hay, Jack lost his footing. Delaney broke free. He sprang toward her but she dodged him, narrowly evading the swipe of his hand. "Dammit, get over here!"

Pulse pounding, she swiped the hair from her eyes. Sadie reared up, hooves hitting the gate to her stall. Delaney's heart went out to her mare. *Stop, Sadie. You're going to hurt yourself!*

But the animal seemed to be working off the adrenaline of the others. The stables were layered in panic, horses distressed by the shouts. Delaney bent down for her gun. Jack came after her, but his movements were slowed by drink. She sidestepped him, but he caught part of her pant leg. She whipped out the pistol from her boot. "Stop or I'll shoot."

Comprehension blazed in his gaze as she leveled stiff arms. Chest heaving, she said, "I mean it, Jack. Not another move."

He eyed the weapon in her hands, a sardonic smile curling his lips. "Still packing heat, I see. Moved up to an automatic, huh?" He nodded casually, as though he weren't wearing a target on his chest. "Nice move."

"I swear I'll shoot you."

From his crouched position, he chuckled. "You don't have it in you."

"Try me."

"In case you hadn't noticed, that's what I was trying to do."

Delaney didn't like Jack's sense of ease. Allowing him space to regain his wits wasn't wise. Operating under the influence, he was likely to make a dumb move, a move that could cost her. Staring down the line of her arms and over the black metal gun, Delaney slowed her breathing. "Get out of here."

He ran a hand through his hair. "Not until I finish what I started."

"You are finished."

He laughed again, as though he didn't take her seriously. "Remember the days when we used to do it in the stables? As I recall, you enjoyed it. One of your favorite spots."

Finger curved around the trigger, she muttered, "I'm warning you, Jack."

"They were some good times." He eased back onto his heels, set a hand to the ground to steady himself. "Before you got all flighty, that is." Jack pulled a gun. Delaney hesitated.

A dark figure lunged.

In the split second, she screamed. "Troy!"

The gun fired. Troy connected with Jack mid-air, two bodies hitting the ground with a thud. Horses shrieked. Cries pierced the rafters. Shock streamed through her limbs.

Oh no... *Troy*!

Chapter Fifteen

Fear curdled in her stomach. Had she hit Troy? Had she hit Jack?

Troy sunk a fist into Jack's face. A thunderbolt of relief coursed through her. Rising up again, Troy slammed another one into Jack's head.

Troy—where had he come from? As he proceeded to beat the living daylights out of Jack, Delaney grabbed at his shoulders. "Stop, Troy, stop!" She didn't see any blood. Not on him or Jack. "Let him go!"

Jack rolled them, careening the two men into her. Delaney jumped but the momentum of their bodies caught her on the ankle. She tripped, slammed to the ground. The gun tumbled from her grasp. Like a crazed maniac, Troy continued pummeling fist after fist but Jack broke free. Spotting Delaney's gun, he dove for it. Troy twisted.

"Not so fast, boy."

Delaney's pulse kicked at the sight of Jack's gun aimed at Troy. On hands and knees, Troy remained immobile, his hand inches from her pistol. "Get up," Jack commanded.

Slowly Troy rose. Delaney leapt up and rammed shoulder first into Jack. Troy snatched her gun from Jack's hands as he went down. Standing over him, Troy trained the gun on Jack's head.

Delaney shrieked, "Troy, no!"

Dark eyes blazed hot with fury. "Give me one reason."

"Casey!" she cried out. "*Casey*," she repeated breathlessly. "Casey is your reason."

In a sudden fit of movement, Troy kicked at Jack's unconscious body. Whipping the hair from his brow, words seemed to hang on his lips, but he didn't utter a sound. He didn't have to. The combination of innocence, shock and anger in his eyes said it all.

Delaney's heart broke. "I'm sorry, Troy."

Confusion slammed into his expression. "You ain't got nothin' to be sorry for," he snapped angrily.

Delaney bowed her head. But she did. She had almost shot a man.

Jack.

Moaning, he writhed on the ground beside her. She had almost killed Jack. Almost shot Troy by accident. A shudder passed through her, shockwaves rippling in its wake. Leg muscles withered as a wash of light-headedness knocked her off balance.

"Miss Delaney? Are you okay?"

No. She wasn't okay. She needed to sit. She needed to breathe, *to think*.

Troy shadowed her to a wooden bench parked against the wall. Broad chested, the black T-shirt strapped tightly across his torso, he gingerly set the gun down beside her on the bench. He shot a glance over his shoulder, concern swamping his gaze. "You want me to get you a glass of water?"

She shook her head. No. She didn't need water. She'd almost killed Jack. She'd almost killed Felicity's father. Flashback images inundated her—his cocky grin, his disgusting breath, his disturbing moves. Delaney closed her eyes. "I almost killed him."

Troy was calm, even-toned. "You did what you had to do."

Did she? What would have happened if Troy hadn't stepped in when he did? Would she have killed Jack? Would she have been justified?

"I heard enough to know he would have got what was coming to him."

Jack emitted a long groan. From the periphery of her vision, she saw him roll to his side, reach for his face. It was bloody. Bloody from the beating Troy inflicted and not from a gunshot wound. Peering up at Troy, she mumbled, "I think he was going to rape me."

His face reddened. "Don't talk that way. It ain't necessary."

Because it was over. She glanced at Jack. For the time being, it was over. Would he try again?

A sliver of fear poked at her. Nick was gone. He'd be gone for days. Turning, she took in the sight of Jack's battered body. If she'd killed him, he wouldn't be back. Ever.

Delaney didn't say another word. Troy, gun in hand and a guarded eye on Jack, went to calm the horses. At Sadie's stall, she could hear him whispering soothing words to her mare. He went to the next and the next, systematically reassuring the animals. Then he called Cal. In the quiet of the stables, she could hear his every word. "Yes, Mr. Foster. She's here. They're both here. Yes, sir. I think you need to come quick."

Cal arrived within ten minutes. Resting her head against the wall, Delaney watched him go to his brother, held in place at gunpoint by Troy. The two exchanged harsh words. Then Cal conferred with Troy. She felt detached from it all, as though she were watching a movie play out before her, a movie in which she didn't have a starring role. She wondered idly where the bullet landed. Was it in the ceiling? Entrenched in hay? Implanted in a wall? Thank God it hadn't hit a horse.

Cal walked over to her, his features steeped in concern, his fair skin tinged pink. He seemed calm, tranquil, unsullied by the scene splayed out before him. Neat and tidily dressed in his business khakis and white button-down, he looked too clean. Out of place. "Delaney, are you okay?"

She nodded. "I'm fine."

"Do you want to press charges?"

The question dropped out of the sky. Confusion swam in her skull. "Press charges?"

"Jack attacked you. I can call the police but you'll need to provide a complete statement."

A statement. She would have to relay the details of what happened. It would become public knowledge. Nick would find out. Felicity would find out. Delaney shook her head. She didn't want to do that to her daughter. She'd have to confide in Nick but she didn't have to add injury to her daughter's current suffering. "No." She stared at Jack, standing now, flanked by Troy. The man wasn't going anywhere until they said so.

"Are you sure?" Cal pressed.

"I had a gun. He had a gun."

"Yes, but he attacked first."

"And I almost ended it. I almost killed my daughter's father."

The severity of her confession lodged deep in his gaze. Clearly, Cal wanted to dispute the fact. He wanted to defend her, but he couldn't. She had drawn her weapon first. She had intended to kill. Explaining that in a court of law would amount to "he said, she said." Delaney could feel emotion churning within the man before her, words brimming on his lips, but Cal simply replied, "I can't let this pass. I can't let this go." Then his gentle brown gaze nearly undid her. "So help me God, I would have killed him for you, Delaney, I swear I would have."

The breath escaped her. "*Cal.*"

Hazel-brown eyes shining, he shook his head. "I mean it. I'm ashamed of him."

Delaney pressed her lips in a firm line and nodded. She understood. Cal Foster was a proud man, a respectable man. A decent human being. His brother was not.

"I have to do something," Cal said.

"Hurry up, brother! Time's a wasting," Jack's voice taunted.

Rage iced Cal's compassionate gaze to arctic stone. Fixing on Delaney as if to retain a piece of his sanity, he said, "If you change your mind, you let me know."

"Sure thing." Glancing at Jack's swollen face, she added, "But can you take him away from here? I can't stand to look at him."

Cal set his mouth in a stony line. With one last look at her, he turned, marched over to his brother and slammed a fist across his jaw. Jack reeled. "That one's from me."

Troy grinned.

Jack came back at him and Cal thrust his chest forward, cocking a fist in a show of force Delaney didn't think him capable of. Cal had grown into a quiet, peaceful man with no resemblance of the bluster and brawn of his younger days. "Go ahead and give me a reason to beat the crap out of you."

Apparently sensing there was more to his meeker brother than met the eye, Jack held back. He wrenched his face and spat, "You aren't worth the effort."

Troy stood waiting and ready. If Jack hit Cal, it was clear Troy would welcome another round with him. Delaney dropped her head back against the wall. He would have beaten the man to a bloody pulp and left him to die. Visions of Jack's attack assaulted her mind—hand, nails, digging—it was the last thing she expected. The man was unpredictable, yes, but a rapist?

Her daughter came to mind, the reason for this visit, and Delaney cringed. If Felicity knew what had transpired this evening, it would crush her, destroy her. She already believed he was a monster. Believed her mother was one, too.

Overwhelmed by a heavy sadness, Delaney closed her eyes, warding off images to painful to allow. Felicity hated her, might never forgive her. Nick's image steamrolled into her thoughts and she groaned. She hadn't been worried about handling Jack but Nick had been. *Don't confront Jack about Felicity.* At least she'd kept to her word. He confronted her, not the other way around. But still...

She had believed she could handle him. Visions of Jack at the other end of her barrel recharged her nerves. She'd been prepared to shoot. Sure as she was sitting here, she would have shot him. Did, or so she'd thought.

*I heard enough to know he would have got what was coming to him.*

How long had Troy been lurking in the shadows? How much had he seen?

Shame slinked through her. Troy was a good kid. He was doing his best to make up for his past mistakes. Witnessing the ugliness between her and Jack was the last thing he needed. While the boy was good at heart, he had a grenade of a temper. Short-fused, it didn't take much to set him off.

Invariably, it seemed to be his temper that landed him in trouble. Thank God she didn't shoot him by mistake.

## Chapter Sixteen

After refusing escort to her cabin, Delaney hiked the steep incline alone in the dark. No flashlight was needed this evening, not with a nearly full moon floating in the sky overhead. Leaves and trunks were cast in a pale glow, the ground dark and narrow beneath her feet. Katydids pulsated rhythmically in the night, her skin chilled by the moist damp air. Placing a hand to the knotty bark of a tree, she stepped from rock to rock, then pushed off from a massive root embedded in the clay. She knew the way by heart. Every stone, every branch—she could hike this path with her eyes closed. Tonight she wanted to do just that, close her eyes and shut the world away. Immerse herself in the comfort of the familiar, the safety of these woods, her cabin sanctuary above.

As the shock wore off, the reality of what happened trickled in. She'd been shaken by the incident more than she realized. More than almost killing her ex-husband—a thought that unsettled her—his outrageous behavior disturbed her. Could he attack Felicity? Was he unstable enough to attack his own daughter? It was too horrible a thought to consider. She and Jack had their issues, but Delaney always believed he drew the line at Felicity. After tonight, Delaney wasn't certain whether that line was eternally blurred.

Reaching the top, she paused. Boulders were pillows of gray, the gravelly road a sheet of silver carpet leading up to her home. She'd taken her time climbing up, yet she was winded, her energy drained from the ordeal with Jack. After a few moments she pushed herself forward, recovering her breath as she walked the gentle incline to her cabin. Inside, the lights were on. A brief hope bloomed. Felicity's car was parked down in the lot, but it didn't mean she was home. She could be with Travis. Grabbing the stair railing, Delaney hauled herself up the few steps, opened the screen door and strode to the front door, peering inside as she passed. Inside, Felicity was seated on the couch reading a book. A decisive misgiving twisted in her gut. Delaney knew she should keep the evening to herself, but couldn't shake the words from last night.

*You're as big a monster as he is. How could you do that to me? Where was the overprotective mother when I needed her?* Felicity had been angry, hurling insults as hard and fast as she could. Delaney wasn't a monster for keeping the truth from her. Funneling her line of vision on the lone strawberry-blonde head, she wondered, *Was I?*

Tugging the boots from her feet, Delaney transferred the pistol to her waistband and opened the door. Felicity's head jerked at the sound. Instantly she rose from the couch, circled the end and headed for the stairs. She wouldn't even look her mother in the eye.

"Felicity, wait." Delaney reached out and grabbed her by the arm. "Stop, I need to talk to you."

Flames licked at Felicity's green eyes. "I don't want to talk to you."

"I almost shot your father." The words spurted from her lips before she could rein them in.

"*What?*"

In the space of a second, Delaney realized she had to tell her. She had to tell Felicity what happened. It would eventually get out anyway and if she learned the truth from someone else, Delaney's fate as liar and truth-withholder would be sealed. "He came by the stables. He accused me of turning you away from him."

Felicity slackened within her grasp. No longer angry, she stood gripped by confusion. "What are you talking about?"

Heaving a sigh, she dropped her hand. "He thinks I'm the reason you're not returning his calls."

She screwed her expression. "You have nothing to do with *that*."

Relief swept through Delaney. "I know. But he was angry. He had to blame someone and that someone was me."

A sudden fear bridled in her eyes. "Did he hit you?" Studying her face as though seeing her for the first time, Felicity stared at her mother, hard. "Did he? Did he hit you again?"

"No." Delaney felt the weight of the evening press squarely on her shoulders. "But it wasn't pretty." Cradling her daughter in her gaze, hating what she was about to tell her but knowing there was no way around it, Delaney bolstered her resolve with Nick's advice. *Don't sell your daughter short. Felicity is made of strong fiber.* Yes. Yes, she was. "Come," Delaney murmured. "I'll tell you everything."

She plodded to the couch, dropped to a seat and watched as her daughter follow, sitting on the opposite end. She was near but not too close. Because Felicity remained at odds. Taking a deep breath, Delaney began, "Jack"—she refused to grant him the privileged term of father—"came by the stables to make trouble. He was angry and drunk. He accused me of filling your head with poison, then he jumped me." It was an ugly picture she was painting, but an honest one. "He was drunk and unstable so I was able to get away from him, but he didn't give up. I pulled my gun, warned him to back off." She paused, tormented by the horror wrenching the fine features of Felicity's face. "He drew a gun. I pulled the trigger but I didn't hit him."

Luckily. Delaney inhaled, calming a spurt of adrenaline, and continued, "Troy jumped Jack and sent him to the ground."

"Troy?"

She nodded. "He must have been working late. He heard the commotion and took action." Delaney was indebted to him for it. He saved her from making the biggest mistake of her life. Compounding Jack's abuse with his untimely death at the hands of her mother would only have made things worse for Felicity. "Troy called Cal. Cal came and removed his brother from the property."

Felicity absorbed the information in silence. Digesting it, turning it over in her mind, her heart, Delaney understood her daughter was working to cope with yet another ugly facet to her father. Delaney felt responsible, regretting the day she married the man yet accepting that it was another time, another place. A place she couldn't return to, a decision she couldn't change. *Wouldn't*, if given the chance. After all, she thought. Felicity was the product of their union.

Felicity was her treasure.

"I don't know what to say."

"You don't have to say anything, sweetheart. If you'll listen, that's all I ask." At the silent consent in Felicity's eyes, Delaney took the first step, crossing the chasm that had opened between them, "I'm sorry I didn't tell you about the divorce, the reason for the divorce. But you were young, an innocent." Delaney recalled the freckle-faced girl of eight, the shining strawberry-blonde curls, the bright-eyed innocence. "Ernie said we could stay in the cabin." It was a fight at first, but because Felicity reminded him of Susannah, he had agreed.

"Ernie took to you like a bear on honey, inviting you to visit him and Albert any time you wanted." A smile tugged at Delaney. "You thought it was an adventure. You were excited by the prospect of living in Grandma's tree house. That's what you called it. Her tree house." Delaney pulled a foot onto the couch cushion and tucked it beneath her. This wasn't a conversation she ever wanted to have, but now that she was, she was grateful for the chance to remember the good, heal the bad. For both of them. "At the time, I told you Daddy had to go out of town for a while so we were going to live at Grandma's until he returned. Weeks passed and I eventually told you that we weren't going back, that Daddy and I were getting a divorce." Her heart ached at the memory. "Do you remember any of it?"

Felicity shook her head, tears brimming in her eyes.

"As you grew older, you were so smart, so wise. I always thought you were wise beyond your years. Part of me knew you could handle the truth, but a bigger part knew it would hurt. Jack used to call and promise you things and when he didn't deliver, you were crushed. I could tell you were still hoping for his return. So I let things lie. Someday, I told myself, we'd discuss it. But truth was, I didn't want to ruin the little life we had created. When you took up the flute, I think Ernie thought he'd died and gone to heaven, thanked God for the first time in his life." Delaney paused. "Do you understand what those evenings meant to him?"

She tilted her head. "I think so."

It was but a whisper, but the first crack in her daughter's shell. Delaney yearned for the shell to split wide open. Brushing hair behind an ear, she continued, "It meant the world to him. He adored hearing you play, sharing in your enthusiasm. You reminded him of my mother." Felicity smiled. Ever so slightly, but it was there. "My mom was the sugar in his tea, the butter on his bread. She made everything in his life better, sweeter."

Truth be known, Susannah made Ernie's life worth living. When she died, Delaney swore she took a piece of Ernie with her. It was one of the reasons Delaney had tolerated his verbal abuse. He'd been hurting something fierce, and living with Albert didn't help. The man did little more than warm the seat of rocking chair when he wasn't swiping the pantry shelves clean. He proved no comfort to Ernie and vice versa. Looking back, Delaney thought it a miserable existence the two men shared. Breathing in deeply, she released her breath in a ragged stream. "As the years passed, we settled into a routine. You were my world, my everything. Life rose and set with you. I watched over you like a hawk."

*Where was the overprotective mother when I needed her?* The accusation rose like bile. It was true. She'd gone against her better judgment and allowed her daughter to go with Jack.

"Whenever I thought about telling you," Delaney paused, "I thought about how it would spoil your innocence, hurt you. It was an ugly business between Jack and me, not the kind of thing a girl wants to hear about her father, even if he was only in your life on the sporadic occasion. In the rare event he sent a card or called, you were thrilled. You lived and breathed him for days."

The tears filling her daughter's eyes pulled her back to those days when Felicity literally ran through the cabin, singing and dancing. "I couldn't ruin that for you. I couldn't take away the only joy you had with regard to him."

Felicity's face was filled with pain. Tears flowed freely, unleashing her sadness. Staring at her, Delaney always knew this is what the truth would do. This is what telling her daughter would have done all those years ago. "I'm sorry, sweetheart. I honestly thought I was doing the right thing. If I was wrong, I'm sorry. So terribly sorry."

Felicity's gaze shot to the side, her cheeks flushed red with emotion. She hugged her arms to her body and shook her head. "No, it's me. I'm sorry. I shouldn't have come down on you like that without knowing...without..." Her voice broke.

Delaney's heart ached at the sight of her daughter. Felicity was drowning, struggling to wrap her head around a sordid past of lies and deceit she couldn't comprehend. She was mature, but she was young, idealistic. Her dreams were still firmly attached to the clouds.

It was a flight reality had a way of sinking. "You were angry, sweetheart. You didn't know the history. Which is my fault." Delaney wanted to ask who told Felicity, wanted to know what awful person thought it wise to share the information but refrained. It didn't matter. The damage had been done. "If I could take it back and do it all over again, I would. I would have found a way to tell you, to share the truth with you."

"You don't have to say that."

"It's true. Nick was right."

"Nick?"

Delaney smiled, inundated by a stream of warm pleasurable thoughts. "He thinks you're a strong young woman. He thinks I should have told you, that you could have handled the truth."

"You told him?"

She nodded. She told Nick everything. Twisting the ring on her finger, she mused, why wouldn't she? He was her husband. There was nothing she would keep from him. It was the way a real partnership was supposed to work. A marriage. Something she and Jack had in name only. "He thinks you're amazing and he's right." She grinned. "You are. Totally."

Felicity erupted into a giggle and rolled her eyes. "Mom."

It was the first hint of the old Felicity, her baby, her girl. *Young woman*, Delaney corrected. Felicity was growing into an incredibly bright young woman, and her mother needed to start treating her that way. "It's true. You are amazing."

Felicity scooted near and Delaney's heart ripped open. As she reached out for her, joy gushed from Delaney's soul as she welcomed her daughter back into her arms. "Oh, Felicity." Squeezing tight, Delaney relished the warmth of her child, the familiar scent of her. This is what living was about. This is what mattered.

Holding on, locked as one, there was no place Delaney would rather be than right here.

Chapter Seventeen

"Now that Troy knows about the baby, do you think his family history will have a bearing on Casey's pregnancy?" Annie asked.

All morning long she'd been running through the possibilities, hardly able to concentrate on her clientele. Several times she caught herself mid-swipe on a finger nail she'd already done! It was crazy, but she was consumed. Concerned. Casey had told Troy about the baby, and Annie couldn't help but think there was a connection. At her first break, she decided to seek the counsel of her husband. Cal was smart about most things. Maybe he'd have an idea.

"Not sure that a man's contribution comes until after the baby is born," he replied, one eye on her, the other on the goings-on in the hotel lobby. Situated to one end of the front desk, tucked close to the backdrop wall of river rock, Annie didn't mind his divided attention. She was so proud of Cal and the way he was managing the hotel. In the salon most guests didn't realize he was her husband, and she'd overhear them rave about him while sitting for their manicures.

"From what I've been reading online, it's possible Troy's genetics can play a role. What do you think? Should I get Casey to ask him to see the doctor?"

Cal smiled indulgently. Today's heather-green button-down complemented the light brown of his hair, enhanced the sensitivity in his eyes, softened the lines of his clean-shaven face. "I think we should let the doctor decide if and when he's concerned."

"Aren't you the least bit concerned?"

"It's like I told you before. Women have been doing this for years." He pulled her close, a drift of his crisp cologne tickling her desire for him. "Now why don't you tell me why you're as worried as a first-time momma? Is there something I don't know?"

Annie peered up at him. Was he right? Was she being overly concerned? Before she could reply, Cal stiffened within her grasp. "What?" She turned and recoiled. Jack Foster strolled into the hotel lobby boasting a bruised and swollen face. Horribly out of place next to the cheering splash of fountain, the atmosphere of peaceful retreat, he drew stares from a few nearby guests. "What happened to him?"

Cal leveled his gaze. "It's something I was going to mention to you."

Annie turned on him. "*Mention to me*? Do you know something about what happened to him?" Dread peppered her senses. "You didn't have anything to do with it, did you?"

Jack sauntered up to the front desk, dropped a hand to the sleek wood countertop. "Hello, brother."

Cal stood speechless.

"What, no warm welcome?" Jack glanced sideways down the counter.

Two young female reception clerks dutifully ignored him, clearly assuming their best professional detachment though it was obvious they were shocked by his face. Annie tried to pull her focus away but couldn't. He really did look awful. "And I thought this was a fancy establishment, complete with helpful, courteous staff."

"You have no business here."

"Don't I?"

"You don't."

Annie clung to Cal's side, a determined foreboding settling in.

"I'd like to see the manager."

"You're seeing him."

Resentment glinted in Jack's dark eyes. "The real manager. I'm here to press charges against one of your employees."

Annie flung a hand to her neck. Her throat closed. An employee did this to him?

"I'd advise against it."

Jack chuckled. "Of course you would. But since I don't take orders from you, I intend to do as I please."

Malcolm Ward emerged from the back office. Located just to the rear, one could hear everything when the door was open as it had been. Access was inconspicuously fashioned into the rock wall, a discreet vantage point from which he and Cal could be on site yet unobserved by guests. Annie thought it must have been designed with episodes like this one in mind.

Dressed similar to Cal, Malcolm's cool blue eyes, a near match to his pale blue button-down, leapt from his tanned complexion, fixing on Jack in a penetrating gaze. His shock of white hair was combed back giving him an older, authoritative appeal, underscored by a lean, solid build. As hotel owner and husband to Annie's sister, Lacy, Malcolm had been forewarned about the likes of Jack Foster and understood the full extent of what he was dealing with at the moment. "Is there something I can help you with?"

"Yes." Shooting a smug smile toward Cal, Jack said, "I'd like to put you on notice. One of your employees assaulted me last evening."

"Which one?" Malcolm asked pointedly.

Cal interrupted, "You're out of bounds, Jack."

"Am I? Is that what you called it last night when you spoke to Daddy? Told him I was out of bounds?" When Cal didn't respond, Jack continued, "For your information, I didn't try to rape Delaney. She pulled a gun on me."

Annie gasped. Malcolm stilled.

Cal hardened his edge. "I have no intention of litigating this matter in a hotel lobby. If you intend to press charges, call the police."

Jack shifted his weight and tapped his hand to the front desk. "Oh, you're a big man now, are you? Tough and cocky.

Instead of punishing me, you might want to ask what Delaney was doing alone late at night with a stable boy."

Annie's hearing became of vacuum. *Delaney fooling around*?

"Get out before I throw you out," Cal growled.

Jack leaned a shoulder forward and snarled back, "Don't tempt me, brother, or I'll include you in those charges as well."

Malcolm stepped in, leveling in no uncertain terms, "I'd do as the man says. If you have charges to press, call the authorities. Otherwise, I'll have to ask you to leave the premises."

"Really?" Jack laughed, a gesture Annie could tell was forced. "I haven't done anything. How's that going to look for your reputation, kicking out a member of one of the town's most prominent families?"

"Move on, Jack." Singularly focused on his brother, Cal advised, "I think it's time for you to pick up stakes and get out of town."

"Like you did, Cal?" Jack flicked a glance toward Malcolm. "Does your new boss know about your accident?" Annie's heart squeezed as he said, "Drunk driving is a crime. A real shame when you cripple a man."

Eyes darting to Cal, then Malcolm, Annie wanted to lash out and strike Jack on behalf of her husband. She wanted to cut him to the quick for the venom he was spewing.

Cal stood immobile, anger heating his gaze. Malcolm appeared oddly cool. "Another word and I call the police," Cal warned.

Jack laughed, confident he was back in the saddle. "What, can't handle a rowdy cowboy on your own?"

Malcolm stepped around Cal, but Cal stopped him. "Don't. He's not worth it." Then to his brother, "Get out, before I throw you out."

"I'm going," Jack said, pushing off from the desk. "But I'm putting you on notice. Smear my name again and it's the last thing you do. Same goes for Delaney and Troy. Those two haven't heard the last from me."

Annie gaped. *He's* the stable boy?

Jack shot one last smirk their way, then pushed out through the front doors of the lobby. Annie felt tiny, wishing she were trapped in a dream rather than standing in the center of reality where her husband was about to lose his job, her daughter about to have her heart torn to shreds. She closed her eyes, warding off the tawdry images. But it couldn't be true. Delaney and Troy were not together.

Cal said, "I'm sorry, Malcolm."

"Not here." Malcolm signaled his staff with a nod of thanks, then retreated to his office. Cal duly followed.

Annie debated. *Was it her place?* Reaching out for Cal's arm, she blurted, "I'll be in the salon if you need me."

He merely nodded, but the gloom inked in his eyes gouged her heart. He looked like a man on his way to the guillotine.

Malcolm took a seat, indicating Cal should take one himself. He did. Continuing to digest the scene that had taken place, Cal ran through his options. Jack had left him no room for escape. No room to detour. Separated by a simple wooden desk, papers neatly assorted to one side, a computer and keyboard to the other, Cal had to give it to Malcolm straight. Resisting the urge to look at the security images on screens overhead, he tensed. There was a security camera trained on them, recording a conversation he never hoped to be having. It was a closed chapter in his life. A wound that had healed. Until his brother Jack decided to tear it wide open. "Listen, Malcolm, I'm sorry about what happened out there."

"Disgruntled guests are a fact of the business."

"Jack is more than a disgruntled guest." And they both knew it. "I need to explain about the accident, about the drunk driving—"

Malcolm silenced him with a hand. "No need."

"I can't let it pass. I need to explain."

"You don't," Malcolm corrected. Surprised by the finality in his tone, Cal stared at Malcolm, fighting to make sense of it. "I know about the accident."

Cal shot forward. "You what?"

"I know about the accident, I know about the other driver. I know about what you tried to do for him and his family."

"But how?" Malcolm closed his expression, undercutting Cal like a blow to the chin. "I don't understand. You can't know. I haven't told anyone except for Annie."

Malcolm almost looked guilty as he said, "I checked your background before I hired you. I made calls to your boss, I searched the public records, did a full search on your name." He added a half-smile. "You'd be amazed by what the Internet will reveal these days." Cal dropped back into his seat like a ton of lead. Something told him he was about to find out. "When I learned about the accident from the papers, I made some discreet inquiries to your attorney." He raised a hand between them and said, "The man didn't break client-privilege, but he did reveal in so many words how you were trying to help the family. I checked into it. The hospital bills, the medical care..." Blue eyes softened. "I respect what you tried to do."

Met by compassion, Cal hardened. "It was my fault."

"Culpability wasn't proven."

"Still. It was my fault. I'd been drinking." Words he didn't have use for these days, but remained stuck to him from the past. He glanced at the security monitors and found lobby activity had returned to normal.

"You made a mistake. You tried to own up to it. I respect that in a man." Malcolm heaved a sigh, holding Cal firmly within his sights. "I've made some mistakes in my life. Everyone has. What I've learned is that I'm more interested in where a man is going then where he's been. You're a good man, Cal. You're rock solid. I need you by my side running this hotel."

"Thank you," he murmured, too shocked to say anything more.

"But I also need honesty from those around me. Jack was pretty battered. He made a pretty nasty accusation." Malcolm narrowed his gaze, one that nailed Cal to his seat. "What happened between Jack and Delaney? How does Troy fit in?"

Cal started from the beginning, from the minute he received Troy's call to the moment he dumped Jack at his parent's home and the subsequent conversation with his father about the incident. He didn't leave out a single detail, not an inch of what he knew. He owed Malcolm that much. He owed Malcolm a whole lot more, but he'd begin where he could. "I didn't expect him to have the audacity to press charges."

Malcolm returned a contemplative stare. "Nick will have to know."

"Don't you think Delaney will tell him?"

"Did you tell Annie?"

*Ouch.* Apparently Malcolm picked up on Annie's surprise.

No, Cal had not told her. Delaney had wanted the ordeal kept private so as not to hurt Felicity. Cal gave her his word. It wasn't Annie's business. It wasn't anyone's business but Delaney's and Jack's and Troy's.

Troy. Hopefully this wasn't going to ruin his second chance. From what Annie said, Casey had taken him back. She'd told him about the baby and the boy was reportedly thrilled. If Jacks persisted, Troy could end up in jail.

"Delaney asked me to keep her confidence and I gave her my word. I figure it's her business who she tells."

"Do you know what really happened?"

"Only what Troy told me."

"Troy." Malcolm furrowed his brow. "How did he manage to get mixed up in this mess?"

"He was working late, overheard the commotion. When Jack went for Delaney, he intervened."

Malcolm shook his head. "That boy has an amazing ability to find trouble."

"I'll give you that," Cal agreed, "but he did the right thing."

"Maybe." Caution entered Malcolm's gaze. "But it might be the end to his career with Harris Hotels."

Outrage rippled through him. "You're not going to fire him, are you?"

"The decision might be out of my hands. Depending on whether or not Jack goes through with pressing charges, Troy might find himself with a legal battle."

"It won't come to that, I promise you."

"How can you be so sure?"

Cal couldn't. He simply knew he couldn't allow it to happen. There was too much as stake for his family—his wife and step-daughter, his soon to be son-in-law.

"Either way, Nick needs to know."

"You don't think Delaney will tell him?"

"Can't be sure. But now that I know, I can't hold her secret." He paused. "I'm sorry, but Nick and I go way back. We don't keep important information from one another no matter who wants it so."

Reluctantly, Cal nodded. Jack attacking Delaney on hotel property counted as important when it came to Nick. As owner of the hotel, Malcolm would have to be concerned. Troy was an employee. His actions had consequences.

Chapter Eighteen

Annie rapped lightly on Casey's bedroom door. "Sweetheart, can I come in?"

"Yes," came the muffled reply from somewhere inside.

Annie pushed open the door to discover her daughter whisking hangars from one side of her closet to the other, a dull array of tops and dresses swinging from the force. Casey wasn't known for her bright clothing. She wasn't known for caring about how she looked. "What's the matter? Did you lose something?"

"I'm having breakfast with Troy today and I don't want to wear a tent dress."

"Tent dress?" Annie asked, venturing further in. "Those are maternity clothes, not tent dresses."

Casey glanced over her shoulder with a stony eye. "They're tent dresses, Mom. They make me look big as a house."

Annie nearly laughed. "You couldn't look big as a house if you tried."

Casey groaned loudly. Hands slid hangar after hangar along the metal bar as she pulled each piece of clothing out, inspected it, shoved it back in. *Plink.* She thrust another back in dismay. "What am I going to wear?"

Annie savored a private smile. It was nice to see her daughter care about her appearance. She couldn't remember the last time Casey fussed with her hair or clothes. She didn't wear makeup, no nail polish. Her toe nails were painted, but it was only under duress. The techs needed practice during their soft opening the week before Memorial Day, and though Casey had wanted nothing to do with it, obliged on their behalf. Annie was happy her daughter had found reason to care. She feared it was a joy soon to be extinguished.

She doubted the girl knew anything about the incident with Delaney. "Well..." Annie meandered closer. "Why don't you try that sundress Lacy bought for you?"

Casey halted mid-motion. "What sundress?"

"Remember, the aqua blue one she said would bring out the color of your eyes?"

Visibly searching her memory, Casey replied, "I don't know where it is?"

"Maybe in the box? You never opened it." Casey had said it was too bright and would call attention to her figure.

"Oh yeah—I almost forgot!" Racing across the room, she yanked out an ivory-painted dresser drawer and pulled the dress free. Tags dangled from its spaghetti shoulder straps, wrinkles creased lines down the skirt. "Do you think it will be too much?"

Annie smiled. "I think it will be adorable."

Casey lashed her with a dose of suspicion. "You're not just saying that, are you?"

She chuckled. "No, I'm not just saying that. I think you should wear those silver hoops Cal gave you for your birthday, too. Maybe a pair of sandals?" she prodded, unsure if any of her open-toed shoes still fit. Casey practically lived in her boots these days.

"I'll try it on."

"Okay." Pleased she'd been able to help, Annie re-traced her steps. "Let me know when you're ready. I'd like to see it."

"Okay," Casey replied distracted by the row of shoes on her closet floor.

Annie returned to the living room where Cal was reading the Sunday morning paper, folds of newspaper piled by his side on the sofa. Comfortably dressed in jeans and T-shirt, legs kicked up on the coffee table, reading glasses perched on the end of his nose, he looked up. "Well? What did she say?"

"Nothing. I wasn't about to bring it up." Annie circled the couch and dropped to a seat next to her husband. Reaching for her cup of coffee, she cradled the warm ceramic in her lap.

"Why not? I thought you were curious."

She chucked a sideways glance at him. "Curiosity killed the cat, you know."

"Old wives' tale," he countered.

Most of which were true, Annie wanted to retort. But it was neither here nor there. Heaving a sigh, she replied, "Casey wouldn't have heard me, anyway. She's in a whirlwind over having breakfast with Troy, trying to decide what to wear."

Cal lowered the newspaper in hand. "Ah."

"Do you think Troy's going to tell her about the incident with Delaney?"

"No reason for him to tell her."

Annie nodded, relieved. Casey didn't need the added stress. "Do you think Jack will really press charges against him?"

"Doubt it. It would open him up to a litany of charges from Delaney, and I think he's smarter than that. Evil, but smart."

At the sound of Casey's bedroom door opening, Annie turned in her seat, watching her daughter breeze out into the living room of their small apartment. Their new house wasn't finished yet, the plans for which Cal had surprised her with over Christmas. They were building it on Casey's half of Ladd Springs with her daughter's blessing. Not only had she changed her mind with regard to family ties, she seemed eager to stay close. Cal must have seen it, too, refusing to rent a larger place for the interim. He insisted living here would give Casey a sense of stability, continuity. The quarters seemed cramped to Annie, but at the moment, she was grateful. The arrangement kept her close to her daughter.

"Well, what do you think?" Casey spread the skirt with her hands. "Do you like it? Do you think it's too much?"

Cal pulled the glasses from his face and let out a slow whistle. "That's a mighty pretty dress on you, really brings out your eyes."

Pleased by the compliment, she asked her mother, "What do you think?"

Warmed by Cal's response, Annie agreed. "I think Cal said it all. It suits you perfectly and Lacy was right. It does make your eyes pop."

Casey beamed. "Do you think Troy will like it?"

"If he doesn't, he needs to have his head examined," Cal said, matter-of-fact.

Casey giggled, a sound filled with girlish delight. "I'm meeting him at ten."

"Care if we join you?"

Casey and Cal both looked to Annie in surprise.

"Well..." Casey hemmed, holding the lengths of her skirt close to her body. "It is our first breakfast together since I told him about the baby."

"What do you say your mother and I find our own booth," Cal said, silently urging Annie to agree.

"Of course," she said. "You two will have a lot to talk about." Like your high blood pressure, your lack of weight gain, his family medical history—none of which would likely make it into the conversation. "We'll find our own booth," Annie muttered under her breath.


Troy spotted Cal as he held the door to the diner for Casey and Annie. Sitting at a table in the back, Troy stood, weaving through tables crowded with people as he automatically headed for Casey. Sunday morning was a hive of activity at Fran's, most diners dressed for church services while a few remained casual like him. Unfortunately, Troy didn't remember the last time he'd attended services. But with a baby on the way they were going to have to rectify that and quick.

As he neared Casey, his mouth fell open. "Dad gum, woman. Where did you get that dress?"

"Do you like it?" she asked, her expectation stamped on her grin.

"Like it?" He inspected her attire with open desire. "I love it."

"Thank you!" she chirped, blue eyes shining with pleasure as she practically lifted from her toes.

Taking her by the arm, Troy leaned over and kissed her cheek. "I mean I really love it." The dress was bright blue with frilly trim, totally opposite to Casey's normal boots, jeans and sneakers—or lately, her oversized maternity dresses—and it showed off her bare shoulders. Her really smooth, creamy white bare shoulders. "I've never seen you in anything like it before."

"Aunt Lacy gave it to me. She said a pregnant woman was the most beautiful kind of woman and should dress like it."

Troy chuckled. "Well, you ain't gonna hear any disagreement from me!"

"How goes it, Troy?"

Troy looked at Cal's knowing eyes, instantly wondering if Casey or Annie knew about the business with his brother but realizing at once they did not. Casey, anyway. She was too cheerful. "Fine. Real fine."

"Good." Cal placed a hand to the small of Annie's back. "Mrs. Foster and I are going to enjoy a bite of breakfast."

Troy nodded. *Why else would they be here*? Leading Casey by the elbow, he guided her back to his table. Jimmy Sweeney was in the back, sulking. Once Troy told him the news about him and Casey getting married, Jimmy had closed his mouth and turned on his heel.

Like he should. Trying to step in on his woman the way he did, the boy ought to run scared. He'd also better get the hint that Troy didn't approve of male friends hanging around his wife, either. "Are you hungry?" Troy asked Casey, helping her to a seat and then sliding in next to her.

"Starving."

Giving her the onceover, he commented, "You don't look like you been eatin' much."

Casey groaned. "Now you sound like Fran and my mother."

"Well, are they right?" He slid an arm around her shoulders and said, "I thought pregnant women were supposed to get big and round when they were carryin' a child."

She skewed her expression. "Not all do. My Aunt Lacy hardly gained an ounce."

Troy pinned her with a skeptical gaze. "Well you're gonna eat with me," he told her as a waitress delivered two glasses of ice water. Looking up, Troy said, "We'll have a stack of pancakes, scrambled eggs and grits, side of bacon and two biscuits."

Casey gaped at him. "Who's going to eat all that food?"

"You and me," he said, then directed the waitress, "You can set it anywhere you like. And two OJ's, too, please." He looked at Casey and tapped the top of her stomach. "The baby needs some vitamin C."

Warmth flooded her. He was being so protective, so caring. Casey didn't know what she'd expected when she told him about the baby other than she'd been concerned about his reaction to the added responsibility. She never dreamed he'd take to it like a fussy old woman. But it pleased her. "Troy, you don't have to fuss."

The waitress left and he settled on her, a silly grin peeling at his eyes. "What? I ain't fussin.' All I'm sayin' is we have a baby to care for now. We have to start thinkin' about these things, make sure the baby is healthy."

Doubt petered through her limbs. Casey reached for her glass. "The doctor said I'm fine."

"Good. I aim to keep it that way. Now listen, I didn't tell you about Vegas."

"Vegas?" she asked absently.

"Remember that horse I helped deliver? I saw him at the stables. He's a real strong one, maybe even a fast one. Miss Delaney has a winner on her hands with that one. Then there's that horse I was training when you walked up the other day."

"The big brown one?"

Troy nodded. "His name is Spirit and, boy, I tell you he's chock full of it. He came to us from another ranch where they claimed he wasn't suitable for ridin.' But you know Miss Delaney. When she has her heart set on something, she ain't hearing nothin' else. She knows a good horse when she sees one." Casey smiled, pulled in by the depth of his pleasure. It was hard not to feel the things Troy felt about his horses. His love was visceral, contagious. His entire demeanor lit up as he spoke. "Well, I've been workin' with him and I think he's gonna be ready for riding next week!"

"So soon?"

"Yes, ma'am." Troy squeezed her to him and drew his glass of water near. "Just goes to show most folks don't know what they're talkin' about when dealin' with horses."

"Not like you."

Troy took a sip, beaming in light of her praise. Setting his glass back down, he said, "You know, I've been thinking..."

When he didn't continue, Casey wondered at the hesitation softening his gaze. It wasn't like Troy to hold back. "What?"

"Well, I was wonderin'... When I save up enough money, what would you think about me training horses?"

"Training them how? Like you are now?"

"Yeah, you know, training them how to be around people, gettin' them ready for others to enjoy but also maybe breeding. I know a fine horse when I see one. We could make a nice living makin' a business of it."

"Isn't that what the Fosters do?"

"It is."

"Sounds great!" she replied, uncertain as to what was involved but trusting him. Horses were his department and she believed there was no one better. The Fosters had been pleased with his performance, except for his drinking.

"Do you want to work them with me?"

She pulled back. "Me? I don't know anything about horses." She liked riding them, but that was as far as her knowledge went. Her interest lay in science, not horses. Stars, constellations. What would she do with a horse?

"I could teach you. I bet the horses would love you."

"Well, er..." She glanced away, rubbed a hand over the swell of her abdomen. "I'm going to college now and—"

His brow shot up. "You are?"

She nodded. "Jimmy and I are taking a few classes—" She paused at his instantaneous glower. "What? Is that bad?"

Capping the lid on his temper, Troy glanced back toward the kitchen. "Naw, it ain't bad."

"I'm sorry." Anything that had to do with Jimmy was bad in Troy's eyes. "But when you left, I didn't think you were coming back. My mom convinced me I should go to college, take a few classes, see how it went. Jimmy agreed to go with me."

"You don't have to explain," he said, though it was clear they were words he was using to placate her, not words that reflected his true emotions.

"I'm sorry. I thought you were gone for good."

The hard edge in his gaze melted away. "It's not your fault. I thought you understood. I thought you knew I was coming back." He paused, placed a hand over hers. Staring at the tabletop connection, he said, "It's my fault."

Shame filled her. Sinking her mind into the din of conversation around her, the banal normalcy of the life and people she'd always known, Casey wondered if she should have known better when it came to Troy. Her mother said not to waste her time on him. Her mother said to look ahead to the future. But then again, she never much approved of Troy. That was Casey's role. She's the one who should have believed in Troy when everything and everyone pointed to the opposite. Swallowing over a knot in her throat, she was grateful he'd come back to her. If he hadn't, Casey could have lost him forever.

The waitress delivered their juice, vivid orange liquid with bits of pulp suspended in the glass. The sight made Casey's stomach rumble. "Ya'lls order will be out soon," the woman clipped on her way off.

"So you're going to college." Troy shifted gears, elevated his tone. "What are you studying?"

"I'm taking a few science courses."

"Science?"

"Astronomy."

A knowing grin lit up his eyes. "You're studying the stars in school?"

"I am."

Troy laughed softly and swung his head away. "Dad gum, Casey. It figures."

"Is that a bad thing?"

"No. But now I'm gonna have to remember all those galaxies and things floatin' up there. You're always pointing them out and now I'm gonna have to learn them."

"Why?"

"Because you like them."

Her heart sang. *Because she liked them*. Those were about the sweetest words she'd ever heard in her whole life. Because she liked them, he was going to learn about them. Leaning over, Casey kissed his cheek. "Don't worry. I won't give you a test or anything."

"I hope not," he replied with a sheepish grin.

Casey perked up at the sight of Felicity and Travis walking in the front door. Her hands instinctively went to her belly. "Your brother's here." Troy shrugged a glance toward the door, "He's been real nice about the baby," she said.

"If he's so nice, why didn't he tell me about the pregnancy? I would have come home sooner had I known."

"I asked him not to tell you. I didn't want you coming home because you felt you *had* to."

"What's that supposed to mean?"

Casey's throat became suddenly dry. One arm resting over her stomach, she reached for her orange juice and held it between them. "I wanted you to come home because of me."

Troy leaned close, his movements cautious of her enormous midsection. "You listen to me. There's only one reason I'm home and that is because of you." Hitching a thumb towards Travis he said, "Mr. High and Mighty might think I'm a screw-up, like I was trying to shirk my duties, but that had nothin' to do with it. I would have come home if I knew. I didn't, I came home anyway. Because of *you*, you hear me? Because of you."

Suddenly trembling, Casey nodded, then downed a small sip of her drink, the sweet taste cold and soothing as it flowed down her throat.

Troy smirked. "The baby's an extra benefit."

Casey almost choked on her juice. "Benefit?"

Troy's cocky grin unleashed a smile. "Yeah, *benefit*. We were gonna have babies one day anyway. Why not get them out of the way now?"

Casey smiled. While it wasn't the most beautiful of compliments, she understood what he meant. Troy was happy. Pleased. She was silly to have ever doubted him. Nudging Troy, she said, "They're coming over."

He turned as Felicity and Travis strolled up, hand-in-hand. Travis acknowledged Casey, then cast a reproachful gaze over his brother. "Troy."

"Travis."

Felicity waved hello, strangely preoccupied with Troy. She looked normal enough, dressed in her usual denim cutoffs and brightly colored T-shirt, her strawberry blonde hair braided in a line down her back. But her green eyes glistened, like she was about to cry. "Thanks for helping my mom," she said softly, almost pained.

*Helping her mom*? Casey's gaze sought Troy, who seemed as surprised as she by the comment. "It wasn't nothin'," he replied, easing away from Casey's side.

"It was, and thank you. I can never repay you."

Troy shrugged it off. "Your mom has been good to me. There isn't anything I wouldn't do for that woman."

Felicity nodded, appearing to be on the edge of tears.

"Let's go," Travis said. "I'm hungry."

The couple turned and Felicity froze. Casey spotted the cause.

Jack Foster stood at the front entrance to the diner, his face a horrible mess of purple and red bruises. People collected around the cash register concealed awkward glances, though it was hard not to stare. His eye was swollen shut, his skin marked by red and purple. It was horrible. "Oh my, what happened to him?"

Troy said nothing. Travis said nothing, though she noted he squeezed Felicity's hand, drawing it close to his side. Intuition clanged like church bells in Casey's brain. The man's battered appearance reminded her of the day when her own father walked into the diner after a beating. She locked on Troy. Jeremiah had accused Troy of the beating. *Did he have something to do with this one*?.

Chapter Nineteen

"Ignore him," Travis advised her.

Casey tensed. That was going to be difficult, considering the man was headed directly for their table. She could feel Felicity's nerves fire and pop while Troy remained a statue next to her in the booth. Travis stood strong, his muscular body edging in front of Felicity's.

Swaying hips in and around tables, Jack Foster had eyes only for Troy as he made it tableside. A flurry of questions zipped through Casey's mind. Please don't let this have anything to do with why Felicity thanked him. Please make it a coincidence that her father is staring down her boyfriend. Casey wanted to close her eyes, pretend this was nothing but a dream.

Jack entered their midst. Briefly glancing at Travis and Felicity, the man drilled into Troy. Casey detected a soft spot in the callous demeanor as he gazed at his daughter. His face looked awful, but his hostility slipped. "I've been trying to call you."

"I know," Felicity stammered, leaning into the safety of Travis, his body a shield between her and her father. He was a gallant knight, wielding his shield for his damsel in distress. And Felicity was clearly distressed by her father's presence. After their conversation the other day, Casey could understand why. She stole a peek at the man. *He hit Delaney.*

"She doesn't have anything to say to you," Travis stated.

"Don't interfere, boy. This is between me and my daughter."

Felicity remained a frightened fawn, but Travis pushed out his chest as though he were looking for a fight. "She wants nothing to do with you."

"And I told you to stay out of it."

Troy was on his feet in seconds, standing shoulder-to-shoulder with his brother. Together, they looked like twin guards. Glancing between the two, Casey thought Troy every bit as tough as Travis, and with far less effort.

Jack merely chuckled. Giving Troy the onceover, he remarked, "Surprised you're still walking the streets. Won't be long, though. The police are looking for you."

Casey's pulse quickened. What? *Police*?

Thankfully, Cal Foster walked up behind his brother. "Jack," he said in a very calm voice, "why don't you leave these kids alone?"

"Why don't you stay out of my business."

"These kids *are* my business."

He scowled. "Not my daughter."

Cal glanced to Felicity. She stood immobile, Travis silent. He exchanged a glance with Troy. It was as if everyone was communicating via ESP, everyone except her. Casey's insides began to unravel. What did the police have to do with Troy? Who had beaten Jack Foster? What did Cal have to do with any of it?

Cal turned to Felicity. "Are you interested in a visit with your father at the moment?"

Visibly trembling, her pink-toned skin pale, she shook her head.

"You have your answer," Cal said to his brother. "It's time for you to leave."

Like a cornered rat, Jack made a quick assessment of the situation and decided the odds were against him. Three men against one. And he was already injured. Looking as if he were about to spit, Jack replied, "You're gonna be sorry for this."

Casey shuddered. If words could kill, her stepfather would be lying in a pool of blood right now. As Jack walked away, Troy stood rigid by Cal's side. Felicity reached for Travis and he pulled her close, mouthing, "It's okay."

"You okay?" Cal asked Felicity.

"Yes."

Travis led her away from their table, not bothering to say goodbye to anyone. Cal looked to Troy and then offered a small smile for Casey. "You two enjoy your breakfast, you hear?"

She swallowed hard. Not hardly!

Troy sat down and Casey whirled on him. "What was he talking about? Why are the police looking for you?"

Clearly agitated, Troy replied, "It ain't nothin' to worry about."

"Nothing to worry about?" Was he insane? He just got back in town, just got a new job and the police were looking for him? She didn't call that nothing to worry about—she called that a big problem! "Did you do that to him?" she blurted, gripped by a sudden need to know. "Did you do that to Felicity's father? Does it have anything to do with why she was thanking you?"

Troy didn't answer. He clamped his mouth closed as though forcing the words to remain unspoken. Casey wanted to shake him, shake the words from his lips. Their waitress arrived with their breakfast, sliding plates of steaming food before them. Moist heat rose from the pancakes before her, mixed with the scent of buttery yellow eggs and grits, half a dozen strips of rusty-red bacon and two fat biscuits. A mountain of food.

Food she couldn't stomach the first bite of. Casey clutched hold of her belly, reassured by the warm round feel of her baby. She had no appetite—not for food. She needed answers and lots of them.

"Will there be anything else?" the waitress asked.

Troy looked to Casey but all she could think about were police, his job, a beating.

"I think we're good," he told the girl.

"Okay. Holler if you need anything!"

"Troy." Casey's breathing grew shallow, her chest tight. She didn't want to know but she had to know. "What happened?"

He unrolled his silverware. "It's nothin' you should be worried about."

"I am. I am worried. Are you in trouble?

"No."

"No?" Casey didn't believe him. Not the first breath. "How can you say that?"

"'Cause it's true." He jabbed a fork into his eggs.

"Then why would that man bring up the police?" she demanded, the aroma of his eggs sending tingles of hunger pains through her stomach. "Why would he come here and say that?" she cried, quickly unraveling beneath his calm.

"He's trying to make trouble."

"Trouble for whom?"

"Everyone."

Frustration wedged a lump in her throat. Troy was being evasive, dodgy. He wasn't telling her the truth—a truth that could cost him. Without thinking, she sought her mother across the diner. Her blue eyes were glued to Casey. Concern and distress rippled through her features. Her mother knew something. Something Casey didn't know.

"Eat your breakfast, Casey."

"I'm not hungry," she replied. She wanted answers, not food. From the corner of her eye, Casey caught sight of a uniformed policeman. Her heart stopped, then thudded against her ribs. Mindless chatter ran on around her, utensils clinked. Shiny buttons gleamed from his starched uniform. *Was he here for Troy*?

Removing his hat, the blond-haired officer surveyed the restaurant. Vaguely familiar, Casey had a bad feeling. A knot lodged in her chest. He was staring at them. Them! Casey became frantic, flashing a look to her mother and Cal both tuned in to what was happening. Everyone except Troy seemed to get the severity of what was going on.

Casey wanted to jab him, alerting him to the impending trouble. But she couldn't move the first muscle. Pinning her gaze to a rising Cal Foster, Casey silently implored him to come, to fix this mess before it got out of control.

Troy set his fork down as the police officer arrived at their table. "Troy Parker?"

"Yes."

Skimming over Casey, the officer asked Troy, "You have a minute?"

"What for?" he asked innocently.

"I have some questions I'd like to ask you."

Casey released her breath in a rush as Cal showed up politely inquiring, "Is everything okay here?"

The officer addressed Cal. Man-to-man, they were nearly the equal in height, equal in coloring. Although Cal was a bit darker in looks with his medium brown hair, the officer *felt* darker in his black uniform. "I have some questions for the boy."

"Sure thing." Cal nodded, silently gesturing for Troy to get up and take this outside.

Troy glanced sideways, a shaft of regret stabbing his dark gaze. "It won't be but a minute." He tossed his napkin to the table and walked outside with Cal and the police officer.

As if on cue, the scene controlled by an unseen director, Casey's mother appeared at her table. She slid into the booth beside her asking, "Sweetheart? Are you okay?"

"I don't know what's happening," Casey murmured, oddly comforted by the scent of her mother's perfume as she watched the men take her boyfriend outdoors. "What's going on?" She turned to her mom. "Do you know?"

Annie nodded. "It'll be okay," she assured, wrapping an arm around Casey's body. "Everything will be okay."

Really? Folding arms over her stomach, Casey continued to stare at the three men standing outside. Because it felt like her world was toppling over.

Delaney led Sadie through the empty stables, walking in sync with the gentle fall of her Palomino's hoof-step. Sunday afternoon was quiet, most guests retired to the hotel or the outdoor Serenity Scape, a gathering beneath the trees where guests were treated to the sights and sounds of nature infused with a mellow taste of local music performed alongside an open fire pit. In Tennessee that meant a medley of acoustic guitar, violin, harmonica, banjo and the occasional rap from a drum. Delaney and Nick sat in for the first evening, and she'd been floored by the powerful combination. She never imagined the combination would have such an effect, but then again, she wasn't Malcolm Ward. The man was a creative genius.

Nearing Sadie's stall, Delaney reflexively scanned the walls around it for signs of her bullet. Where had it landed? For two days she'd searched high and low but found nothing. She dropped her head back and searched the ceiling. Could it have ricocheted into the rafters? Lodged itself into the tin roof?

"There you are."

The deep masculine voice startled her. Whirling, Delaney snapped, "What are you doing here?"

"I live here?" Nick posed nonchalantly, his playful tone betrayed by an intensity lining his eyes. Her heart thudded at the sight of him.

Dropping Sadie's lead, she hurried to him. Nick swept her into his arms and hugged her tight, then pulled away, dipping his head for a kiss. Deep, fierce, it was the kiss of a man who'd been away too long. Succumbing, she dissolved into the strength of his embrace, the stress of the past few days vanishing from her heart. Solid, warm and strong, Delaney needed his comfort, his touch. "I missed you," she said breathlessly, consumed by his presence, the muscular arms encircling her, the firm wall of his chest. "But I didn't expect you until tomorrow."

"Change of plans."

She detected an edgy undercurrent of displeasure. Peering up at him, she asked, "Did you get everything taken care of in St. Kitts?"

"I did."

"Good." She placed her cheek to his chest. That meant there would be no reason for him to dash off again anytime soon. Jack's assault had unnerved her more than she expected it to. It was taking a toll on Felicity as well. The two of them could use Nick's calm, staunch, even-handed support. Knowing he was near eased her mind, calmed her spirit.

"Is there something you want to tell me?"

"Tell you?" she squeaked, hating the weakness in her voice.

"Jack Foster?"

Delaney pulled back in alarm. "Did Cal tell you?"

He shook his head.

"He had to—he's the only one who knew!"

Nick held her, cords of discontent running through his dark gaze. Muscles in his jaw jumped but he didn't respond.

Delaney glanced away. "I'll tan his hide..."

"Why? Because he was willing to keep your dirty little secret?"

Stunned by the razors cutting between them, she stumbled, "Nick—"

Nick held her firm. "Don't worry. Cal had your back. Malcolm had mine."

"Malcolm?"

"Yes. Jack came to the hotel to cause trouble and Malcolm told me everything."

Shame filed in, filling her with a guilt she deserved. Malcolm had Nick's back when she didn't. She was his wife, his life partner, yet it was his business partner who came clean with him. Not that she wouldn't have. But...

Nick's hands tightened on her arms. "You have to let me take care of you. You can't continue to take chances like this, don't you understand that?"

"I left him alone, I swear." Delaney dropped her head forward, shook it gently. "He came out of nowhere. It was totally unexpected."

"So help me, Delaney, if he laid a hand on you, I'll kill him."

She raised up to face him, torn by the emotion clenched in his eyes. "I nearly did."

The statement defused the ball of rage in his gaze. "So I heard."

Sliding her arms around his waist, Delaney melted into him. She needed the strength of his body, the shield of his love. She needed the intimidating rock of a hard man with a soft center.

Nick held her for a minute, erasing the pain, the fear, rejoining the bond between man and woman. Releasing her, he brushed the hair from Delaney's face, gingerly touched her brow, her cheek. "If anything happened to you..."

He didn't finish. He didn't need to. Everything he felt was etched plainly in his eyes. Nick loved her. From the bottom of his soul she felt his love pour into her.

With a glance to her horse, the animal content to linger in their presence, Nick asked, "You know he's making trouble for Troy, right?"

"What do you mean?"

"Cal told Malcolm that Jack paid a visit to the diner this morning, followed by your police officer friend, the one who showed up on your doorstep a year ago with questions about Jeremiah."

"Gavin?"

"Yes. Cal said it's pretty serious. Jack's charging aggravated assault." Nick cupped her chin and forced her to face him. Dark eyes reached out and grabbed hold of her. "Which I don't understand—why would the man charge assault as though Troy started the fight? Didn't you set the record straight?"

Delaney slumped, glanced to the horse at their side. "Oh, no..."

Hard lines formed around Nick's eyes, his gaze devoid of cheer. "Talk to me. What's going on?"

The weight of Troy's predicament landed squarely on her shoulders. This was her fault. It was her fault they didn't know the truth. "I wanted to talk to you first," she said dully. "This will end up all over town, and the hotel will be dragged into it..."

"Forget the hotel—you need to put the guy behind bars where he belongs."

Yes, of course. Did she expect Nick to say anything different?

But this would also affect Felicity. She'd been appalled by her father's behavior, not only from the other night but from a decade ago. It cut deep, raw. Exposing his attack would invite gossip and add to her pain.

Delaney had hoped the incident would have ended with Jack's departure the other night. He'd been drunk. He probably didn't remember half the evening. Apparently she thought wrong. "It's his word against mine."

"Wasn't Troy a witness?"

She shrugged. Pushing from Nick's arms, she gathered Sadie's lead, removed the bit from her mouth and replied, "I can't say. I don't know how long he was there, how much he heard or saw."

"Have you asked him?"

Unhooking the latch for Sadie's stall gate, Delaney opened the door and gave a pat to her horse's rear "Go on, girl." She secured the door, turned back to Nick. It embarrassed her to think Troy might have seen the worst of it, but he could have. She simply didn't know. "Not really. Cal said he was going to handle it."

"Doesn't seem to have done a very good job."

Delaney leapt to his defense, "Cal's a good man. This isn't his fault. I intended to talk with Troy but haven't gotten around to it." Nick thrust a cynical glance down his nose at her. "I mean it. Between the shock over what happened, sharing the news with Felicity..."

The whole thing had gotten away from her. And, besides, she wanted to discuss it with Nick first. She needed him by her side before she took the steps to reveal the gory details.

"You talk to the police. I'll talk with your ex."

"Nick"—she reached out to him—"do you think that's a good idea?"

"Any man touches my wife is going to hear about it from me."

"But Nick," she protested, knowing his temper the way she did, "don't you think that will make things worse?"

"Don't care. Jack struck the first blow. I intend to finish the fight."

While she liked the idea of Nick defending her honor, she didn't want to consider the ramifications should his actions slide out of control. With the hotel, Felicity, there was too much riding on it. Nick could jeopardize everything in one simple act of revenge. "Shouldn't you consult with Malcolm first?"

A wry smile pulled at the corner of his mouth. "He already knows."

Delaney groaned inwardly, rolling her eyes upward before settling on Nick. As he stared down at her, his gaze no longer hard and angry, Delaney detected a fatigue. Nick had to have traveled all day to get here. He must have had to make excuses to his staff in St. Kitts. Must have dropped everything and come home. Gratitude and remorse swirled together as she thought about what that meant to her. "I'm sorry about not telling you. It wasn't a call I thought you needed to receive while a thousand of miles away."

Nick pulled her into his arms. "How about you let me be the judge from now on?" He nipped her nose. "Okay?"

Delaney nodded dutifully. "Okay." Nick was right. She needed to stop making decisions for everyone around her—choosing—"what" they needed to know and "when" they needed to know it. She only seemed to foul things up.

"Next on the agenda is Felicity. Is she home? Have you talked with her yet?"

Relief loosened the tangle of emotion inside her. "Yes. She's forgiven me. She understands, but she's having a rough time dealing with it."

"Can't say as I blame her. No young woman should ever have to deal with such business, especially from her father.

But we'll fix it, and in time she'll be able to move on. How about Troy? Do you know where he is?"

"I don't know. Didn't you say the police came by to question him? I would assume he's at home by now."

"Where's he staying?"

"I guess with his parents."

"Good. I'll need to talk to him."

Delaney sighed. "Should I join you?"

"No. You'll be engaged in more important discussions with members of the police department."

Chapter Twenty

Frustration boiled, spurting from her pores as Delaney stood before her friend and police officer Gavin Shore. Gritting her teeth, she tried to remain calm but her patience was quickly draining. Gavin had arrested Troy on aggravated assault. It was a serious charge and he wasn't budging, wasn't listening to reason. She didn't know what to do other than shake some sense into him. A move that would likely land her in jail. "How many times do I have to tell you? It's what happened. Jack tried to rape me."

Gavin sat on the corner of his desk, one leg hitched up over the end of it. He was dressed in his full uniform, the black clothing adding an authoritative air to him. His office was plain, the bureaucratic basics consisting of a metal desk and file cabinets, rolling chair, computer and a miscellany of manila files. One probably had Troy's name on it. Easing his weight backward, Gavin said, "Mr. Foster told me you'd probably come in here and stick up for the boy."

"Gavin, I'm not sticking up for Troy, I'm telling you the truth!"

"He said you pulled a gun on him and he was trying to defend himself."

"He pulled a gun on me!"

"He said you drew first. Said you took a shot at him."

"Jack attacked me, Gavin. I pulled a gun because he attacked me. Attacked me and then drew his gun."

Gavin roamed her figure with a cautious gaze, searching her body from head to toe. "I don't see any marks. Unlike Mr. Foster." Pulling a paper from his desk, Gavin read from it. "I was standing in the stables, having a private conversation with my ex-wife when Troy Parker jumped me, proceeded to attack me with his fists before using Delaney Wilkins' gun to threaten my life." Gavin looked to Delaney. "Which goes to intent. No self-defense." Setting the paper down, he asked, "Do you know that's considered a Class C felony, carrying three to fifteen years in prison?"

Prison. The single word gutted her. Troy could go to prison because of her. He'd have a permanent mark against his record. Would Nick keep him on at the hotel? Could he keep a convicted felon on the payroll? Friendship aside, business was business. Nick had a company to think about. Then there was Casey. Delaney didn't even want to think about what this could do to Casey and the baby!

Staring at Gavin, a man she'd known since grade school, Delaney was stunned. She couldn't believe he was being so difficult. Sure, his mother was friends with Victoria Foster, the two families closer than blood, but to defend Jack's heinous actions was disgraceful. Gavin was an officer of the law, not a kingpin in the good old boy network!

Steeling her resolve, Delaney tamped down her temper. "Gavin, what can I do to convince you? What can I say to make you understand it's the truth?"

Gavin looked at her, an odd mix of curiosity and distance coalescing in his hazel gaze. A smile tipped the corner of his mouth. "How about we start from the beginning?"

"I told you everything."

"Did you, now?"

She didn't appreciate the sarcastic roll of his tongue. He was mocking her. He was treating her as though she were the criminal here. She was beginning to grasp the reluctance women experienced in coming forward. If a friendly face could do this to her, make her feel awkward and embarrassed, what was a stranger capable of? It was enough to drive her home and lock the doors, never to breathe another word of the incident again. But she couldn't. Troy's future depended on it. "I did, Gavin. I told you everything that happened."

"Are you having an affair with Troy?"

The question knocked the wind from her lungs. "What?"

"You heard me."

"Of course not—that's sick!"

Gavin smiled. "C'mon now, Delaney. You're an attractive woman, your husband spends a lot of time traveling..."

Delaney recoiled at the picture he was painting. "You are way off base."

"Am I?"

"Yes," she replied, and it took all she had not to smack the smirk into his skull bone. Gavin was being rude and disgusting, and it felt like she was being violated all over again.

"What was the boy doing in the stables at that hour?"

"Working late."

"Hm. What kind of work does a stable hand have at night on a Friday?"

"I don't know," she said, regretting the words the instant they slipped from her tongue. "He's trying to do right by his girlfriend. They have a baby on the way and—"

"So I hear. Makes it all the more ugly that he's stepping out on her again, doesn't it?"

*What was Gavin doing?*

"As I recall, he did the same with Jeremiah's girlfriend."

"Gavin—"

"And the developer lady? I heard they were pretty cozy when she was in town, too."

Amazed by the spread of false information, Delaney assumed Gavin was referring to the events of Whiskey Joe's where Jillian Devane tried to publicly seduce Troy. According to Lacy, Jillian was running her hands all over him. Unfortunately, Casey walked in and witnessed the entire thing. But to hear Gavin smear it into something ugly and intentional was over the top, like he was gunning for a fight.

Gavin lifted from his desk, circled back to his chair. "I see a lot of holes in your story, Delaney. And you want me to take you at your word over Jack's?"

"Yes," she replied flatly. "I've told you everything—the truth."

"Funny..." He placed a pointed finger to his desk. "But I remember a time when you saw fit to withhold details from me. What's to say you aren't doing the same now?"

"What are you talking about? I haven't withheld anything from you."

"As I recall, you didn't see fit to fill me in on the details of Jeremiah's situation when you had the chance."

Blind-sided, she gaped at him. "But that's different. You know Jack abused me—it's the reason I left him!"

"You never reported him for it."

"I had a daughter to think of!"

Gavin shrugged in what felt like a horribly insulting gesture. The whole town knew why Delaney left Jack. Walls talked. Families protected their own. She knew for a fact there'd been a collective sigh of relief when Jack left town for Nashville. Gavin did, too. He knew all this yet stood here resisting her. Why?

"If you'd a told me about Jeremiah ahead of time, I could have saved the department a lot of grief. Instead, you forced the authorities in Las Vegas to call my boss who then *directed* me to bring him in." Gavin sat in his chair, rolled forward to his desk. "Go on home, Delaney. Let the justice system do its job."

She stared at him. Was she missing something? Gavin scratched the side of his head, waiting for her to leave.

Overwhelmed by an imploding sense of futility, Delaney was rendered immobile. Where was the justice? The common sense of decency? Gavin was seriously telling her to let him and the justice system handle it? He wasn't even listening!

A half hour later, Delaney slugged up the stone steps to the lobby entrance. Heedless to the beautiful surroundings of Hotel Ladd, the luscious bloom of hydrangea, the thriving fern and rhododendron, she couldn't see past her failure. Despite her best effort, she had failed to make Gavin see the truth. More than her failure, she was disturbed by his reception. In no uncertain terms he had shut her down, basically accused her of making up a story to save her employee, an employee Gavin implied she was sleeping with.

It was sick. The whole situation was twisted, a convoluted mess of false allegations and disgusting tongue-wagging lies. It was enough to send a weaker woman running, but dammit, she couldn't run. Troy was depending on her. Through the front glass panels, she caught a glimpse of Nick. His imposing stature towered over the young women beside him at the front desk as they discussed something. His image of strength was emphasized by the wall of river rock behind him, the navy of his button-down making him a standout against the girls dressed in white. To the right, several guests milled about the gift shop, perusing a jewelry case filled with gold pendants formed in the shape of wishing wells. It had been designed as a symbol of eternal hope and spiritual fulfillment, neither of which she felt at the moment.

Hesitating on the threshold, Delaney didn't feel like going in and putting on a pleasant face for guests. She didn't feel like hashing out her failure for others to see. But Nick wasn't looking outside. Sleeves rolled up, he was working. As he should be. As Troy should be.

Pushing through the door, Delaney was struck by a wave of cold air. Chilling the perspiration on her naked arms, it quickly swallowed her whole. Nick glanced up, papers in hand. As he held her in his gaze, his demeanor cooled several degrees. Could he sense the results of her meeting with Gavin? Was she that transparent?

Rather than going to him, she hovered near the indoor fountain. Its water gurgled and splashed, dropping delicately from one tiered basin to the next. Instead of calming her, the sound irritated. Nick neared and drew her off to the side, near a pair of lounge chairs. Neither sat. Lowering his voice, he asked, "Well, how'd it go?"

"Horrible."

"Horrible?"

"Yes. Gavin has arrested Troy and won't listen to my side of the story. Thanks to you and Malcolm, he thinks I'm some kind of conspirator against him, not to mention he's falling for that con artist of an ex-husband of mine's bull crap—"

Nick grasped her shoulders. "Slow down. You're not making any sense. What do you mean, *conspirator*?"

Delaney flipped her face up to meet his, a whorl of emotion funneling through her. "Because you and Malcolm didn't tell him about the warrant out for Jeremiah's arrest, the one he had to learn about from his police chief, he thinks I withheld evidence from him. Information that could have helped him nab Jeremiah."

"But he did get Jeremiah, arrested him and held him for the Vegas DA."

"He doesn't see it that way. He thinks you should have told *him* what you knew so that he could have brought Jeremiah in on his own, without the direction of his boss."

Realization registered in his eyes. "And be the hero."

"Exactly."

Casting a glance around the lobby, shadows formed beneath the line of his dark brows, and Delaney felt as though he were moving his forces out of sight, going underground. She placed an arm to the muscular round of his forearm. "Nick? What are we going to do? I can't let Troy be charged for something he didn't do. I mean, he did hit Jack but only under duress. If he's charged with assault and battery, it will stay on his permanent record."

"We're going to fix it."

"How? Troy's parents are working against us."

"How so?"

"By letting him sit in jail! They think it will teach him a lesson."

Nick raked a hand through his hair, waves of brown clipped short and neat. He looked at her in astonishment. "Don't they understand the circumstances? That he did the right thing?"

"I told them, but they're angry. Upset."

"How the hell do they think *you* feel?" he erupted under his breath.

"It's complicated, Nick. The Parkers are good people. They raised eight kids and only one has caused them any trouble."

"That one being Troy."

"Yes. But he's a good kid. This time he's caught up in bad circumstances that are beyond his control."

Nick pulled the cell phone from his pocket. "I'm going to bail him out."

Relief swept through her. "Thank you. I don't want to fire him, Nick. He helped me, and he's back on the mend with Casey. I don't want any of this to interfere with his job here."

"Who said anything about firing him?" he asked, dialing as he spoke.

"So that means you won't?"

"It means I intend to clean up this mess so that a firing isn't warranted."

"How?"

"I'm calling Lanny."

Lanny, his attorney, the man Nick and Malcolm went to for anything and everything legal. "But isn't he a corporate lawyer? What does he know about criminal law?" *Criminal law*. Troy was no criminal—he was a defender, a protector! Visions of Jack's assault trickled in. The man had pointed his gun at her yet Troy was the one sitting in jail. A wave of nervous energy tumbled in her gut. It wasn't right. It wasn't fair!

"Lanny will put us in contact with the best criminal lawyers in the country," Nick said, holding the phone to his ear. "We'll have Troy out and free of these charges in no time with a few of our own to file."

"Against Jack? But I told you, Gavin doesn't believe me."

"Well, we'll have to make him believe you."

"How? It's not like Jack is going to confess."

"Don't be so sure about that." Into the phone, he said, "Nick Harris. I need to speak with Lanny right away."

"Nick," she urged worriedly, "you can't jeopardize the hotel by beating a confession out of him."

"I don't intend to." Then to his lawyer's office, he replied, "Have him call me on my cell. Tell him it's urgent."

Watching him end the call, Delaney wasn't convinced. Nick wasn't the type of man to let others handle his business for him, not when it came to revenge. Hadn't he flown to South America to exact his revenge on Jillian Devane? Rather than call her father and gather his information, he'd personally flown to Brazil to meet with him in person, in the flesh.

Flesh.

Beating.

"I'm going to get Troy," Nick said, "and then I'm going to settle matters with Jack."

"You can't handle Jack on your own. You need law enforcement involved. It has to be legitimate."

Nick said nothing, casting his attention to the front desk. Delaney turned, surprised to see Malcolm emerge from the office. The two men shared a glance. Behind the black of Nick's gaze she could see a thousand thoughts swirling. The lines in his face had deepened, hardened. Whatever Nick's plan, it wasn't going to be pretty. Distracted by a couple crossing the lobby, a blonde couple who appeared Norwegian or Swedish with their fair skin and naturally rosy cheeks, urgency clawed at her. Once again, Delaney was consumed by the surreal turns her life was taking. First Felicity learned the truth, cursing her mother's decisions, and then Jack's attack, Troy's arrest and Nick's promise to "fix it." It was too much. Nick was unpredictable. "Settling matters" with Jack could mean any number of things.

"I want you to go to the stables," he said to her, pulling her into a hug. "Take your mind off this business and let me handle it from here, okay?"

Cheek pressed firmly to his chest, Delaney soaked in the feel of him. She trusted Nick but feared the circumstances might prove beyond his control. Jack would taunt and bait and try to lure Nick into a compromising position.

"I'll let you know when I have something concrete." Nick kissed the top of her head.

She nodded dutifully. Did she have a choice?

## Chapter Twenty-One

"Please, Casey," Annie pleaded. Clipped to the edge of the sofa in their apartment, her daughter sat resistant to reassurance of any kind. She wouldn't eat, wouldn't drink, wouldn't listen to reason. She wouldn't do anything but wait for Troy's phone call. Annie didn't like the situation any more than Casey, but there was honestly nothing they could do.

"He said he'd call. But he hasn't! I have to go to him!"

"We have to wait for Nick to take care of things."

"Troy's in jail—his parents won't bail him out! How can I just sit here and do nothing?"

Annie hated the panic in her daughter's voice. She was losing control—understandably so—but it couldn't be good for the baby.

Brightly dressed in a blend of green and blue and swipes of eye shadow to match, Ashley Fulmer stepped in. Her rhinestone-studded wardrobe felt wildly out of place in the fluster of upset, but Ashley only did bright and glittery, and this morning was no exception. "Now calm down, darlin' before you come apart at the seams. Mr. Harris is going down to bail him out and he'll be home by lunchtime. There's no sense in your going, too."

"What if he can't? What if the police won't let him go?"

"Bail only takes money, darlin' and Mr. Harris has it spillin' from his pockets."

Casey's gaze darted between the two. She didn't trust them. She didn't trust Nick. She didn't trust anyone at the moment. Annie couldn't blame her. No one had told Casey about what happened between Jack and Delaney. Why shouldn't she think they were holding back from her now?

"What if he can't prove Troy is innocent? What if no one believes him?"

"He will. Delaney said Nick's lawyers will fight and Troy will be cleared of these charges, you wait and see." Ashley exchanged a solemn glance with Annie, communicating a concern that went beyond the pregnancy. She was worried about Casey's past. High strung on a good day, she had taken to drugs in the past and Ashley feared that if Troy were found guilty of the charges and sent to prison, Casey would skate off a cliff. Annie couldn't refute the notion.

Annie squeezed Casey's hand. "Nick will take care of it, sweetheart, you've got to trust him." Delaney said as much when she called this morning, though Annie still couldn't believe Gavin was defending Jack. Everyone knew the history. It wasn't a secret. But when Candi said Jack's and Gavin's mothers were close, Annie hadn't realized she meant closer than two kernels on a cob! It was ridiculous to think they would collaborate to protect a criminal like Jack but they were. "They'll call us as soon as they know something. Worrying about it now won't help."

Casey stared at her like a frightened cat, a kitten dangling from an electrical line over a pool of water. Just when Casey allowed herself to believe the future was bright and happy, Troy could be ripped from her life and sent to jail. "I'll ask Cal when I get to the salon, okay?" Annie had to work, the schedule stacked from open to close. She didn't want to leave Casey alone which is why she called her godmother. Ashley would stay with Casey and keep her calm.

But still Annie was concerned for Casey's health and the health of the baby. She couldn't shake what the doctor had said about stress. *Stress is a killer. You must make sure she keeps it to a minimum.* Easy for him to say. He wasn't living the nightmare!

Drawing her purse close to her body, Annie looked to Ashley. "I've got to go."

Ashley nodded and walked with her to the front door of the apartment. "Go on. I've got it covered here."

Her heart looped around Casey, Annie murmured, "I wish I didn't have to leave. It doesn't feel right."

"You have to do what you have to do. You sittin' here isn't gonna wind the clock any faster. We're gonna hear when we hear and that's all there is to it."

"But she needs me."

"And so do your employees. You've got a job to do so get to it. And try to relax, darlin'." Ashley inched closer. "You're wound up tighter than a possum on a freeway."

Annie blinked. Staring into blue eyes, lashes heavily coated in mascara, she asked meekly, "Can you blame me?"

"No, but it's not helping anyone." Ashley rubbed a hand up and down her arm. "You've got to stay strong for the child. She needs you to be calm and steady not unraveling like a ball of quilt yarn."

Everything she didn't feel. "You're right. I'll try."

Ashley whittled her gaze to a fine-tipped point. "You've got to do better than try. There are people dependin' on you."

"I will." Annie nodded dumbly. "I will. Will you talk to Ida?" Ashley and Ida went way back. Her sister was married to Booker's first cousin. It was possible she could talk some sense into her and in turn, get Ida to convince Gavin to settle this mess.

"I told you I would and I will, first chance I get." Ashley ushered Annie toward the door. "Now git. You've got re-sponsibilities waitin' on you."

Annie was already running behind, but she couldn't shirk the entire morning. It was true. People were waiting on her, clients included. "Thank you."

"You don't have to thank me. We're family. It's what we do."

Family. A word growing by leaps and bounds in Annie's world. With one last glance to Casey, Annie was determined her daughter wouldn't suffer because of Jack Foster or Troy. She was determined the incident with Delaney would not serve to ruin her child's and grandchild's lives.

Casey sniffled, the sound tugging at Annie's heart. Taking a step back into the living room, she said, "Sweetheart, I'll call you the minute I know something."

A bleary-eyed Casey nodded.

Annie accepted Ashley's kiss and hug. Swathed in a rush of heavy perfume, she allowed herself to be pushed out the door, a reluctant call to duty weighing on her mind.

"Call us, you hear anything, okay?" Ashley asked. "We'll be fine until then."

The door closed, leaving Annie alone on the second-story balcony, awash in a bath of bright morning sunshine. Turning, she cast a glance out over the parking lot. Quiet, most spaces empty, the bulk of apartment residents were already up and out the door for work. Work. She loved the new salon but at the moment not a cell in her body wanted to be there. She turned back to her front door. Every fiber of her being wanted to be at home with Casey.

Nick, Malcolm and Cal drove to the county jail. Seated in the backseat, Cal had a bad feeling as he listened to Malcolm's phone call. He was on the line with the attorney for Harris Hotels, coordinating a plan to defend Troy on the charges—charges Cal couldn't believe had made it this far. According to his father, his mother was digging her heels in on this one and squeezing her contacts for favors. Momma was protecting Jack, insisting Gavin Shore charge Troy to the fullest extent of the law. Daddy said she wouldn't listen to reason but then again, Cal doubted he would push. Gerald understood this was Victoria pitting Jack against Delaney in a silent play for revenge. While the town would see the Fosters versus the Ladds in a court dispute, very few would know that Foster versus Foster lay at the heart of the battle.

"Thanks, Lanny." Malcolm ended the call and reported, "Lanny suggests a guy out of Chattanooga. Says he's the best in the state when it comes to criminal defense."

"Good," Nick replied, one hand firmly on the steering wheel. "Call him. See how fast he can get on Troy's case."

"It might take some time," Malcolm advised. "The police are claiming he's a flight risk which might pose a problem with bail."

"That's ludicrous. Troy's no more flight risk than you or I. Pay the man extra. We need Troy out and back on the job."

Malcolm's pale blue eyes changed to near gray as he asked Nick, "Have you thought about the repercussions down the road?"

"What repercussions?"

"We can't employ a convicted felon."

"He's not going to be convicted."

Malcolm's voice was quiet, level. He was giving Nick a reality check. "I agree. But in the unlikely event that he is, the fact remains. It goes against stated corporate policy."

"To hell with corporate policy—we'll change it!"

Malcolm remained calm, the steady stream of river to Nick's crash of waterfall. Cal had come to learn it was a rhythm the men had established. Nick was the scorch of flame, Malcolm the intensity of embers. Nick crashed and pushed, Malcolm eddied and flowed.

Flashing a glance in the rearview mirror, Nick asked him, "Do we know any judges around here?"

Cal nodded. "A few."

"Can we talk to them? Will they listen to reason?"

Malcolm turned reproachful. "You're not planning on bribing any judges, are you?"

"I plan on doing whatever's necessary." Nick looked into the mirror for a long moment. "Including speaking with your brother."

Cal understood. You didn't attack a man's woman without hearing from him personally. Jack was family but Cal wasn't going to excuse his behavior. Unlike his mother. "You might want to wait on that count."

"Wait?"

Cal looked to Nick, aware of his displeasure. "My mother seems to be backing Jack on these charges. If you add your feelings to the mix, she might corral you into the same pen and press charges."

"On what grounds?"

"I assume you meant a face-to-face confrontation with Jack."

"I did. But I know how to stay out of legal trouble when I do so."

Cal glanced out the window. Rural landscape was transitioning to cityscape, homes and buildings becoming more frequent. They were houses and structures he recognized, businesses entrenched in the community of his childhood. This particular stretch of road was one he'd traveled many times, mostly due to his own stupidity, egged on by his wild-haired brothers. Cal had sat where Troy was sitting now. As had Jack, both Foster boys intimately familiar with the town jail and local police force. "Maybe so, but Jack's not above lying. With my mother involved, he might be emboldened to make something up."

"Cal might have a point," Malcolm agreed.

Nick's expression tightened. "You leave Jack to me."

Malcolm paused, then shifted in his seat. "On another note, I have some news."

"What news?" Nick was quick to ask.

"My pal in Vegas called to inform me that Jeremiah has paid his marker."

"What?" He glanced sideways. "How'd he manage that?"

Cal shared in Nick's surprise. He knew the story. Jeremiah Ladd had returned to Tennessee a year ago to grab his share of Ladd Springs, only to find the welcome mat hadn't been set for him. He and Ernie got into it, not to mention he and Delaney. Shoot, from what Cal heard, Jeremiah had been causing trouble for the whole damn town, including enlisting the help of jailbird Clem Sweeney to ferret out gold from land deep in the forest. Cal wasn't surprised. Folks turned crazy when they heard the word gold and Clem had baited Jeremiah like a topnotch fisherman.

Only he didn't count on his ally double-crossing him or winding up in jail on a bad gambling debt. Malcolm Ward was responsible for that stroke of genius. Once Lacy—currently married to Malcolm but ex-runaway cohort of Jeremiah's—revealed his gambling troubles, Malcolm wasted no time calling the Vegas authorities to sweep Jeremiah off the streets and into jail where he belonged. The fact that he was out couldn't be good. For any of them. Jeremiah was Annie's ex-boyfriend and Casey's father. If he came back he was sure to cause trouble somehow. From what Cal understood, Jeremiah had managed to do a fine job of it the last time he'd been in town.

"Don't know, but according to my guy, he's paid up in full."

"I don't like it." Nick shook his head. "I don't like it at all."

"Didn't think you would."

"No, I mean I think something's up. Someone had to help him pay that money."

"Who?"

Nick fired a glance to his partner. "I'll give you one guess."

Malcolm honed in on Nick. Cal could feel the wheels turning, the blades sharpening. "You don't think Jillian had something to do with it, do you?"

"Wouldn't put it past her."

Malcolm twisted fully in his seat, glancing askance. "Seriously?"

Nick nodded. "She's a spiteful one, with the memory of an elephant and the claws of a tigress."

"What the heck did you do to that woman?" Malcolm exclaimed, clearly upset by the possibility that Jillian Devane—arch rival to Harris Hotels and vindictive ex-lover of Nick Harris—could be back in the picture. "I thought we were finished with her."

"So did I." Nick looked away and Cal detected disquiet in the reflection of his dark-eyed gaze. It gave rise to one of his own.

"Aw, hell." Malcolm slammed a hand to the passenger-side door jamb. It was a rare display of emotion for him, one that signified he was worried.

"How would Jillian know anything about Jeremiah?" Cal asked. "She wasn't around when he was here, was she?"

"Jillian is as resourceful as they come," Nick replied. "She arrived on the heels of Jeremiah's departure, but she spent enough time in this town to dig up dirt on everyone in it."

"Yeah," Malcolm put in unhappily, "except there's only one person's grave she's interested in digging. Yours."

Nick chuckled. "Well, she's gonna have some trouble with her shovel because I have no intention of going in the ground anytime soon."

Malcolm looked at him. "If she's teaming up with Jeremiah, you might go down unwittingly."

Nick circled his hand more tightly around the wheel. "You're not worried about him, are you? That guy was child's play."

"I'd call him a grown child with a chip on his shoulder and a mountain of support in his back pocket if he's hooked up with Jillian. Jeremiah has nothing to lose, which makes him a dangerous man."

"Except his freedom."

Cal didn't like where this was going. From what Annie said, Jeremiah had changed a whole lot since they were kids. He was harder, meaner. Visions of him marching Annie and Lacy through the woods, threatening them with a gun rose in his mind.

Bile rose in his throat. If Jeremiah thought he was going to lay a hand on Annie he had another thought coming.

Nick turned sharply, bumping the three men inside the truck as they pulled into the lot for the county jail. The single-story building hadn't changed in decades, save for the peeling gray paint. It was drab, cold, as unappealing as it always had been.

"Let's say we focus on Troy's freedom first, shall we?"

Agreed, Cal thought. There was plenty enough time to deal with Jeremiah Ladd later.

## Chapter Twenty-Two

"Thank you, Mr. Harris." Troy eased from the backseat of Nick's truck and closed the door. Speaking through an open window, he said, "I owe you one."

"You don't owe me a thing, Troy. I'm merely repaying my debt of gratitude to you for stepping in on Delaney's behalf."

"Yes, sir. Thank you, sir." It wasn't like he could have avoided it. Hearing Mr. Foster's brother talking to her the way he was, seeing the look in his eyes, the gun... Troy had no choice.

"Tell Delaney I'll call her later," Nick said. "Right now, we have some business to attend to."

Troy wondered if any of that business included a visit to the real criminal, Jack Foster. The scum. Troy hoped it did and he hoped they made it hurt. Cal Foster was a decent man but his brother deserved no mercy. Attacking a woman was unacceptable, as low as a man could get. Man, hell. Jack Foster was no man. He was a liar, the devil incarnate. "I'll tell her," Troy replied.

With a tip of his hat he watched the truck pull out of the hotel's parking lot and onto the road. They were kind enough to drop him at the hotel so he could get his things. Travis had picked up his truck from Fran's Diner yesterday and driven it home. Was supposed to be driving it here to the hotel for him, now. He'd said it'd be about an hour, which would give him enough time to collect his stuff and say goodbye to the horses. Goodbye. He didn't want to think it could be permanent because of that liar.

Troy took the turn for the stables and headed up. Ejecting thoughts of Jack Foster from his brain, Troy focused on his job ahead. The sun overhead was blazing hot, but he couldn't care less. Sitting in that cell had taught him to appreciate the outdoors, hot or otherwise, his freedom to go where he wanted, when he wanted. The fact that his parents left him there rubbed raw. His father's message had been clear. *Maybe this will give you time to think about your future.*

Troy picked up his pace, a layer of perspiration building beneath his T-shirt as he entered the shaded section of trees. The air was noticeably cooler. Alongside him the creek was a babble of noise, calming for a man who needed to think, but Troy wasn't that man. He didn't have anything to think about other than how to care for his baby, his new wife. He loved his parents but they were wrong on this one. His future was about horses and about marrying Casey, soon as he could. He'd realized it while sittin' in jail. No baby of his was gonna be born a bastard, but where was he going to get the money to buy a ring? His parents sure as heck weren't going to loan it to him. Would Cal? Maybe Delaney?

Stepping over a fallen branch, he hated the need to ask, but the only money he'd saved up had to go to pay rent— first, last and a security deposit. He and Casey couldn't live in her mother's apartment. It was already crowded with Mr. Foster moved in. They couldn't live at his parents' house. He planned to move out of there himself this evening, seeing as how they couldn't support their son when he needed them. He surely wasn't gonna need them.

Emerging into open pasture, Troy glanced up at the stables. The late afternoon sun warm on his face, longing pricked at his heart. He wasn't kidding himself. With no job it was gonna be tough. Mr. Harris told him he had to take some time off until things settled. They couldn't keep him on the payroll with the charges pending. Guests might get uncomfortable knowing there was a criminal among them. Alleged or otherwise. Troy ground his jaw.

Shoving the thought from his mind, he hiked the fenced incline until he reached the stables. Catching his breath, he rounded the building and saw Delaney walking Sadie into a stall. His heart caught as he recalled the fear in her voice. Normally strong and tough, she'd been struggling against Mr. Foster as he attacked. Anger threaded through him. She didn't deserve that. No one did.

"Hey, Miss Delaney."

Delaney turned, and smiled. "Hi, Troy." Tentative, but it was a smile all the same, a welcome home. Grateful for the friendly face, Troy headed for her. "How are you?" she asked casually, absently stroking the horse at her side.

"Fine." Troy glanced at the Palomino, the golden-haired animal beautiful, alert as she assessed his presence. "Sorry about all the trouble I've caused."

"Trouble you've caused?"

"Yes, ma'am. I don't mean to be causing trouble for the hotel."

She straightened, pushed her shoulders back and said, "Let's get one thing settled right here and now. You did me a favor, Troy. You stepped in before God knows what could have happened, and I can't thank you enough. I'm only glad I didn't shoot you in the process."

Affection welled into a grin. "Your aim is better than that."

"Except that I didn't see you until it was too late."

"As you can see..." Troy tugged at his T-shirt. "I'm plenty fine. Not a scratch on me."

A smile slipped onto her lips. "Jack didn't have a chance against you. You're an amazing guy, Troy Parker. One of the good ones."

Startled by the compliment, he stammered, "If only my parents held your opinion."

Sadness changed her smile. "They do, Troy. They're simply struggling with your choices, that's all."

"Are you?"

She hesitated for the briefest of seconds. "No." Confidence worked slowly into her gaze. "I'm not. I trust you know what's best for your future, but to be honest, I'd have been upset if Felicity decided against college. It's a detour every parent has trouble with. Give them time. They'll come around."

Troy kicked at the ground. "I know you mean well, Miss Delaney, but not everyone comes around. Some bridges are burned crisp."

"That might be, but in all my life I've never seen a bridge that can't be rebuilt, including the one between you and your folks."

Emotion pulled at him. Delaney Wilkins was one of a kind. Strong and sure, she didn't waver in her support. If she was on your side, you could count on her staying put. "How come you couldn't have been my mother?"

Delaney erupted into a laugh. "And erase one of Felicity's dearest childhood friends? I don't think so!"

Troy grinned. Growing up, Felicity, Travis and he sure had been cinched together tighter than a freight train on high speed. They played together, rode together, swam together—even studied together, though he didn't take part in a whole lot of studying. Nobody dared tried to separate the trio. Except for Travis. An odd sensation uncoiled in his gut. In high school it had become clear that Travis wanted Felicity all to himself. It was also when most of their troubles began. "Yeah, that would have been weird."

"Definitely weird." Delaney gave a pat to a restless Sadie and the horse returned a low rumble of a nicker. "Go on, Sadie." Delaney gently pushed her toward her stall. "I'll be back for you this evening." The animal obliged, plodding in without protest. Troy waited as Delaney closed and latched the stall gate. Pausing, Delaney focused on Troy. Brown eyes turned velvet soft, matching the silken sheen of her long sleek ponytail. "I'm glad you're back, Troy."

"Er—I'm not actually back." Angst split his calm. "Didn't Mr. Harris tell you?"

"He did. But you're back enough for me."

Affection swelled. She didn't care about any fake criminal charges. She was glad to have him home and out of jail.

Unlike his parents. It was a show of support that meant the world to him. "Thank you."

"We'll get through this, Troy. You wait and see."

He nodded. It was the "wait and see" part that was going to be the hardest. Without a job, with criminal charges hanging over his head and no place to live, he wasn't sure how he was going to make ends meet, let alone tie them together in the middle.

When Delaney walked over and enfolded him in a hug Troy was overcome by uncertainty but duly wrapped his arms around her slender body and returned the gesture. It felt good to be appreciated. Respected. Miss Delaney was like a mother to him. She'd always looked out for him and Travis and probably always would. Delaney Wilkins cared about his wellbeing, she cared about his future. He wasn't going to let her down. Not today, not ever. Which brought him to someone else he wasn't going to let down. Releasing, he asked, "Do you mind if I use a phone? My cell battery is dead."

"Of course. Use the one in the office." With a knowing smile she added, "Take your time, Troy. There's no hurry."

Leaning forward, Felicity gently squeezed her inner thighs into the muscular midsection of her black mare, Blue, as the horse navigated the narrow trail along the mountainside. Riding since she was ten, Felicity had a sense of peace and calm. Blue felt like a best friend, a family member. The animal was like an extension of her. Travis had suggested a ride would get her mind off her troubles. Felicity had resisted all day, but once her mom called to tell her Nick had Troy in his truck and they were pulling away from the jail, Felicity tossed a bridle and reins onto her horse and decided Travis was right. A bareback ride on her mare might do her good.

The constant hoof-step, the rhythmic bob of Blue's head as she followed behind Travis' beefy brown horse was soothing. A canopy of green overhead, the earthy scent of clay and bark, the cool misty rise of the river water combined to remind her of better days before her father made life in Ladd

Springs miserable. Not only had he attacked her mother but he was accusing Troy of a crime he didn't commit. He'd had Troy thrown in jail—jail!—where his parents let him sit until Nick bailed him out. She couldn't believe the Parkers would do such a thing, not when Troy was innocent. Travis hadn't been surprised though. He'd actually had the nerve to agree with them.

Felicity could only pray that Nick would get the charges against Troy dropped. She prayed he would put an end to the madness her father created. But stone-cold reality could prove very different.

Travis glanced back over his shoulder. He wore no hat at the moment, his dark brown hair falling freely across his brow. "Wanna take them swimming?"

Peering at her boyfriend, the one and only boy she ever thought she could love, the best looking boy in school with his tanned smooth-skinned complexion, gorgeous chocolate brown eyes, overgrown layers of hair skimming past his strong brow, Felicity shook her head. Swimming like they had in the past held no appeal. At the moment she wasn't sure she liked Travis, let alone loved him.

He turned forward and continued to ride in silence. Felicity dropped her gaze to his back, the gentle sway of his body as it moved in sync with his horse. Like her, he rode bareback. Like her, he loved these woods, these rides. Unlike her, he wasn't a fan of Troy's. Something she didn't understand.

How could he be so callous toward his brother? Knowing what he knew about Troy's innocence, Travis had sided with his parents agreeing the best thing for Troy was to sit in jail for something he didn't do. He had it coming, Travis said. Maybe it would be the wakeup call he needed. Felicity vehemently disagreed. Troy might have his problems but this wasn't one of them. This was Travis' problem—a fact that was becoming more apparent to her each day.

As they rode, Felicity dropped her gaze to the massive brown flanks ahead of her, dwelling on the cause. Ever since the two of them made their feelings for one another public, Travis had grown angry with his brother. Where she would have thought it would be the other way around, it wasn't. Felicity knew both boys had been vying for her attention over the years. She wasn't blind. While they were young, it hadn't been an issue, the three satisfied to hang out together. But as they entered high school, the divide became obvious. Troy was hurt to learn she'd chosen Travis. For a while he didn't speak to her. They shared words, but not with the same ease and intimacy. Travis told her not to worry about Troy. He was jealous, angry.

Felicity didn't like that she'd hurt him but it was unavoidable. She couldn't date both of them, though they'd kidded about it numerous times. Eventually she had to choose. Moving her gaze from the shiny rear muscles of the Quarter Horse to Travis' navy blue jeans and T-shirt, Felicity settled on the thought. *She had chosen him.*

As though sensing her gaze was plastered to his back, he twisted his body around. Setting a hand on the back of his horse to keep steady, he asked, "Are you still mad at me?"

Staring into his dark eyes, pools of affection held only for her, she thought, *no*. Disappointed was more like it. Unfortunately, it was a concept Travis didn't seem able to comprehend. "I don't want to talk about it."

"So you're going to punish me instead?"

"I'm not punishing you."

"Yes, you are. You're not talking to me because you think I'm wrong about Troy." His horse missed a step as the animal began its descent down a slope, causing Travis to turn, regain his balance until hitting level ground whereby he twisted back. "I'm not, Felicity. You don't know my brother as well as I do. Troy needs a wakeup call. He needs to learn that he can't keep running off half-cocked just because he's mad."

Felicity leaned back as Blue gingerly made her way down, stepping over a rock to reach flatter ground. Resting hand and reins against her thigh, Felicity returned, "Justifiably so in this case, don't you think?"

"Maybe in this instance, but what about all the others? He gets drunk because he's mad. He quits his job because he's mad. The boy needs to learn about impulse control. I'd think you'd agree, considering how you feel about Casey these days."

Bringing Casey up felt like a slap in the face. Travis wasn't a big fan of Casey either. He lumped her together with Troy in the "immature and unstable" category. They weren't going to college. They were making a mess of their lives. Felicity believed differently. In her mind they were two young people trying to find their way. She also believed they loved each other and love could see them through anything.

As the trail curved sharply to the right, Travis turned forward, angling clear of a jutting tree branch. Felicity could hear the river before she saw it. Knowing their special place was located just ahead, special feelings began to take on a new coloring. She was beginning to doubt when it came to her and Travis. All he seemed to care about was being right. Raising her voice as they neared the rushing river, she said, "I think Troy is learning about stability *because* of Casey. I think he's made some mistakes but he's owning up to them. He's back, isn't it?"

"'Cause he quit another job," Travis said, riding his horse down to a clearing by the water's edge. Behind him, fast-moving water careened over massive boulders scattered along its path.

Pulling her mare up beside him, Felicity leaned forward and stroked the meaty neck of her mare, finishing with a few solid pats. Blue raised her head and shook her mane. "He quit to be with Casey. What part about that don't you understand? In one breath you act like he's supposed to do what's right by Casey and in the next you won't give him the chance."

"Troy doesn't know his head from his butt."

Felicity grimaced. It was as if Travis refused to see any good in his brother, any bright spots, potential... Something she wasn't seeing a lot of it in him at the moment either. Sitting back on Blue, heedless to the dampness of her jeans, she replied dully, "Whatever."

*Why were they riding again*? This conversation certainly wasn't getting her mind off anything.

"Felicity." Travis reached out for her, but she pulled out of reach, nearly causing him to topple from his horse. He scowled. "Why are you being like this?"

Collecting leather reins firmly in hand, she said, "I could ask the same question of you, Travis."

"Listen, when I see Troy making progress I'll be the first one to give him credit. But I don't. All I see is a hot head."

The glimmer in his gaze irked her. Sitting astride his horse, both man and animal magnificent in their beauty and brawn, Travis appeared arrogant. He made no allowance for error, no adjustment for life's pitfalls. "You act as though you've never made a mistake Travis. You're not perfect, you know."

"Never said I was," he replied, though it was clear he thought he was pretty darn close. "But take your father."

"What about my father?"

"You thought he was worth a second chance and look what happened."

He wasn't—is that what Travis was trying to say? Was he trying to rub her nose in it? Beside her, the powerful river seemed to flow right through her, escalating a surge of emotion. "Those are two totally different situations."

"Are they? I told you not to go see him because he hadn't changed. My daddy said he came back from Nashville because of problems at work. Because he *quit*, same as Troy."

Working off Felicity's energy, Blue shook her mane as though irritated, rearing several steps. "I can't believe you're linking the two together like that," she said, pulling her mare under control. "Troy isn't an abuser. He's passionate. There's a difference."

"Yes, and speaking of passion, look where it got your parents. They thought they knew what they were doing when they were young but they didn't. Your daddy let his emotions get the best of him and hit her."

Felicity stared at him. "How do you excuse his behavior as an adult?"

Travis almost smiled but seemed to hold himself in check. "He never learned the lesson when he was young. His parents let him get away with stuff and now look at him. It's exactly my point about Troy. That's why I'm right about him."

Anger and disbelief cascaded in her heart, swirling around rocks and boulders of resentment. That's what this was about—Travis being right. Felicity tugged abruptly on the reins and squeezed her legs against Blue.

"Hey—where are you going?"

"Home." Felicity urged Blue along the riverside terrain as quickly as she could, refusing to look back. She didn't want to see Travis. Didn't want to speak to him. If he couldn't see the good in people, the potential, then maybe he wasn't the guy for her.

"Felicity!" he called out to her. "Don't be like that!"

"Like what?" she shouted back. "Someone with a different viewpoint than yours? Someone who believes enough in people to give them a second chance?"

Travis caught up with her and pleaded, "C'mon, Felicity. I'm sorry. I didn't mean to make you mad."

Since when was it a bad thing to believe in people? Since when did it make her gullible and naïve?

Or stupid. That's how Travis was making her feel. Ignorant, as if she didn't know people. Well, he was wrong. People had good inside them. Sometimes it was hidden but it was there. People could change. If only someone close would put a little faith in them, let them know they cared, it would allow the individual to reveal their sweeter side. Take her Uncle Ernie. He was crusty on the outside as week-old bread, but on the inside he was soft and kind. He'd never said a cross word to her, never raised his voice in anger. For years he'd been dead set against giving the property to her or her mother, but in the end he did. He changed his mind. He changed his heart and everything else changed right along with it.

Timing her body's movements with Blue as she trotted, Felicity ignored the pound of hooves close on her tail. Travis didn't get it, but he didn't want to get it. Troy could change. He'd changed his heart because of Casey and he could change his behavior, too. Felicity believed in him. Casey believed in him. Why didn't Travis?

In a fit of anger, she pulled Blue to a stop. Travis' horse yanked up its head as it detoured to avoid running into her. "Maybe I chose the wrong brother," she snapped. "Maybe Casey's the smart one and I'm the loser."

Travis stood stunned, his mouth agape. His horse snorted. "Felicity, you don't mean that."

"Don't I?"

Hurt thrashed in his dark gaze, underscored by the torrent of whitewater churning in the river. A set of waterfalls rose lay ahead, falls they used to frequent as youngsters. The animal beneath Travis side-stepped impatiently as he said, "You're mad, is all. You're lashing out."

"What I *am* is tired of you telling me what I think and feel all the time. For once in your life maybe you should put a cork in it."

Chapter Twenty-Three

As they made the drive into the Foster homestead, lines of wood board fencing glimmered, enameled from a late afternoon sun. This was Cal's family home, hills and mountains that stirred fond memories. Born and raised here, he and his brothers spent many a day riding this land, galloping far and wide, entertaining girls from school with elaborate picnics supplied by their housekeeper Thelma, evading trouble when one of them shot his mouth off one too many times. Casting his glance to the distant ridge, rounded mounds of green that were the Appalachians, he recalled the first time he'd declared his love for a girl. Melanie Lynn Barker. Warm memories cooled as the house came into view. Cal tensed. This wasn't a pleasure visit. More like a showdown.

When he'd called ahead, his brother Beau informed him that Jack was in the house. He didn't elaborate. He didn't say what decisions had been made. The two brothers kept it short and sweet. Neither Beau nor Cal wanted to admit their brother was a loser, but they wouldn't defend him. Only their mother was prepared to shelter a man gone wrong.

"That's his car." Cal pointed to the black truck parked in front of the house.

Nick nodded that he'd heard, circled around the drive. Malcolm looked to him and said, "We keep this to a minimum. No raised voices, no fists. We say our piece and move on."

Turning to face his partner, Nick erupted into a chuckle. "Are you worried I'm going to take him out back and whoop him?"

Cal noted the mocking tone with a measure of relief. Nick was kidding. He was in control. Last thing they needed was an ugly confrontation. Cal might not agree with his mother's position with regard to Jack, but she was still his mother. Upsetting her was not on his agenda.

"I want to be clear on our goal," Malcolm said. "We're here to inform him of our intentions with regard to Troy Parker's defense and Delaney's subsequent charges, should he prove resistant."

Nick flashed a sardonic smile. "I guarantee he'll prove resistant."

Cal agreed.

"That may be," Malcolm returned evenly, "but we have too much riding on this for you to jeopardize it with your personal feelings."

Nick tossed the truck gear into park. "You know he deserves a square one across the jaw."

"I don't disagree. I'm only clarifying that this is not the time or place. Are we clear?"

Cal marveled at the way Malcolm handled Nick, as though he were speaking to a child and not the head of an international hotel chain.

Nick laughed. "Oh, we're clear all right. So long as you know Jack Foster is going to get what's coming to him."

"I do," Malcolm replied, a quiet glance over his shoulder.

Cal gave a double-take. *Was Malcolm concerned with his feelings because it was his brother they were discussing?* "Don't hold back on account of me," he interjected. "Jack's responsible for his actions and should pay the consequences, whatever those might be."

Nick cut the engine. "I appreciate that, Cal."

For a brief moment, the three men sat silent. Each understood the stakes were high, each harbored a different reason to see the meeting through to a productive end. Nick's motivation was personal, Malcolm's straddled the personal and professional. Cal's was a jumbled mess of the two. Jack was family. Nick was his boss. Troy was the father of his wife's grandbaby. Annie and Casey and Troy were family. If Troy went to prison for a crime he didn't commit, it would ruin the life of a child before she ever entered the world. Cal knew something about ruining a child's life. He'd done of good job of ruining his own daughter's life. At least Emily was speaking to him these days. She didn't attend his wedding to Annie, but at least she'd opened the door to a new relationship and for that he was grateful. His ex-wife had made it happen. Now that he was one year sober, Caroline was beginning to realize he was serious about starting over, making things right. His ex-wife had gone so far as to indicate she'd be open to Emily spending summers with Cal and his new family in Tennessee. They had the first visit scheduled. She'd be arriving in two months. *Two months.*

Inhaling the sight of his home, he suppressed a swell of nerves, a myriad of memories, and grabbed the door handle. He was about to make things right in a different way. Jack lied about Troy's involvement with Delaney, claiming Troy pulled a gun on him. Jack claimed he was the defender and not the aggressor, which Cal knew was a lie. One look at Delaney that night told the story. She didn't take crap from anyone. To see her shaken meant she'd walked to the brink. Jack was the liar here, and Cal didn't take kindly to liars, blood relative or not. "Let's go," Cal said, and pushed out of the truck before any more thoughts could slow him down. It was time for action.

Leading the way into the house, Cal glanced about. Heavy wood beams dominated the interior, an enormous antler chandelier hung from the ceiling above. Wood floors and leather furniture were lit by the subtle glow of lamplight, lending the room a country elegance. Quiet, empty, everything was in its place, appearing picture-perfect, much like his mother's life. Settling on several photographs adorning the mantle, Cal understood what was at stake.

Momma was defending Jack for more reasons than protecting one of her own. She was preserving her pride.

"You have a beautiful home," Malcolm said.

"Thanks," Cal answered the nicety, distracted by the sight of movement in the kitchen. Beyond the living room, someone passed by the doorway. If instinct served him, it had been Jack. Cal headed for him. Nick and Malcolm wordlessly followed.

Cal rounded the corner of the spacious kitchen as Jack switched on a sink faucet. Pulling an arched nozzle, he rinsed a plate, setting it aside on a kitchen towel. The faucet hose retracted with a zip, he shut the water off and turned—and froze. Alarm dashed the calm in his dark gaze but he recovered quickly. "Hello, brother." Jack summoned a smile. "To what do I owe the honor of this visit?"

"We'd like to have a little chat with you," Nick replied.

Jack's gaze sprang to Nick. His smile grew while his eyes remained suitably wary. "Come to apologize for your wife's tawdry behavior?" He snickered. "Inviting another man to her stables late at night isn't conduct becoming of a lady."

Nick stiffened. "You're a piece of work, aren't you?"

"Delaney seems to think so."

Circling the kitchen island, Nick stopped in front of a massive double-door refrigerator, stainless steel gleaming in the overhead lighting. As he faced off with Jack, Cal instantly thought the cookware hanging from a rack above them could act as makeshift weaponry. One whack from a heavy pan could knock a man cold.

Cal stepped forward. "This isn't a game, Jack."

"Who said anything about games?"

Despite Jack's jovial expression, neither Nick nor Malcolm appeared amused. Quite the opposite. "We're challenging your charges against Troy," Cal informed him. "They won't hold up in a court of law."

Nick moved closer to Jack, Malcolm shadowing his movements. Cal noted Nick was within striking range, escalating the adrenaline pump through his system.

But Jack seemed unfazed, despite the fact the imposing Nick Harris now stood feet from him. "I think they will, brother. I have the injuries to prove it. Troy and Delaney have nothing."

"Wrong." Nick stepped forward. "They have me."

Jack's bravado cracked a hair, clearly aware the six-foot-four Mr. Harris could inflict severe injury. "Would you like to add some assault charges of your own?" Jack smirked but Cal detected a hint of fear.

"Yes, I would." Nick leaned down, bringing his face to within inches of Jack's. "Very much so," he added under his breath. "But I won't give you the satisfaction of witnesses."

"Big man afraid?" Jack taunted.

Cal was amazed by his brother's cool, apparently confident Nick wouldn't lay a hand on him. It was a feeling Cal couldn't share. Perhaps Jack had been drinking.

"Smart. Big man is smart," Nick replied, "and putting you on notice. Drop the charges against Troy or Delaney charges you with attempted rape, compounded by aggravated assault with a deadly weapon."

"I never touched her."

"I have two people who say otherwise."

"You're going to have a hard time proving it in court. Unlike me. I have photos to document my injuries."

"Injuries that are going to look pleasant compared to what I have in store for you."

"I think I've heard enough."

Cal whirled at the sound of his mother's voice. Four men stood motionless, staring at the petite Victoria Foster. Across the kitchen she linked arms across her chest, the shimmery cream of her blouse oddly at home in the commercial grade kitchen. Hair swept into a French twist, her neck and ears adorned with diamonds, she glared at Nick and Malcolm with a severe expression.

"Cal brought a couple of thugs for the purpose of intimidation," Jack piped up. Shoving a shoulder toward Nick, he crossed the kitchen and took up residence next to his mother. "Apparently they don't understand that's a crime here in Tennessee."

"The only crime that's been committed has been by you," Cal thrust angrily, irritated by his mother's presence. He had wanted to avoid this scene altogether, but she was making that impossible. "We're here to tell you it won't stand. We will reveal you for the liar you are."

Victoria set her sights on Cal, a glittery mix of anger and determination in her heated gaze heated. "Don't tell me you're going to continue this charade on behalf of your wife's new family?"

"It's no charade. Jack assaulted Delaney. With a gun."

"Because Delaney said so?" Jack laughed, clearly comfortable under his mother's wing. "That woman has had it out for me ever since the divorce, everyone knows that."

Cal wanted to spit. He wanted to smack a stiff one across his jaw. Jack had always been a hell raiser, a short-cut taker, a man skating the field of responsibility, but an abuser? That crossed the line. "What happened to you, Jack?"

His mother responded for him, firing her disdain with both barrels. "What happened to your loyalty to family, Cal? Why have you forsaken your kin for the Ladds?"

"This is about right and wrong, momma. It's not about taking sides."

"So you intend to slander our good name with these false charges against your brother?"

"They're not false."

"They won't withstand the scrutiny of a judge. You and I both know what will happen if you proceed. Without physical proof you will only succeed in smearing our good name." Taking a step toward him, she said, "We have a reputation in this town, good standing within the community. Do you seriously want to ruin that for an old grudge?"

Seemed to him that's exactly what his momma was doing—acting on an old grudge. "Jack is out of control. He needs help."

Jack belted out a laugh, puncturing the room with contempt. "It's not *me* who needs the help. Everyone in town knows it's that Parker kid who's trouble. Why don't you focus some of your attention on him?" Erasing all ease, he added, "Screwing around with your girlfriend's father's lady is pretty sick, if you ask me."

Nick flinched. Malcolm seized his arm. Cal balled his hand into a fist by his side. "You're walking some treacherous ground, Jack. I'd watch your back, if I were you."

"Threatening me again?" Jack looked to their mother. "Tsk, tsk, tsk...when you will you ever learn?"

Victoria glowered, frosty lines carved into her face. "Cal, I think you should leave."

Something in him closed. Hearing those words spoken from his momma's lips sealed it for him. This was a wasted effort. Her stake in this went deep, deeper than he'd realized. Maybe deeper than he could fathom. She was banking her reputation and family's future relations on this one battle. For better or worse, she was fully vested. "I'll go, Momma, but I can't let Jack get away with what he's doing. It's not right, and I intend to do everything in my power to stop him. I'm sorry if it causes you pain, but it's the right thing to do." As he said it, Cal glimpsed sight of his father. His heart pitched. Standing several yards behind her, he'd been listening to the entire exchange. The guilt in his eyes said it all. This was about him.

And he knew it.

Victoria's defense of Jack was an assault against her husband. It was emotional retaliation for the years of hurt she'd endured. Cal hadn't realized until this moment how hot the memory of Susannah Ladd still burned in his daddy's heart. Perhaps he hid it well, perhaps Cal hadn't been looking, but now, in the dim light of the dining room, it was there, clear as mountain river stream.

Casey smacked the steering wheel of her car, cursing the vehicle ahead of her. "The speed limit's forty-five not *twenty*-five!"

A brown station wagon lumbered along at an agonizing twenty miles per hour, blocking her passage on the two-lane

highway. Black pavement was marked by a double yellow
line, lined by heavily-wooded trees, constantly curving. There
was hardly anyone out here, with only the occasional mailbox
jutting out from a hidden drive. Still, there was no way she
could pass. Not without risking a head-on collision.

A tiny spasm cramped in her abdomen. She'd been having them for the last few hours. They were minor. Nothing
more than nerves, but she didn't dare tell Miss Ashley. As it
was, it took thirty minutes of "convincing" to keep her from
driving Casey to the hotel herself. *A woman in her condition
shouldn't drive. She was too upset. It wasn't good for the baby.* Casey wanted to scream at the top of her lungs, "I'm fine!
I'm pregnant. It's fine!"

Ashley had been insistent but Casey was determined she
was going alone. Troy needed her. He'd been let go. Not
fired, he assured her, but "let go." Company policy. Harris
Hotels wasn't permitted to employ criminals or people arrested for crimes. Which was totally unfair. Troy wasn't a criminal. He was arrested on bogus charges made by a man with a
vendetta against Miss Delaney.

And Casey thought *her* sperm donor was a creep. Felicity's father was right there with him! Jack Foster was acting
like Troy attacked him when Felicity said it was clearly the
other way around. He'd been attacking her mom and Troy
had stepped in to protect her.. After Troy left the diner with
officer Gavin, Felicity came clean and told her everything.

At least Mr. Harris was able to get Troy out of jail.
When Felicity told her the Parkers were letting Troy stay in
jail to teach him a lesson, Casey had wanted to cry. They
were going to let him sit in jail for something he didn't do?
What kind of lesson was that? Don't step in and help others
in need? It made her sick. What kind of parents did that to a
child?

Not her. She would never do that to her kid. Ever. Her
daughter was going to be loved. Her child was going to know
she mattered. Troy wouldn't do that to his child, either. He

was going to be a good dad. Brake lights illuminated as the station wagon in front of her slowed for a sharp curve.

Growling under her breath, Casey cursed the car. If she didn't hurry, Troy was going to leave before she got there. "Get going!"

## Chapter Twenty-Four

Regret pummeled her heart as Delaney paced the confines of her office. Nick sat idle, watching her work through her emotions. He was supportive, patient, exactly what she needed. Trail rides were finished for the day, a few men working to tidy up and prepare for tomorrow. Nick had relayed his meeting with Jack, his mother, Cal's interpretation of it all and Delaney was sick about it. This was her fault. "I should have gone down to the police station. I should have gone first thing and pressed charges. That way Jack wouldn't have been able to make it look like I only went down to protect Troy."

"You were trying to protect the hotel. You didn't know he was going to fabricate a story to frame Troy."

"I underestimated him. I should have suspected Jack would try and pull something like this." But in all honesty she'd never seen it coming. She'd been too busy with concerns over Troy and Casey, the initial shock, the near fatal shooting. Casting a glance through the plate glass window, she zeroed in on the scene of the crime. Images from that night swarmed—Sadie, Jack, Troy, shrieks, gunfire—the bloody mess of the fight that ensued. Sure as she was sitting here, Delaney knew that if Troy hadn't stepped in when he did, Jack would be dead. A shiver raced through her. Pulling her gaze from the window, she quieted the flutter of pulse. "I wish I could go back and change it, go down and file the charges. At this rate Gavin won't even listen to me."

"Gavin isn't the only officer on the force," Nick said. "The police can't ignore you. A woman comes in and makes attempted rape charges, someone will have to follow up. There will be an investigation. Troy will be questioned,

you… Trust me, they'll find inconsistencies in Jack's statement. The truth will come out."

"They'll find my bullet lodged in a wall somewhere."
Despite her best efforts, Delaney had been unable to find her
bullet. She'd scoured the walls, the ground, but it was nowhere to be found. Vanished. Disappeared. She bet the police
would find it, and it would go to Jack's claim that she drew
first and fired her weapon.

"Self-defense," Nick stated matter-of-factly.

"Prove it."

"Whose side are you on?"

She dropped to a seat on the edge of her desk, the metal
edge cutting into her tailbone. "Reality. It looks bad for me.
I'm not the one sporting bruises from the encounter. I don't
have any physical evidence to prove my claim."

"You have Troy."

"A young man with an unstable past." A past with marginal personal judgment—very public marginal personal
judgment—including two well-observed dalliances with older
women, one of them Jeremiah Ladd's girlfriend. When
Delaney learned that Jack had insinuated Troy was there after
hours to have an affair with *her*, she'd almost doubled over.
Jack was disgusting. He was a disgusting human being with
no sense of decency. Groaning aloud, she muttered, "Oh
yeah, jurors are going to *love* the two of us."

Nick walked over and took her by the shoulders. He held
firm, looked her square in the eye and said, "I love you.
You're not going to go through this alone. You have me, and
together we'll give Jack exactly what he deserves."

Including a messy battle between two well-established
families in town, she mused soberly. While she appreciated
Nick's declaration of love and support, she didn't share his
confidence. Jack Foster had eluded the consequences of his
behavior for twenty years. There was no reason to believe
that would change.

"You have to believe you're the one with the power
here. Don't give it away so easily."

Delaney blinked, realizing at once he was right. But it was past tense. Shame poked at her heart. She'd been the one with the power a decade ago yet she'd neglected to exercise it. She never pressed charges against Jack for his abuse, instead, opting to run home, taking shelter in the shadows of her mother's sanctuary, just as her mother had done before her. Delaney ran, hid from her assailant. She hadn't done anything wrong yet *she* was the one in hiding. She wouldn't make the same mistake again. "You're right. I'll go to the police station tomorrow morning and give a complete statement."

"Good girl." He kissed her forehead. "Want me to go with you?"

"No." Delaney didn't want Nick to be subjected to anymore ugliness than need be. If Gavin wouldn't listen, she'd find someone who would. This was about doing what was right, not giving into tawdry insinuations and accusations. "It won't take long," she said, and mentally began to prepare for the day ahead, the consequences to come.

"Okay. Now let's get out of here and go home."

Cal and Annie stepped outside the lobby, pausing. Off to the side of the front entrance near plump hydrangeas, their round blooms a soothing periwinkle. A collection of irises surrounded their base creating a lovely effect yet Annie couldn't enjoy them. Not when her husband was hurting. Troy was no longer employed by Harris Hotels—a technicality of sorts, but a fact—a shock that still stung. Cal felt responsible which was ludicrous. He'd done nothing wrong. It was his brother, not him. Circling a hand around his arm, Annie secured their connection. "At least ya'll were able to get him out of jail. I know he's grateful to you for that. Did Troy say what his plans were? I mean, if the Parkers weren't willing to bail him out, will they let him move back in?"

"He didn't say. He was pretty beat up about losing his position at the stables."

"You assured him it's only temporary, right? Until Nick gets it cleared up in court?"

Cal gazed down at her, a deep sadness wedged in his hazel eyes. "Yes, but that can take months, especially if Jack proves to be difficult."

"Do you think he will?"

"Yes, but the rest is up to Delaney."

"She's going to officially press charges, right? Won't that help?"

"I imagine so."

"But what?" His reticence was distinct. "What's troubling you?"

"It's my mother."

Annie balked. "Victoria? What's she got to do with anything?"

"She's taken up for Jack."

As a mother, Annie understood. A mother couldn't forsake her child. Couldn't abandon them in their hour of need. Even when they made poor decisions, a mother would be there for her child. "But surely she understands the severity of the situation. This isn't a bar fight. Can't she support him without allowing him to lie?"

Cal stepped away from Annie. Locating the nearest bench, he lowered to a bench, dropped his elbows to his knees, burying his face in his hands. Annie hurried to his side, placed a hand to his back. "Talk to me, Cal. What's going on?"

"It's ugly. Momma is fighting Jack's battle because of Daddy's past with Susannah."

Annie dropped to a seat next to him, the rich scent of pine infusing the air around them with a serenity she needed but did not feel. A beautiful mountain evening was unfolding, but it was stained by an unfortunate turn of events. Victoria couldn't possibly be holding a grudge over Susannah Ladd after all these years. The woman was dead. Gerald and Susannah were ancient history—they'd been teenagers, for

Heaven's sake! Annie honed in on Cal's face as he raised his gaze to hers. *Could she?*

"Daddy is caught in the middle and I'm afraid it's his fault."

"His fault?"

"I think he's been pining for Susannah more sharply than we realized."

Oh, no... Annie looked away, settling on a clump of ferns. Realization settled in like a barrel of cold molasses. She recalled his offer to buy her share of Ladd Springs. He'd been quick to offer, excited by the prospect. At the time Annie had chalked it up to his passion for land, his admiration for the beauty and abundance of Ladd Springs, the rivers and streams, the wealth of natural springs. She tried to remember Victoria's reaction but nothing stuck out as memorable. Victoria didn't cringe, she didn't protest. The woman didn't so much as blink.

Could it be true she'd been harboring a stubborn jealousy all these years?

The pain in Cal's gentle eyes tore at Annie's heart. This cut deep for him. Jack was his brother, Victoria and Gerald his parents, Troy his soon-to-be son-in-law. Cal was caught in the middle, tangled in a web he had no part in spinning "I'm sorry, Cal. This can't be pleasant for you."

"It's not pleasant for anyone. Momma was angry. When we were there to confront Jack, convince him to change his mind about these assault charges, Momma appeared out of nowhere and told us where to go and don't waste time gettin' there. She didn't know it, but Daddy was standing behind her. He didn't say anything but the look in his eyes..." Cal looked away. "It was sadder than a lonesome breeze through a cold forest of pine. It was a look I saw for the first time, but Momma"—he shook his head—"I think it must have been something she's been living with for too long. The dam on her emotions finally broke."

It never occurred to Annie that Gerald and Victoria could be the ones hurting the most right now. The two had built a life together, had four sons, a reputation as a loving couple. Annie had always thought the rumor mill was churning because folks were jealous of Gerald's and Victoria's ideal marriage. Annie never suspected it was due to a deep-rooted truth. "Do you think she would listen to reason? Could you talk to her?"

"What kind of reason speaks to a woman scorned?"

Annie pulled back. He had a point. "But she has to, Cal. She has to understand the repercussions of this decision."

"She might be a woman tired of patchin' together the threads of her heart. Jack is moving out of the house, but I don't know how far he'll get."

"If we're lucky, he'll make it across the state line and never look back."

"Don't count on it. Not with Momma's support."

Distracted by movement, Annie turned, searching a cluster of rhododendron rising behind the hydrangea. She searched for signs of an animal. Had it been a bird? A squirrel? Running her gaze up the trunk of a nearby tree, she sifted through leaves and branches but saw nothing. Returning to Cal, she asked, "What about family? Don't you think it would matter to her to know she's tearing apart the family by supporting Jack?"

Cal dragged his hands down his face, raked them back over his head. "Maybe." Blowing a ragged sigh, he turned to Annie. "Family's always been important to her. Maybe it will make a difference this time."

Felicity ducked further behind the bushes, careful to avoid detection by Casey's mother. After returning Blue to the stables, she'd come here looking for Casey, prepared to offer her help in any way. But while eavesdropping on her mother's and Cal's conversation, an idea had formed. Victoria Foster was a mother, a woman. Her family was being torn apart. Naturally she wanted to stick up for her child, grown adult or not. Only in this case it was misguided. She didn't understand what actually happened. She only understood what she'd been told. Of course her son was going to lie to her. He was trying to protect himself.

Moving away from the entrance, Felicity retreated and headed for her car. Travis was right about one thing. Passion had a way of making people do things. In the heat of the moment, people said and did things they wouldn't ordinarily do or say. She'd done it with her mom. She'd said hateful things the night after her botched dinner with the Fosters, none of which were true. But she'd been angry, hurt. Maybe her father had been drunk the night he hit her mom, like at the stables the other night. Maybe alcohol was the real problem and not the man. It could be true. It was possible. Felicity pulled keys from her purse and centered on the notion. Without the alcohol her father could prove to be a decent person.

Look at Troy. His poor decisions had been due to drinking. He'd been fired because of it. Now that he'd quit drinking, he was back home, back with Casey. He was rising above his past to be the man he was meant to be. If Troy could do it, maybe her father could too. Maybe Jack Foster could beat the bottle and live the life he was meant to be—father, community leader—whatever he wanted to do he could, so long as he quit drinking. Victoria Foster didn't want her son to be a drunk, did she? Especially not to the point of misconduct. A shiver passed through her. Criminal misconduct.

Yes. Victoria, like any mother, would want what's best for her son. She'd want him to be the best he could be. She'd want him to have a relationship with his daughter. She'd said as much during their dinner, making a fuss about the importance of family—of blood—and how they needed to stay close. If Felicity could convince Mrs. Foster that Jack was hurting the family, preventing any potential for a relationship between Felicity and the Foster family, maybe she'd drop this misguided support for her son. She was a reasonable woman. She had a heart. She cared about family, about people. Withdrawing her support in this case wouldn't mean she was abandoning her son, quite the opposite. She could help him change. Like Troy, maybe Jack Foster could change his ways. If only someone was there to extend a hand in forgiveness. Why shouldn't that person be her?

Seated on the edge of a hay bale, Troy decided to call Casey. If she was on her way, he was gonna tell her to stop, meet him at the diner instead. He was hungry and tired and in no mood to face his parents, not without first discussing his options with Casey. The two of them needed to talk before he made any final decisions. *Decisions.* Big decisions like where to live, how to earn some money. Angst skirted through his pulse. They had a baby on the way and he was responsible. He had to find a way to provide for both her and Casey.

Casey told him it was a girl. A little girl. His heart swelled. He was gonna be a daddy to a baby girl. Glancing around the barn, the horse tack, the feed—this was the core of his life, a life he was gonna share with a child. Envisioning a chubby little face beaming up at him, dark curls of hair covering her head, Troy reaffirmed his need to provide. Only for the time being, that paycheck wasn't gonna come from Harris Hotels. Troy accepted Mr. Harris' decision about hotel policy. It was a good policy. No one needed criminals working the grounds of a fancy hotel.

*Criminal.* The word snaked through him. He was no criminal. Jack Foster was the criminal. Heading for a phone in the barn office, he dialed Casey's number. When she didn't pick up, he left a message, "Case, I'm leaving. Meet me at the diner." On second thought, "Call me, will ya?"

Ending the call, he cursed. He forgot that his cell phone was dead. Hopefully Travis had dropped his truck at the parking lot but without a phone, there was no way to confirm. Shaking his head, he walked out of the barn, headed out. Dad gum truck better be there.

Suddenly Casey's car began to slow. "What the—" She pressed the accelerator but the car continued its deceleration. "Oh, no... Not now!" The car had been acting up over the last few weeks, starting and stopping in fits. At the moment, it was a complication she didn't need.

Darting a glance to the rearview mirror, Casey checked for oncoming cars. No one was behind her. Ahead of her the slow-poke station wagon put distance between them. She jammed a boot to the gas pedal. No response. Casey scanned the roadside for an area to pull off. Trees, ditches, mailbox, there was no space large enough for her car. "Dang it!"

Wheels continuing to slow, the car rolled ahead like a lead balloon. Tugging at the sluggish steering wheel, Casey's glance raced across the dashboard. Red arrows indicated engine temperature, oil pressure, battery strength, gas level. *Gas level.* Her spirits crashed.

The tank was empty! Casey aimed for the nearest driveway, praying her car would make it. How could she run out of gas? How could she have missed it? But missed it she had, the car coasting past a ditch before settling safely on a gravelly driveway. Hopefully no one would be coming out any time soon because she was completely blocking their way.

Not like she could do anything about it. At a complete standstill, she watched in dismay as the tail lights of the station wagon disappeared around a wooded corner. Grabbing her purse, Casey pushed out of her car with an angry shove. No car trouble was going to stop her from getting to Troy. She'd darn well walk if she had to. Crawl if it came to it. Nothing was going to keep her from seeing her man.

Tossing the door closed, she stood, peering up the road. Trees leaned over the street, branches hovering in a green canopy of shade. It couldn't be that far. This was the last turn before the Sweeney property. But as she walked, her spirits dipped when she registered where she was. She wasn't on the curve she'd originally thought. Taking in her surroundings, the lack of driveways, the scarcity of flowered dogwoods, Casey realized she was a mile or so farther away.

Her heart fell. She couldn't walk that far!

She'd have to get a ride. She'd call her aunt, her mother—she'd call Troy! Someone would give her a ride. Pulling the phone from her purse, Casey sagged as she looked at the tiny screen. No signal. There was no signal in this stretch of the mountains! Slinging a glance in both directions, Casey wanted to cry. Living in the mountains meant intermittent signal. No signal. No car. She was left with nothing but empty road.

No one coming. No one going. Nothing but pavement.

Shaking it off, Casey continued toward Ladd Springs. Eventually someone would drive by. This area was rural but it wasn't desolated. Five o'clock in the evening there'd be *someone* driving home from work. Granted talking to strangers wasn't a great idea, but no one would mess with a pregnant woman. That would be plain sick.

Chapter Twenty-Five

Jack Foster placed a pair of folded jeans on top of his suitcase, then closed the lid, pulling the zipper closed. There hadn't been a whole lot to pack. He'd only intended to stay through the holidays until his mother convinced him to stay indefinitely. He had no job waiting for him, no family. Why not stay on at the ranch until he figured out his next step? When Daddy didn't object, the matter was settled. Like she said, Jack had nowhere else to go.

So he stayed here, in the guest room. It used to be Clint's room, but all hints of masculinity had been wiped clean, replaced by an immaculate antique desk and four-poster bed, the mattress covered by a patterned quilt and stylish throw pillows. Jack's room had been remodeled into a suite for Thelma. Now that she was getting on in age, the housekeeper stayed over on the nights she worked late, as opposed to driving home.

"You don't have to leave," his mother said. Appearing in the doorway, she fixed an unsteady gaze on him. Dressed in an ivory silk blouse and linen slacks, her hair pulled back into a twist, she wore a complete face of makeup and diamond jewelry as if she were headed out for a night on the town, though he knew she wasn't going anywhere this evening. Victoria Foster always dressed to the hilt because one never knew what a day held in store.

Jack smiled at her logic. "I don't want to cause you and Daddy any more harm than my being here already has."

"This is your home. You shouldn't be run out of here like a scalawag."

Jack chuckled at the old-fashioned term. His mother was so proper, so prim. Initially her adamant defense had surprised him. He hadn't looked forward to revealing the incident involving Delaney for fear his mother would kick him out. After the fiasco with Felicity, her sterling image of him was steadily coming under fire. Another smear and Jack had thought she'd show him the door. But to his astonishment, she had done nothing of the kind. Instead, she came to him, wrapped her arms around him and hugged him. *We'll get through this together. Those Ladds will pay for what they've done.*

Victoria Foster never cared for the Ladds. Jack knew it was due to Daddy's old relationship with Delaney's mom, but they were feelings never publicly aired. His mother had consented to Jack's marriage, offered to host the ceremony and reception at their home. Old Ernie Ladd didn't offer the first dime. His beloved sister's daughter was getting married, yet he refused to spit out a cent. He didn't attend, never sent a card. Nothing.

It wasn't until years later that Jack learned the depth of animosity between Ernie and his father. Before then he and his brothers were too busy prowling the town to concern themselves with others. But a few years of marriage to Delaney had opened his eyes. The rumors were true. Gerald Foster and Susannah Ladd had been romantically involved. Lovers, many said while others refuted the fact. Only friends, platonic, they claimed. But all agreed the two had been in love—a fact that royally incensed Ernie Ladd.

Jack's gaze settled on his mother, gathering her close. When had she learned the truth? It couldn't have been before she met Daddy because he courted her from afar, while she still lived in Chattanooga. Jack smiled inwardly. Smart man. The only women around these parts interested in tangling with the Ladd-Foster feud were after his money. The stately and elegant Victoria Guthrie had money of her own and no knowledge of the events prior, making her the perfect wife for Gerald Foster. Now she was staking her marriage to a fence post for all to see. She was taking sides.

Against her husband.

Jack smiled indulgently. "No one is going to mistake me for a scalawag, Momma. Your reputation will remain intact." Disapproval glinted in her eyes, forcing Jack to walk the statement back. No sense in alienating his only ally. "Forgive me, it was a joke. Your reputation reigns far and above anything I could be involved in disputing."

"I don't like what they're trying to do to you. Cal is letting a job come between him and his family and it's not right."

"Fine way to repay you after everything you did to help him return home from Arizona, tail between his legs and his butt on his shoulders."

"Jack."

"Sorry, Momma, but you know it's true. He didn't have a pot to sit on as far as friends, and here you opened you doors to him. Ungrateful bastard."

She unwound her arms and entered the guest room. "Enough about Cal. I don't want you to go. What are you going to do? Where are you going to live?"

Jack throttled his temper. His mother didn't deserve his wrath. She was one of the good guys. "I'll get a place at a local hotel—a decent one," he underscored, "and nowhere near the Ladds."

"How long will you stay?"

Jack shrugged. "Until I decide my next step." He'd been in town since Thanksgiving, doing nothing but drifting save for a brief stint with the gorgeous developer lady, Jillian Devane. Jack felt a surge of arousal at the mere thought of the woman. Unlike any woman he'd ever known, her looks were sleek and exotic, her touch silky smooth but beneath her beautiful exterior was a woman of stone. Cold, calculating. Jack had the sense she viewed him as a conquest rather than an enjoyable diversion but he could care less. It was all the same to him. Too bad Delaney's new boyfriend ran her out of town.

"But Mr. Dakota said the trial wouldn't happen for weeks. What will you do in the meantime?'

Yanking the suitcase from the bed, he set it to the floor. Lately Daddy had been pushing him toward a job with Beau on the ranch, but sweating outdoors wasn't Jack's thing. Back in Nashville he'd been selling cars, dating a few country singer wannabes. He had no ambition for any more. But when he was arrested for a fist fight with a manager from one of the bigger music labels, his boss fired him. Charges were dropped on the condition he leave town. *Don't let the door hit you on the way out.* "I'll figure something out," Jack said. Right after he nailed Delaney's little friend to the wall. Troy Parker had messed with the wrong man, and Jack was damn well going to see that he didn't forget it. "Besides, like you said, we've got to make them pay."

A tentative smile eased onto her lips. "Let me get my purse. I'll give you some money."

Malcolm emerged from the office behind the front desk. He looked as drained as Annie felt, and for good reason. He'd accompanied Cal and Nick for both their trip to the jail and to Cal's family's home and Annie was certain this small town feud was more than he ever bargained for. Malcolm was a city boy from Los Angeles. He seemed happily married to Lacy, overjoyed by the birth of their baby Emma Jane, but now he'd been drawn into Troy's mess and its potential re-percussions for the hotel. Settling hands to his hips, he said, "Why don't you two go on. It's been a long day."

Cal and Annie looked to him. "It's only five o'clock," Cal replied.

Glancing back toward the recessed office door, he nod-ded. "True, but I have a few more hours of work left to do. No sense we're both here."

"Where's Lacy?" Annie asked.

"With Fran. The two are having dinner at the diner with Emma Jane. They're not expecting me. Fran is trying to give Jimmy more responsibility so she's sitting the night out, watching while he works as a pseudo manager. Lacy says it's about time."

"I agree," Annie said. "Fran might be Chief Cook and Bottle Washer, but the woman needs a break now and again."

"More like she's looking for a chance to play with the baby," Cal corrected.

Malcolm grinned. "Agreed. Something you two are going to have yourself in a couple of months."

Thoughts of Casey's baby pulled mixed feelings from her. "Yes. Soon." Looking up at Cal, Annie sighed. "I need to call her." She wanted to know how Casey was dealing with Troy's situation, the future. Annie was concerned she wasn't going to take the news well. Ashley reassured her that Casey seemed fine, but was she? Would she want to talk?

"Do one better and go home to her," Malcolm said. "She'll need her family to get through this situation with Troy."

Malcolm didn't mention Jack. Annie wondered if it was purposefully not to offend Cal.

Cal seemed hesitant, but at Malcolm's insistence, acquiesced. "Okay. Thanks, Malcolm." He clapped him on the shoulder. "I'll be back first thing."

"You mean pre-dawn."

The comment drew a small smile from her husband. "Mother Nature's never prettier than when she's wakin' up in the morning." Cal slid an arm around Annie and drew her close. "Same goes for a woman."

Malcolm laughed. "You won't hear any disagreement from me!"

Grateful for the break in tension, Annie leaned into Cal's embrace. Warm, solid, she needed his strength but understood he needed hers, too. Together, they'd get through this mess. *Together*. The word gave her a tingle.

Cal took Annie by the hand and walked her to the front door. "You hungry?" he asked. "Maybe we can convince Casey to join us for a bite to eat and have a visit with Lacy and the baby?"

"Good idea." Annie punched in her home number. No answer. Then Casey's cell. After she waited through the rings, the call went to voicemail. "Casey, it's Mom. Cal and I are going to Fran's for dinner and wanted to know if you'd like to join us. Lacy and the baby will be there. Let me know..." Annie wanted to know where Casey was, she wanted to tell her to call the minute she received the message.

Ending the connection, Annie slipped the phone back into her purse, forcing herself to let the worry go. Casey was an adult. She was going through her own troubles and was probably with Troy this very minute.

Casey yanked branches from her path as she stomped through the underbrush. This used to be a shortcut to Ladd Springs. She remembered it from years ago when she and her friends used to come out here and spy on Felicity and Travis and Troy. Back then it had been an established trail. Now it was nothing but leaves and weeds and vines of some sort. "Ouch!" Glaring at her thorn-punctured thumb, she sucked the red tip. Whipping her glance around, she looked for easier passage. Sunlight slanted through the trees, coating leaves in a gold-white haze. Heat was lifting from the mountain, but it didn't ease her body temperature. She was hot, sweating, her cotton dress sticking to her back. The hike had been more than she bargained for, but once committed there was no going back. Besides, she had to be getting close.

Continuing several more steps, she detected an open space around the bend ahead. Was that the trail? Hurrying, she was rewarded with the sight of a clearing. More a break in the brush, but it might be a section of trail that would prove an easier trek. Propelled by renewed energy, she worked through trees and bushes, boots crunching over fallen branches until she made it to the open space. Relief flooded her as she glanced over the ground of moss-covered rocks and clay. Yes. *This was the trail.* Glancing in the direction of Ladd Springs, Casey knew she was getting close now. Close to Troy.

Felicity tamped down a swell of nerves as she turned on-to the drive for the Foster's ranch. There was nothing to be nervous about. It wasn't like Mrs. Foster was some kind of monster lying in wait to eat her. She was a beautiful, elegant, compassionate woman. She'd raised four boys, had good standing in the community. Everyone in town knew her fami-ly, respected her personally, not only for her medical charity work but because she had taken it upon herself years ago to form a committee and raise money to build a new library. Built of brick and pillars, the downtown facility was not only beautiful but housed a children's reading room and the latest in computer technology including nearly a dozen computers, not to mention any book you ever wanted to read. Most amazing, the small town library rivaled any Felicity had seen at the University of Tennessee.

Yes, Felicity assured herself, Mrs. Foster was decent, noble. Surely she would do the right thing, and who knew? Maybe the two could have a relationship going forward. After all, the Fosters were her only living grandparents. Shouldn't they be close?

It was a question soon to be answered. She drove through rolling fields, four-board fencing lining her way, gorgeous horses grazing idly on either side of her as the af-ternoon sun sank into the western horizon. The heat of the day had gone, leaving a blaze of green mountain landscape in its aftermath. As Felicity pulled around the circular drive in front of the two-story estate, she was hit by a wave of doubt. Should she have called? What if Mrs. Foster wasn't here? She glanced at the dashboard clock. Five-thirty on a Monday night should find her at home, shouldn't it?

Too late now. She was here. Felicity parked and hurried to the front door before she could change her mind. She at least had to try. Ascending the front steps, she crossed the wide veranda and knocked on the door briskly, polished wood bruising against her knuckles. Taking a deep breath, she waited. The door opened and an elderly woman smiled. Mrs. Foster's housekeeper, Thelma. Felicity remembered her from the other night.

Like in the movies, she wore a starched white uniform, her aging skin creasing as she smiled genially. "Good evening, Miss Felicity."

"Good evening," she replied. "I'm here to see Mrs. Foster."

The round, elderly woman knit her brow in concern. "Do you have an appointment?"

Felicity shook her head. "No, I'm sorry. I was in the neighborhood and wanted to drop in and say hi. Is she here?"

"She is," the housekeeper replied as she opened the door wide without question. "I'll run upstairs and fetch her."

"Thank you." Felicity entered, hit by a cool shaft of air-conditioning, the house as she remembered it. Not a stem out of place in the floral display, floors gleamed, pillows and frames sat perfectly situated. The warm ambiance of wood and leather beckoned her indoors.

"Why don't you go on into the living room and have a seat." The woman paused. "Can I get you something to drink?"

"No, thank you. I'm fine."

"You sure you wouldn't like a spot of water? It sure is hot out there today."

Felicity smiled, working to loosen the knot in her chest. "I'm fine, thank you."

The woman shook he head as though Felicity were crazy not to accept, then padded up an elegant spiral staircase, disappearing somewhere above. Felicity's breathing grew shallow as she looked around the empty house. Was Mr. Foster here? Was her father?

Her pulse jumped. She hadn't considered the possibility of running into *him*. But Cal said he'd left, didn't he? Moved out? Sliding a hand down her ponytail braid, Felicity pulled it forward as she walked into the living room, searching adjacent rooms for sight of movement. No one. She didn't hear anyone in the kitchen, didn't smell any food cooking. It was as though the house had been vacated. Didn't they have to eat? She ventured farther inside. Had they gone out to dinner?

## Chapter Twenty-Six

Annie spotted a blue car on the side of the road and pointed. "Oh my gosh—Cal, look! Is that Casey's car?"

"It sure looks like it."

"Pull over!"

Cal slowed, veering off to where the blue car sat parked. Annie didn't wait until his truck stopped before leaping out. "Annie!" Cal called out.

Visions of her daughter slumped over the wheel propelled her forward, ripped through her imagination. "Casey!" Racing over, she slammed into the car, hands hitting windshield and roof as she peered into the interior. Empty. Panic battered her heart. Empty!

Cal appeared by her side. He placed a hand to the hood. "Car's still warm. She couldn't have gotten far."

"Where is she?" Annie cried. "Where would she have gone?"

Cal glanced back in the direction of the hotel. "Looks like she was headed our way."

"Cal—what are we going to do?" Dread filled her. "We didn't see her."

"She might have called for a ride."

Annie yanked out her phone. She dialed Casey's cell number, each unanswered ring compounding her fear. Thoughts of an abductor swirled in her mind. Casey's voice message played and Annie snapped, "Casey, its Mom. Call me when you get this message."

What if it was too late?

Cal placed arms on her shoulders and drew her near. Holding her securely, he zeroed in and held tight. "She's all right, Annie. She probably called for a ride. Troy most likely. Why don't you try his phone?"

"I don't have his number."

"Try Delaney. She's bound to have it."

"Yes, you're right." Annie immediately called Delaney. "Delaney, do you have Troy's cell phone number? I need to call him. Casey's car is broken down on the side of the road, and I need to see if she's with him." Shooting a worried look toward Cal, she responded into the phone, "Yes, she was on her way to the hotel. Okay, thank you." Clutching the phone to her breast, she said, "Delaney said Troy was at the stables earlier. Told me to let her know if I can't reach him and she'll call down for me."

"Good. Don't worry, sweetheart. Casey's fine."

Turning to Nick, Delaney set her phone on the kitchen counter of her small cabin. "Casey's car is on the side of the road. Annie says she was on her way here."

"She abandoned her car?"

Delaney nodded. A disquiet slinked in, rivaling the sudden unease in her husband's gaze. "Annie's calling Troy. She thinks maybe he went and picked her up."

"He probably did."

Delaney couldn't eject her concern so easily. "Should we call him?"

"Didn't you say Annie was calling him?"

"Yes."

"You both don't need to call. Why don't you check with the stable manager, see if Troy has left?"

Delaney picked up the phone and dialed the stables. After speaking with her assistant manager, she finished the conversation more worried than when she began. "He said Troy left an hour ago."

"So we don't know when Casey left her car, do we? He could have grabbed her and gone."

Delaney shook her head, unsettled by Nick's choice of words. "I don't like it. Casey's seven months pregnant. Something could have happened to her."

Nick reached for her. Taking the phone from her vise-like grip he set it on the butcher-block island and took her in his arms. The beginnings of dinner prep on the counter beside them were discarded, their evening of relaxation marred. "Let's not jump to conclusions. Why don't we get in the car and go take a look for ourselves?"

"Good idea."


Walking past the hotel lobby, Troy cursed his brother again. Twenty minutes. Twenty minutes before he could get someone to follow him to the hotel where he would drop Troy's truck. Twenty minutes that were supposed to happen an hour ago. Inwardly, Troy fumed.

"Troy!"

He turned, surprised to see Malcolm Ward waving him over to the hotel. His heart leapt to his throat. *Now what*?

Troy hurried over to the lobby entrance. Tipping back his hat, he asked, "Yes, sir?"

"Annie's on the phone for you."

"Mrs. Foster?"

Malcolm nodded. Troy jogged up the steps and headed through the door Mr. Ward held for him. "You can take the call over there."

"Thanks." Troy went to a phone located on a small table situated between two over-stuffed chairs. He didn't sit, just picked up the receiver and asked, "Mrs. Foster?"

"Yes. Is Casey with you?"

"No, ma'am. She said she was coming to see me but I called and told her to meet me at Fran's Diner."

"You did? What time was that?"

Alarm bells went off in his brain as he checked his watch. "About a half-hour or so. Why? What's the matter?"

There was a long pause. Troy turned from nearby eyes and ears. Staring at a border of ferns visible through floor-to-ceiling glass windows, he asked, "Mrs. Foster, is something wrong?"

"We found her car abandoned on the side of road about three miles from the hotel. It looks like she was headed in that direction."

Troy's blood ran cold. "What do you mean abandoned?"

"It's on the side of the road. I think she was having car trouble."

"Well, where the heck is she now?" he demanded, controlling his tone the best he could.

"I don't know," came her mother's shaky reply.

Troy's entire world nose-dived. Indecision gripped him. Should he go to Casey's car? Should he go to Fran's Diner? Back to the stables?

He didn't have a vehicle—how was we gonna do a thing? Horrible thoughts assaulted him as he imagined a pregnant Casey hitchhiking. Dad gummit! Why didn't she call him?

Casey pulled a crooked twig from her hair and tossed it to the ground. Brushing wayward strands of hair behind her ears—hair damp with sweat—she bent over and recovered her breath. Hands to knees, she inhaled deeply against the pound of her heart. That last trek had been tough, most of it uphill. Lungs heaving, she hoped the baby was okay. The doctor said exercise was good for the baby. Did that include mountain climbing?

Her impromptu hike had been more than she expected.

But she was here. Almost. The level of sunlight was growing, open land visible through the trees ahead. Swiping the back of her hand across her brow, she stood, gently stretched and massaged her lower back. Her legs were wired and tired. She was hot, dehydrated. The muscles around her stomach were tight, cramps occurring at more regular intervals. Stepping over a downed log, she kept her footfall light as possible. Jarring steps aggravated her stomach. She already felt an odd pressure. She didn't want to worsen it.

For the first time Casey was afraid. She had a bad feeling about her baby. She'd read about counting the minutes between contractions was what a woman did when she was determining whether or not to go to the hospital. But she was only seven months pregnant. Her cramps weren't technically contractions. What did it mean if they were happening more frequently? Was it because she'd overdone it?

A brush of light-headedness swept through her skull. Pausing, she waited for it to pass. Yes, it had to be. Too much exertion wasn't good for her. She needed to sit. Relax. Take it easy and let her body recover. But she couldn't. Not yet. After a few minutes, she picked up the pace and continued. The trail widened, opened to a field. In the distance, she spotted a metal rooftop. Her heart sang. Yes! The stables were in sight!

Breathing in, she calmed the rapid beat of her heart. The rest of the trip would be easy. Pulling her cell phone out of her pocket—she'd ditched her purse a while back—Casey checked for signal. One bar. It was worth a try, she thought and dialed Troy's number. The phone went straight to voicemail. "Dang it," she muttered, her throat dry and scratchy. Dropping the phone back in her pocket she supported her underbelly of her stomach with both hands and kicked into motion. It would be okay. She could do this. She'd be there in five, ten minutes, tops. "C'mon, baby. We're going to see your daddy!"

"Felicity."

"Mrs. Foster!" she exclaimed breathlessly, startled by the sound of her name, despite the fact she'd been waiting for the woman. Dressed elegantly, as though she were on her way out for the evening, Felicity suddenly wondered, *Was she*?

"When Thelma told me it was you, I didn't know whether to believe her or not." Victoria Foster neared, concern and curiosity mingling in her light brown gaze. "It's so lovely to see you again. How are you feeling?"

Felicity gulped. She was referring to her hasty departure last week, her unexpected dash from the dinner party. "Fine," she replied. "It must have been a twenty-four hour bug."

"I'm so glad to hear it." Extending a hand toward the sofa, Mrs. Foster asked, "Would you like to sit?"

"Sure." Thankful the lie had been easily accepted, Felicity hurriedly took a seat on a leather sofa. There was no doubt Mrs. Foster didn't believe her but she was being polite, and for that Felicity was grateful.

Mrs. Foster opted for an upholstered wing chair. Rather than relaxing into the cushions she sat perched on the edge, her posture erect. Imperious. "To what do I owe the pleasure of your company this evening?"

Setting hands to her knees, Felicity glanced about her surroundings, uncertain how to begin. "I'm sorry to barge in on you without calling first."

"Please, you're not barging in at all. We're family." Mrs. Foster smiled, emanating warmth, camaraderie. "I'd ask you to stay for dinner, but with no one else home, Thelma's taking the night off from the kitchen."

"Oh, no problem. I'm not really hungry," Felicity replied, growing uncomfortable beneath Mrs. Foster's expectant gaze. With the niceties covered, she was clearly waiting for Felicity to explain the nature of her visit more thoroughly. Clearing her throat, Felicity pushed up a little on a her cushion and said, "I wanted to come by and talk, apologize for the other night and—"

"Sweetheart," Mrs. Foster interrupted, pleasure lighting up her gaze, "you have nothing to apologize for. Please, we all have moments we'd rather forget. It's forgotten. Don't give it another thought."

Felicity settled in on the older woman's face, the pleasant smile, determined eyes framed by fine lines, accentuated to perfection in a shimmery cream shadow and sable liner. Mrs. Foster was a woman of purpose. She wasn't frivolous or stupid. There was no sense in playing games. She'd see right through them, anyway. Felicity took a deep breath and dove in, "I'm here to talk about my father."

Mrs. Foster's expression grew concerned. "Yes, dear, I'm sorry to hear about the trouble between him and your mother. It's quite unfortunate when a child becomes entangled in their parents' problems."

Felicity thought that was putting it mildly. Terms that came to her mind were "*punching bag*", "*tug-of-war*", "*good guy-bad guy.*" Her grandmother acted sincere, while at the same time, oblivious to the facts. "I understand you're supporting him," Felicity put forth, "taking his side against my mom."

Victoria raised a manicured brow and glanced askance. "There is always more than one side to any story, my dear. You should be old enough to understand that."

"Yes, but there's only one right and wrong. My father is pressing charges against Troy for things he didn't do. He went to jail because of it."

She frowned. "Yes, Jack mentioned something about the boy."

"Mentioned something about him? He's in *jail* because of him."

"Sweetheart, you weren't there, nor was I. Can we really profess to know what happened?"

Felicity struggled to keep her cool. The woman was maddeningly calm, talking as though they were discussing a news story from halfway across the globe involving complete strangers. They weren't. They were discussing her father—Victoria's son—and Troy, one of Felicity's best friends. Did Mrs. Foster not understand what was at stake? Did she not know the truth?

"Do you know he tried to rape my mother? That he beat her all those years ago and that's why she divorced him?"

Victoria stiffened, pursing her lips. "Once again, there are two sides to every story. You are only hearing one side, which is most undoubtedly skewed."

The breath escaped Felicity. *Was she serious*?

"He's never laid a hand on you, has he?" her grandmother pressed.

"No... But he hit my mother. Isn't that enough?"

Victoria cast a withering look. "So she claims."

Felicity gaped. "Claims?"

"Sweetheart, I'm sorry to be the one to break it to you. I know how hard it is for a child to hear ill words spoken against their parent, an adult they love and adore, but your mother isn't the most reliable source. She's been known to tell half-truths."

Angered by the woman's patronizing tone, Felicity demanded, "What are you talking about? My mother has never told a lie in her entire life!"

"Really?" Victoria raised her chin. "Perhaps you should speak with Officer Gavin. He might tell you a different story."

"I don't believe you," Felicity snapped. "You're just saying these things so I'll think my father is the good guy here."

"Isn't he?"

At her grandmother's intransigence, all Felicity's hopes for reason and compassion squashed flat. "No. He's an alcoholic. He needs help. I would have thought you'd be interested in helping him."

Setting her mouth in a hard line, Victoria rose from the chair. She stared down her nose at Felicity and said, "I think we're finished here."

Felicity shot up from her seat. She was failing, losing her last chance to save Troy from a horrible injustice being done by *her* family, and she couldn't let it happen. "Don't you care about him? Don't you want to see him get the help he needs? You're his mother. You of all people should want what's best for him."

Victoria linked arms across her chest and replied contemptuously, "What I care about is wasting time listening to a child who thinks she's entitled to insult her father."

"I'm only speaking the truth."

"You're mindlessly spewing the venom of your mother. It's predictable but unfortunate." Flicking an insulting glance, Victoria added, "And just like your mother, you don't know half of what you think you know, yet you insist on throwing your opinion around as though it were the gospel. How stupid of me to think we could actually have a relationship despite her."

Emotions crashed and pitched in Felicity's heart. Optimism popped like a balloon. Victoria Foster was denying her son had any trouble with alcohol. It was as if she had built walls around her, walls between her and the truth. Anyone could see Jack Foster had an issue with drinking. Her own husband didn't permit it anywhere near his home or ranch. Why was Mrs. Foster acting this way?

"Shall I escort you to the door?" she asked.

Felicity shook her head, wracked by despair. "No. I can find my way out."

## Chapter Twenty-Seven

Annie sat rigid in her seat as Cal drove. Hands clenched in her lap, she scanned the roadway for signs of her daughter. With each passing mile, her heart sank deeper into the pit of her stomach. Casey was seven months pregnant. She should not be walking this far. She should not be alone. Who could she have called? Ashley and Fran hadn't heard from her. Troy didn't know where she was. Delaney, Malcolm—no one. Maybe someone she knew drove by and picked her up. It was possible. Maybe she called Jimmy. Fran said he wasn't at the diner. Maybe he was with Casey.

"It'll be okay," Cal said quietly, as though reading her thoughts. Cupping a hand over hers, he squeezed. "We'll find her."

Annie didn't dare look at him. She merely latched onto to his grasp like the lifeline that it was. Reassuring words aside, she understood the reality. It was possible Casey had met with foul play. Unthinkable, but possible.

Troy raced out of the lobby headed for the street. Mr. Foster said he'd check the roads and to sit tight. But if Casey was headed here on foot, maybe she'd made it. Maybe she was in sight from the hotel drive. He stared down the two-lane road—no no sign of her. His pounding heart constricted. Casey's mom said she'd call the diner. If Casey was there, she'd let him know. He glanced toward the hotel, angst mounting. Mr. Ward had not called him back. Translated: Mrs. Foster had not called to tell him she'd found Casey. Turning on his heel, Troy took off running for the trail that led to the stables. It was the last place Casey was supposed to be, but she could have made it there without him seeing her.

An unlikely prospect but plausible. She could have gone up while he was in the lobby.

Running past the history shack that had replaced Old man Ernie's cabin, Troy noticed a few guests had exited, staring at him curiously. Probably wondering why some guy was running through the property. Troy didn't care about the stares. He couldn't waste time walking. If anything happened to Casey, he didn't know what he'd do. He couldn't live without her. They'd been through too much. He'd worked too hard to get back to her, and despite all his mistakes, she was giving him a second chance.

*Third*, but who was counting?

It was a chance he wasn't going to blow. There was too much riding on it.

Racing through the shaded patch of trees, up the incline, Troy drove himself faster. Boots pounded over clay and gravel, every step reverberating in his chest. A barrage of thought thrashed through his brain, most of it ugly. If someone harmed Casey, he'd kill him. With his bare hands he'd kill anyone who laid a hand on her, on his baby. Absolutely— without hesitation—he'd kill them.

Slamming a hand to the barn for support, Casey clutched the door frame for support, groaning as another cramp wound through. Her spasms had grown into full blown cramps, bad cramps, the kind that had to be associated with delivery—a delivery that was too soon!

She might not have ever delivered a baby before, but she knew these cramps were too strong to be casual. Casey lifted her head, sweat dripping into her eyes, stinging. She blinked, wiped them away. She was hot, her bra soaked with perspiration, her legs rubbery weak, but she was here. She stepped inside the barn. *She'd made it.*

Felicity walked into the diner, her mind a jumble of confusion. She didn't know what to do. She hadn't imagined the meeting with Mrs. Foster to go as it had. She'd been floored by the abrupt shift, the harsh words. She never expected the woman to turn ugly so quickly. One minute she was sweet and gracious, the next she was a hissing snake. Quick to insult, quick to bite back. She'd acted as though Felicity had purposely come to insult her and her son and she was fighting back with everything she had.

Ashley Fulmer rose from a nearby booth, leaving Fran, Lacy Ward and her daughter Emma Jane. She hurried to Felicity's side. Dressed in fuchsia from head to toe, Ashley's blue eyes held brevity that seemed misplaced next to the glittery ornamentation of her blouse. "Darlin'? Are you okay?"

Felicity nodded. Tear sprang to her eyes. "Fine."

Ashley hugged Felicity to her. Her generous figure enveloped her in soft cushiony comfort and heavy perfume. Ashley led Felicity to the table of women, gently guiding her to a seat. "You don't look fine. Talk to me. What's the matter? Is it Troy?"

Fran and Lacy looked at her, their faces mirroring Ashley's concern. Fran's brown eyes turned hawkish, sharp and alert against the red of her hair. Lacy's blue eyes became oceans of upset within the porcelain cream of her complexion. A near twin image to Casey's mom, Annie, with her shiny straight black hair and slender figure, Lacy held her baby close, rapt with attention. From within Lacy's arms, Emma Jane smiled open-mouthed and made a squeak as she jabbed a chubby leg into the air.

"I went to see Victoria Foster," Felicity told them. "I thought if I talked to her, she'd understand that supporting Jack against Troy wasn't the right thing to do. That maybe she could get my father help for his drinking problem instead of supporting him in his charges against Troy."

Ashley's thickly-mascaraed eyes rounded. There was no cheer in her gaze. "I'm sorry, darlin'."

"I don't get it. Why is she so blinded?"

Ashley looked to Fran. Both were solemn, both silent, as though they shared a secret.

"Troy could go to jail for something he didn't do. It will ruin his life." Fear returned in a rush, echoed in the quiet of Ashley's razor-sharp expression.

"There's a lot you don't know, darlin', a history that has nothing to do with you and everything to do with Victoria. She's not a happy woman, not when it comes to the Wilkins family, anyway."

Felicity clung to Ashley's every word. She spoke with a calm certainty leading Felicity to believe she held the answers. Fran sat mum, her face a billboard of support. "But why?"

"She and your grandmother share a past."

"They knew each other?"

"In so many words, yes. More they knew *of* each other. They shared a common tie to Gerald."

"To Gerald? What kind of tie?"

"The stranglin' kind."


Troy tore into the stables, searching up and down corridors. Pumped from the run, he peered in and around stalls. "Casey?"

Horse ears perked and twitched as animals turned toward him as he strode through. Was she here? Had anyone seen her? Stopping suddenly, he ran back to the office. Lights out, it was empty. Miss Delaney had gone for the day, but that didn't mean the stables were empty. He knew for a fact some of the staff stayed late. At the moment he saw no one.

Troy ran outside, checked the perimeter of the building. Again there was no one. He dashed back inside, forcing his mind to think. Pressing hands to the sides of his head, he willed an answer to appear. Casey—*where are you*?

His head shot up. The barn. Casey might think he was in the barn. That's where she found him the last time he was here. Troy sprinted from the stables.


Shuffling farther into the barn, each and every step was more delicate than the previous. Through the opposite end of the building, Casey could see the stables. White wood was washed with yellow, the metal rooftop gleaming in soft silver. A beautiful sight to behold. Doubling over in pain, Casey gripped the underbelly of her stomach as another cramp wrenched through her midsection. Wetness warmed between her thighs. "Oh, no!" Casey cried out. "This can't be happening!"

Fear dribbled down into her spine as warm liquid streamed between her thighs. She clutched her crotch, overwhelmed by a dull pressure. Totally soaked. This was bad. This was really, really bad. It felt like the baby was pushing.

She had to get help—now. Easing down onto a bale of hay, one of a pile stacked in the corner, she reached a shaky hand into her dress pocket and seized the square metal of her phone. Hair lay matted against her forehead, her arms and legs slick with sweat A few pieces of hay stuck to her legs as she pressed the number for her mother. Jabbing phone to her ear, she heard it ringing. A cramp cut through her. "Ooww!"

"Casey!" Her mother screamed into the phone. "Where are you? What's happening? Are you okay?"

Too many questions. "I'm in the barn, at the hotel." Tears swamped her lids, blurring her vision. "I think the baby is coming!"

"*What?*"

As expected, her mother's voice was frantic, but Casey was feeling the same. She was worried. It was time to panic. "The baby—I think I'm going into labor. I'm having really painful cramps and they're coming all the time." Another warm surge moistened her underwear. She pulled her hand away to see it tinged with red. "I'm bleeding!"

"Stay where you are. We'll be right there."

"Okay," she stammered, clamping a hand back between her legs. A shiver rocked her body. She wasn't cold. *She was scared.*

"Is Troy with you?"

"No. I don't know where he is," she murmured, the seriousness of her condition sinking in.

"Okay. We're on our way. Stay on the phone with me."

Casey nodded but couldn't speak. Plunking her gaze to the hay-covered cement floor, she envisioned having a baby in the midst of dirt and dust and hay. She cringed, groaned as a sharp pain knifed across her lower belly folding her in two. Deep and severe, it continued for several long seconds while she clutched her stomach with both hands. Pressure to push mounted, like the baby wanted out right now!

This couldn't be happening. This couldn't be happening!

Allowing her gaze to glaze over, Casey could hear muted shrieks from her phone, but had no energy to respond. Every ounce she had was overwhelmed by the baby inside her body, the pain.

The pain was incredible. Excruciating. The phone tumbled from her grasp.

*Is this what all women went through?* It was horrible to think having a baby meant this much pain—why would a woman ever do it twice?

*Baby.* Casey seized on the thought. She was having a baby. More fluid collected beneath her, soaking into the bale of hay beneath her. A fresh wave of fear flowed through her and she began to cry. This wasn't good. She glanced around the barn. This wasn't good at all!


Troy entered the barn and whipped his gaze around the interior. Tractor, tools, hay bales, there was no one here. With several long strides, he called out, "Casey? Casey, are you here?"

Pausing, he thought he heard something. Slowing his breath, he listened. His gaze narrowed. It sounded like whimpering. His heart belted out several beats in rapid succession. Taking a few steps, he surveyed the vicinity. Partially hidden behind the mountain of bales, he thought he saw a dark head of hair. Adrenaline kicked. "Casey?"

Over a lower bale, her face emerged. Anxious blue eyes pleaded for him to come. Adrenaline charged him forward.

Warning flares fired in his chest, his skull as he ran toward her. "Casey!"

"Troy," she cried, her voice shaky and weak. "I think I'm having the baby."

Blood on her dress. Alarm ripped a hole in his chest. Questions fired through him. When did she get here? How had he missed her? As he reached her side, all questions evaporated. He dropped to a knee. "Does it hurt?"

She nodded. "It hurts a lot."

"Okay. It's okay," he said, brushing damp hair from her eyes. His mind raced through options. Towels. Water. He needed something to clean her up. He needed something to clean a baby. "Hold on a second."

"Troy?"

Her panicky tone split his gut, but if he was going to help her, he needed supplies and he needed them quick. "Stay put. I'll be right back."

Grabbing a stack of white towels from a cleaning closet, he dashed to the wall and plucked an empty bucket from a stack by the garbage cans. Next, he ran to a hose bib and filled the bucket with water, all the while keeping an eye on Casey. "One second," he called out to her, controlled panic streaming through his veins. "I'll be there in one second." Wrenching the valve closed, he jumped to his feet, a sheet of water drenching his jeans.

Eyeing the bucket and towels as he neared, she asked, "What are you doing?"

"I'm delivering a baby, what do you think?"

She recoiled. "What—you can't do that!"

"I sure can. If I can deliver a foal I darn sure can deliver a human."

"Troy," she sputtered. "My mom is coming. I need to go to the hospital."

Troy zapped her with a dark-eyed gaze and Casey stilled. "Casey, you don't have time to go to the hospital. This baby is coming *now*."

## Chapter Twenty-Eight

"*Ohmigod, ohmigod, ohmigod.*"

"Shhh," Troy hushed. "It's gonna be okay." Breaking a nearby bale in half, he scattered chunks of hay across the floor to make it more comfortable for her. Taking her gently by the arms, he asked, "Can you move?" She nodded. "I think it'll be easier if you lie down." He didn't know why, but it seemed more natural, like the mare who delivered Vegas. And didn't women lie down at the hospital?

They did. Casey needed to lie down, he decided and he eased her to the ground.

Blue eyes became saucers. "Troy, I'm scared."

Troy felt the same. He was scared—for her, for the baby—but he wasn't about to let on. Casey needed him to be calm. "It's gonna be okay."

"But it's too early!"

Troy shook his head. "Don't matter. When a baby's ready to come into the world, nothin's' gonna stop her." Her. His little girl. Swallowing hard, he gently lifted Casey's dress and winced at the sight of her blood-soaked panties. "I need to remove your underwear, okay?"

Propped up on her elbows, she nodded, her gaze intent on his. Troy lifted her hips, spread a towel beneath her and removed her panties as delicately as he could. His heart pitched at the sight of a dark hair poking out from between Casey's legs. The baby was coming all right -this minute! With a wary eye to Casey, he said, "I need you to breathe." He moistened another towel with water and wiped his hands clean, forcing his pulse to settle. "Push and breathe and go real easy, okay?"

"Okay," she whispered.

"Atta girl. We can do this," Troy said almost as much for his benefit as for hers. He reached for Casey's hand and kissed it. "The baby will work her way out and we'll take it from there, okay?"

Casey nodded, then jerked her hand from his, her face twisting in pain. She sucked in a few quick breaths and sank deeper onto her elbows. Troy divided his attention between Casey and the baby. He hated to see Casey in pain. Hated that their baby was being born in a barn, but there was no other way. "Baby's gonna be fine—"

She cut him off with a guttural cry, her fingers clawing at the ground.

"That's it, keep pushin'." He spoke over her awful grunting noises, assuring himself this was normal. Everything was normal. Women made all kind of sounds when they were in labor. "You got it. Keep breathing. In and out..."

Casey shrieked at the top of her lungs, more howl than cry. Troy checked the baby and noticed a dark-haired bubble of a head emerge. "Okay, Casey, we're gettin' there." He reached down and placed his hands beneath the tiny head, forehead skin brighter than a lobster. Casey tried to close her legs but he wedged his body between them. "C'mon, Casey. We're on the homestretch. You can do this."

"I can't! It hurts!"

"Keep pushing," he said. "You've got to keep pushing. The baby's coming out right now." Casey dropped her head back, moaning and writhing like a dying animal. Thoughts of Vegas' birth flooded his mind. The foal had been stuck for too long, stopped breathing. Clammy fear clamped down on him. "Push!" Troy urged, afraid for his baby if Casey quit. "You've got to push through it!"

"It hurts."

"I know it does, Case, but it'll stop when the baby is out." Troy felt her push but it was weak, fatigued. She was dropping off. Giving up. "Do you have a name picked out?" he asked, drawing her focus back to the moment. "You said she was gonna be a girl. Do you know what you want to call her?"

"Cassidy," she breathed out. "I always wanted to be a Cassidy."

Troy cradled the baby's head in his fingertips, supporting it as it protruded from Casey's body. "I like it." He rallied a grin. "Sounds like a real cowgirl."

Casey rewarded him with a faint giggle before her body arched and she wreathed in pain. "Troy, help me!"

"I'm here. It's okay." Perspiration dripped from his nose, salting his lips. Whipping the hair from his face, he concentrated on Casey. "I need you to push—real hard, right now—I need you to push. Can you do that for me?"

"Yes." Casey clutched at clumps of hay on the ground and pushed hard.

"Atta girl," he said, relieved the head was emerging. Gingerly supporting the newborn with his finger pads, he could feel a little neck and shoulders. They were like sticks. It was the weirdest feeling to know he was touching a live baby—his baby—as it was being born. Completely different than a foal. It was amazing, staggering. Fragile.

Mindful of his hold, he focused on Casey. "A few more and we're done, okay? That's it. A few more and we're home free."

"Uh-huh." Panting, Casey's breathing was audible, strained. She lifted up to her elbows again, like her interest had been re-ignited. Cheeks flushed, she looked him straight in the eyes. "I can do this."

Troy grinned. "You can do this." Closing her eyes, Casey grunted, her face wracked by a grimace. "That's right, *push*," he urged, gently tugging the baby's body as she did so. Overcome by a rush of adrenaline, Troy knew they were close. Holding the tiny human being as she entered a new world, he was struck by how delicate she appeared. Red and squash-faced, her bony limbs were stuck to her body. Casey pushed again and the baby slid out entirely, her umbilical cord the only thing left to connect her to her momma. "She's out!" he declared triumphantly.

Casey's eyes shone. "She is?"

"Sure is," he said, mindful of the cord, the baby's need to breathe. Should he spank the baby like they did on television? Troy blanked. Cut the cord? *What was he supposed to do?*

Troy honed in on baby's chest, looking for signs of movement. He wiped the fluid from around the baby's nose and mouth.

"Can I see the baby?" Casey asked, lifting her body fully.

Troy held the baby up without thinking, the sticky cord dangling against his forearms.

"She's so small..." Casey marveled. Flashing a glance to Troy with renewed panic, she asked, "Is she okay?"

"I think so," he replied, noting the faintest rise and fall of her chest, more a flutter of skin near the rib cage. Leaning an ear close, he listened. Was that the baby's breath sound he detected? Or was it his own?

Holding as still as he could, he continued to listen. The baby convulsed in a tiny sneeze. Casey laughed. Relief swept through him. "I think she's okay!" he announced happily.

"Maybe she's allergic to hay."

"Hope not," Troy said, heartened by the love coursing in Casey's eyes. "'Cause this here girl is gonna learn how to ride before she walks."

Casey looked to him. "Can I hold her?"

"Course you can," he said. Sliding his knees along the ground, he maneuvered his body next to hers. He placed the baby in her outstretched hands.

As though fearful she'd break, Casey cautiously took the infant from him, crossing her legs Indian-style beneath her. As Casey gazed at the miniature figure, Troy tugged the hem of her dress over her knees. "She's beautiful."

"That she is. Most beautiful creature I've ever seen." Concerned with completing the task, he wondered if he was supposed to cut the cord. It looked like it was pulsating. Should he pull the placenta out? Horses allowed it to release naturally. Peering at Casey, Troy decided to let nature take its course. Childbirth was natural. What came next had to be natural, too. Slightly unnerved by the mess of blood beneath Casey, soaking through her dress, he wadded a towel and tucked it between her legs.

"Casey!"

Jarred by the interruption, Troy turned on his hunches. Annie and Cal Foster rush into the barn, Miss Delaney and Nick on their heels. "What happened?"

"We had a baby," Troy said, prouder than he'd ever been in his whole life.

Casey's mom stopped dead in her tracks. "You had a baby?"

Cal grinned. "We have a granddaughter!"

"Sure do," Troy replied. "Most beautiful little thing you ever laid eyes on."

Mrs. Foster rushed over, crouched beside her daughter and locked onto the baby in Casey's hands. Slick from birth, skin wrinkly, the baby was making noises that reminded Troy of a kitten. Casey smiled. "Say hi to your new granddaughter."

Mrs. Foster was speechless. The others gathered around her, ogling over shoulder. Shock was the best word to describe the women's expressions. Pleasure covered the men. Troy felt a healthy mix of both.

"Ain't she a beauty?"

"Troy, she's the most beautiful baby I've ever seen," Nick responded.

Delaney followed suit, her gaze strung tightly around Casey and the baby. "She's amazing, Troy."

Cal grinned. "No different than delivering a foal, huh?"

Troy laughed. "Well, now I wouldn't go sayin' all that. This here was quite a bit different but we managed."

Nick grinned. "You did more than manage. You saved the day."

Casey was staring between her mother and her baby. Eyes glistening, she was mesmerized between the two. "What do you think?"

"Are you okay?" Casey nodded. Glancing to the wriggling baby in Casey's hands, Mrs. Foster started to cry. "Is the baby okay?"

"I think so."

"Ambulance is on its way to take you two to the hospital," Cal informed them. "We called on our way here."

"Good," Delaney clipped. "I'll head over to the stables so they'll know to direct them here."

"How about we call down to the hotel and get Malcolm to direct them back?" Nick asked.

Delaney nodded. "Better idea."

"Can I hold her?" Annie asked.

Casey moved hands and baby toward her mother who, realizing the cord was still attached, seemed to think twice. "It's okay," Casey said. "Take her."

She did, ever so slowly drawing the newborn close to her chest. Gazing down at her, Troy could feel a swell of emotion gush from Mrs. Foster as she said, "She's so light. And tiny, isn't she? But she's two months premature," Annie said, concern gathering in her gaze as she answered her own question.

"We'll get her checked out at the hospital," Cal reassured, "and make sure all is well."

"Yes," his wife echoed the sentiment. She glanced up at him, concern not completely wiped from her gaze. "We'll make sure she has the best treatment available."

"She's gonna be fine," Casey said. "Thanks to her daddy."

Mention of the word daddy zapped through Troy like a bolt of electricity. Daddy. He was a daddy! Everyone turned to him, igniting a hot rise to his cheeks. "I only did what I had to do."

"You did a fine job, Troy." Delaney leaned down and planted a kiss on his cheek. "A really fine job."

Reaching a hand to cover the space on his cheek, he rose. Mildly embarrassed, he replied, "Yes, ma'am. Thank you."

Cal clapped a hand to his shoulder. "Wouldn't have expected anything less."

Troy pushed his hat back. "Thank you, sir. I appreciate that."

Delaney squatted by Annie, taking a closer look. "Have you thought of a name?"

"Cassidy Jo."

Annie looked at Casey over the baby. "Sounds strong and capable."

"Like you," Casey said, her voice whisper-fine.

Tears welled in her mom's eyes. "Like *you*."

## Chapter Twenty-Nine

"Sweetheart," Ashley said. "I have a story to share with you."

"A story?" Confused, Felicity glanced around the table to find all eyes on her in the most disconcerting way. "What story?"

"You know your grandmother was my best friend." Felicity nodded, momentarily distracted by several rapid kicks from Emma Jane. Her mom had said as much before. "The two of us go way back," Ashley continued, "to our elementary school days." She chuckled, momentarily lost in a faraway memory. "I loved her like a sister. She was my other half. Closer to me than anyone in this world," she added fiercely.

Felicity began to relax. "Yes, I think I remember my mom telling me." Now that she was back in the fold of family and well clear of Victoria Foster's presence, the knots in her stomach loosened. She could let down her defenses. Ashley and her grandmother Susannah had been childhood friends. Ashley and her mom were close, too. Like the mother she no longer had.

"Well, when your grandmother was young, she was real close with Ernie. Looked up to him like he was a walkin' angel, and I know he felt the same about her." Ashley nodded, as though confirming it as fact. "But Ernie was possessive when it came to Susannah. He watched her like a dog with a bone, wouldn't let anyone get within two feet of her unless he approved of them."

"Didn't she mind?" Felicity asked, trying to imagine Uncle Ernie behaving in such a way. For as long as she remembered, he'd been twiggy, bony. How did he expect to protect her if someone wanted to do her harm?

Ashley smiled, blue eyes shining with affection. "Susannah adored Ernie and trusted him with her life. If he said no to something, the answer was no. When Gerald Foster started comin' around, Ernie got a little crazy."

"Crazy?" Felicity asked. "But why?"

Leaning forward, absently fiddling with one of Emma Jane's chubby feet, Lacy seemed as intrigued as she. "Was Mr. Foster not a nice person?"

"Aw, no," Ashley said, waving Lacy off. "Gerald was a fine young man. Ernie's dislike didn't have anything to do with Gerald. Not really, anyway. Gerald's only crime was falling in love with the wrong woman and wanting to spend his every waking moment with her. He and Susannah were closer than two peas in a pod, walking to school together, taking picnics by the river... But they were never more than friends—at least on Susannah's part. But Gerald," Ashley sighed, sliding a quick glance to Fran. "He was smitten."

Fran nodded, a stark sadness entering her eyes. "Deacon witnessed it personally. He lived two doors down from Gerald and used to hear him whistling Dixie when he'd walk past his house on his way home. Without fail he'd weave Susannah's name into the song and Deacon thought he was plumb crazy."

"He was," Ashley agreed. "Crazy in love with Susannah."

"Why weren't the feelings mutual?" Felicity asked.

"Susannah was sweeter than a dog in heat, don't get me wrong," Ashley said with a swing of her head, "and she adored Gerald. But she had a wild streak bred deep in her soul that she couldn't ignore. Soaked clear through, like butter in a biscuit, you know what I mean?" Ashley nodded, as though prodding her to agree. "Ernie saw it, too, which made him worry all the more over the two spending so much time together."

When Ashley didn't continue, glancing to Fran like she was seeking permission before she spoke the next words, Lacy beat Felicity to the question. "What?"

Ashley dipped her chin and glanced between the two women seated across from her. Felicity and Lacy held their tongues in anticipation. "Ernie thought Gerald had takin' to supper before sayin' grace."

"Huh?" Felicity looked to Lacy. "What does that mean?"

Lacy clamped her mouth closed, leaving Ashley to reply, "He thought Gerald had stolen Susannah's virginity. Sent his blood a boiling, I tell you he nearly split the man's skull."

Felicity gasped in unison with Lacy who exclaimed, "I didn't know that!" Fran nodded solemnly. "Are you saying Ernie actually went after him *physically*?"

"Yes, ma'am. Ernie took a shotgun to Gerald but when the gun jammed, he cracked him over the head with it."

"Oh my gosh!" Felicity cried out, disturbed to learn her uncle had it in him. "*Are you kidding me*?"

Ashley paused. "I wish I was darlin' but I'm not. As God is my witness, I'm telling you the truth. Ernie was mad enough to hunt bears with a hickory switch that day." Casting her eyes to the ceiling, she rolled out, "Well, don't you know Susannah nearly lost her mind over the incident. She shrieked and she hollered, but Ernie didn't listen to a word of it. He stared her down like a varmint and said, 'No more.'" Ashley brushed her palms together before her. "And just like that, Susannah told Gerald she couldn't see him anymore."

Felicity fell back against her seat, stunned. Shocked, disappointed, but mostly stunned by the ferocity of her uncle. She'd always known Ernie to be crusty and grumpy, but she'd never thought him capable of physical violence. She had discarded all his threats over the years as nothing but talk. Trash talk, angry talk. Why, to think that Uncle Ernie could have killed Mr. Foster was unbelievable! "So that's why Uncle Ernie was angry at my mom all these years. Because she married Gerald's son?"

"Oh, Lordy, he was fit to be tied! Refused to attend the wedding, despite Susannah begging him for days. Not a chance in he—" Ashley flung a hand to her mouth. She smiled sheepishly and said, "Well, you know what I mean. Ernie wasn't going and Delaney was marked from then on."

"I guess," Felicity replied, staggered by the level of hatred a man could hold in his heart.

Yet never once did he direct it at her. Never once did he raise his voice to her. Felicity finally understood what her mother had meant all these years when she said, *You're special to him.*

"After the incident," Ashley said, resuming her story, "Susannah was miserable for a few weeks but she let it pass. Like I said, she was never interested in Gerald in a romantic light. She only had eyes for Harry Wilkins."

"My grandfather," Felicity uttered automatically.

Ashley nodded. "The boy was nothin' but a hayseed plow boy, never wanting any more than a wad of tobacco and a good time. He worked for a local farm, provin' about as useful as a back pocket on a T-shirt but Susannah didn't see any of it. Harry was a charmer. Reckless too, enthralling Susannah with tales of his escapades." Ashley fanned herself as though suddenly warm. "Lord knows I tried to convince her otherwise. Gerald would have made a good husband, a devoted husband. Harry on the other hand was about as reliable as a dime store magic trick." Ashley shook her head. "But Susannah thought he was handsome and charming and her heart was sewn to his."

"Did Uncle Ernie know about him?"

"Not 'til it was too late. Knowin' the same fate would befall Harry as Gerald, Susannah ran off and married the boy on her eighteenth birthday." Ashley shot a hard gaze toward Felicity and said, "I don't like speakin' cross words against your kin, Felicity, but Susannah could have done a lot better than Harry."

"Uncle Ernie wasn't mad about her marrying Harry?" Felicity asked.

"It was too late. Susannah had done the deed and he wasn't gonna force her to annulment. Remember, she was his whole world. And she was married, which meant she was Harry's responsibility."

"Didn't Harry manage the liquor store downtown?" Lacy asked.

"Drank half the profits, too."

"My grandfather was an alcoholic?" Felicity asked, misery sinking into her heart. Was everyone in her family a drunk?

"No, darlin' he wasn't. Harry liked his whiskey but he never let it get out of control. And he was good to Susannah. Loved her with all his heart. Harry just couldn't hack responsibility, always looking for the next thrill." When Ashley's gaze dimmed, Felicity felt it coming. "He died playin' chicken with a freight train. Tried to time it just right but miscalculated."

Felicity closed her eyes, warding off visions of squashed metal and shattered glass. She had no idea her grandfather died in such a manner.

"Was he drunk?" Lacy asked, cradling a wiggly Emma Jane close to her breast.

"Not a drop. It was high noon on a Monday afternoon. But old Harry never met a challenge he couldn't lick and thought he was invincible." Ashley winked. "I think that's where your momma gets it from."

Lacy's cell phone rang. Fumbling through the purse next to her, she snatched an aqua encased phone and pressed it to her ear. "Hello?" Her expression morphed from prurient curiosity to sheer horror. "Oh no!" Angling her head into her phone, she sent a shocked look around the table. "In the barn? No doctor?"

Felicity's heart stopped. Who was she talking about? Her mother? Troy?

Lacy burst into a giggle and squealed to the table, "I'm a great aunt!"

"What are you talking about, child?" Fran demanded.

Ashley gaped. "Casey had her baby?"

*Casey had her baby*? Felicity reeled—but she couldn't have—she was only seven months pregnant! Horrible thoughts and images crashed in her brain. Was she okay? Why was she in a barn? Where was Troy? Was the baby okay?

"She had her baby in the barn over at the hotel," Lacy explained, phone planted to her ear. "Cassidy Jo."

"Cassidy Jo?" Fran asked.

"That's her name," Lacy told them.

"Is she okay?"

Lacy nodded. "Baby and momma are both fine. There's an ambulance on its way to take them to the hospital."

"Well, if that don't put pepper in the gumbo!" Ashley exclaimed. "We got ourselves a barn-birthed baby!"

Nervous excitement sprinted through Felicity's stomach. She had a new cousin! Or did she? What would Casey's baby be to her? Felicity wondered as Lacy delivered a blow-by-blow of the events. Casey's car ran out of gas, she hiked to the stables, never made it, felt cramps, Troy showed up and helped deliver the baby. His baby. Troy helped deliver his own child.

How incredible. How romantic! Felicity leaned in and digested every word Lacy spoke.

Casey had a baby!

## Chapter Thirty

Sitting in a chair, bedside, Troy watched Casey as she held a well-bundled Cassidy in her arms. Perched atop the sheets of a hospital bed, the new Parker mother was feeding her baby as she awaited official discharge. For three weeks Cassidy had to remain under doctor's care. Three long weeks. Casey had wanted to be with the baby every second of the time, a sentiment he understood, but it made it real hard to wrestle her away for a marriage ceremony. Nothing fancy, but Troy had to make it legal. It wasn't right, otherwise.

Swathed in a lightweight blanket, marked by pink and blue stripes, Cassidy sucked from a petite plastic bottle. Her lips moved rhythmically as fingers wrapped around her momma's thumb, holding it close. Troy marveled at his daughter's size. She was like a miniature human being, a tiny person, yet she behaved the same as anyone else. Cassidy drank, gazed at the world around her, wriggled and waved arms and legs. And she smiled. Or what Casey claimed was a smile. Troy wasn't sure how much of a baby's behavior was intentional or instinctual but he knew one thing—Cassidy knew who her momma was.

Reaching over, he gently stroked the feather-fine hair on his baby's small head, the strands dark and dense as they full covered her skin. Caressing the silken strands gave Troy deep pleasure. Roused a deep need to provide and protect. He didn't care how much hair she had, only that she was healthy and happy, though the nurses were convinced Cassidy Jo Grace was going to be the envy of all the girls in school with her thick waves of black hair. Peering into Casey's eyes, her gaze secured peacefully on her daughter, Troy figured Cassidy was gonna have hair like her momma. Pausing on the picture of his wife and child, powerful emotions wound through him. Actually, he hoped Cassidy did everything like her momma. From her looks to her heart, he'd be real pleased if the two were exactly alike. Except that Cassidy was gonna love horses like him.

"Cal said the cabin is comin' along real quick," Troy said.

The comment drew a smile from Casey as she temporarily withdrew her gaze from her daughter and rested it on him. In one gaze she transferred a mountain of love and adoration from Cassidy to him. "I'm glad. I'm ready to get out of here and move into our new home."

Pleasure coursed through him. *Our new home.* Amazing how a woman could affect him like this. A child, his family. Especially after the last several weeks. With criminal charges hanging over his head and a new baby and now a wife in his life, it had been rough going. Miss Delaney wouldn't let him work the stables. Cal Foster couldn't get him a job at his family's ranch. He could work scooping piles of horse crap at a nearby ranch, but he wasn't ready to reduce himself to mindless work. It would hurt too much being that close to the animals and not being able to work with them. It was one thing to invest the time in menial labor with Hotel Ladd where he had hope for a future. It was quite another to accept a dead-end job with a second-rate ranch in the backwoods of Tennessee. Casey had suggested he bus tables for Fran, but Troy couldn't bring himself to do it. Jimmy Sweeney worked there, and now that he was training to be assistant manager, he could potentially be Troy's boss.

*Ain't gonna happen.* While he promised Casey he'd work on his relationship with Jimmy, Troy wasn't going to allow that to include subservience. He might have to accept that Casey and Jimmy were friends and would remain so, but he didn't have to lose his manhood in the process. Troy didn't care for Jimmy. He'd put up with him, tolerate him, even allow him to visit with Casey and Cassidy whenever he wanted, but he wasn't gonna act like they were cool. They weren't.

Instead, Troy accepted an offer from his father to work part-time in Chattanooga. His daddy was a vice-president of operations for a packaging company and said he could use help in his office. He was willing to pay twice minimum wage which Troy took as a peace offering. Not like he'd get rich off the job, but it was a heck of lot more than he'd make anywhere around here at the moment. And he needed money to support his family. His momma encouraged him to take it as a way to end the hostility between father and son. They'd apologized for letting him sit in jail and he should forgive them. Old resentment pulled at him. Only because Miss Delaney marched over and gave them an ear full. If it wasn't for her, his parents would still think the worst of him. Pulling his hand from Cassidy's head, he shrugged it off. Whatever. Cal said they could move into the cabin next week and that's what he was focused on. Moving forward.

Setting the bottle down on the cushion beside her, Casey tossed a soft cloth over her shoulder to prepare for a round of burping. Troy watched in awe as she handled the infant. Only three weeks old, Cassidy was small and spindly. The nurses kept her warm, kept her monitored, but he thought she was too skinny. Cassidy was being released today, something they'd been waiting for, but suddenly Troy wasn't so sure. Would she be okay at home? Would he and Casey be able to care for her?

Placing child to her shoulder, Casey nestled close and began the process of eliminating any gas Cassidy might have ingested while drinking from her bottle. Gone was the uncertainty and doubt he'd witnessed in the immediate days of his return home, replaced by a confidence Troy assumed must come with motherhood. Giving birth must transform a woman's heart and mind as the baby growing inside had done to her body. These days Casey seemed so relaxed, self-assured. After they delivered the baby, an ambulance transported them to the hospital where doctors and nurses flocked to their side, whisked Cassidy away and placed her under intense scrutiny by a twenty-four hour neonatal staff—despite his protest.

But if his baby needed care than so be it. At least they allowed him to be present while Casey was being examined. And while he held her hand the entire time, Casey only wanted one thing. Her baby. Not him, not the doctors or nurses or family but her child. Eventually he and Casey were allowed to visit Cassidy and Troy recalled how sick he felt when he saw her. There were wires connected to her chest, tubes attached to her nose and mouth, heat lamps set up all around her pint-sized crib. It looked awful, like Cassidy was near dead. But she wasn't. The nurse assured him she was okay and this was nothing more than medical assistance to make sure she stayed that way.

Once they decided Cassidy was well enough to be with her momma, Casey took to mothering like she'd done it a hundred times. Forget that it was her first child, she seemed to know instinctively how to care for a newborn. She never stumbled or hesitated, rather reacted as if a whole new layer of knowledge had been packed into her brain with the birth of her child. Troy on the other hand was still getting used to the idea. He was getting better, but a part of him still felt like he was going to break something if he held or hugged Cassidy too hard.

"Let me see that little girl," Troy said impulsively, reaching over for Cassidy.

As Casey released the baby to him, she handed Troy the cloth which he flung absently over his shoulder. He was the daddy and he was determined to care for his baby, too.

Skinny little legs kicked wildly against him and he said, "Hold on, now. I'm gettin' there." He shook his head. "You're gonna have to learn some patience or you're never gonna learn to work a horse."

Casey gazed at him fondly, a soft sheen of love deepening the blue of her eyes. "Cassidy has a mind of her own, something daddy is going to have to get used to else there be fireworks in the household."

"What are you talkin' about?" Troy asked, concealing the swell of a smile. *That* much about kids he knew.

Folding her hands across her flat abdomen, Casey simply smiled.

Cassidy gurgled next to him, tickling the skin at his neck. Tilting his head, Troy gently tapped his to hers. "C'mon, sunshine. You've got this. Give me some gas, baby, gimme some gas."

Casey chuckled and shook her head. "You'd better be careful, or she's going to give you more than gas." Arching a brow, she added, "Her face is turning red."

A distinct sign of bowel movement. "It don't matter. She can poop all she wants. Her momma will get her diaper," he said, suppressing a knowing grin.

"If you can burp her, you can change."

"Oh, no. No self-respectin' man is gonna change a diaper."

"What happens when you're alone with her?"

"We'll wait for her momma to come home."

"You do and I'll whoop your hide."

Troy couldn't help but laugh as he imagined Casey trying to whoop him. She was half his size and scrawny as a stray dog. She couldn't whoop a flea, let alone him. "Go ahead," he teased. "It'll be fun watchin' you try."

Casey crossed arms over her chest and feigned anger. "I'm gonna surprise you one of these days."

"Good. I look forward to it. Now back to serious matters, have you talked to your momma about shopping?"

"Yes. She wants to go next week."

As a wedding gift, Cal and Annie offered to purchase three rooms of furniture for the new cabin—living room and two bedrooms. Troy instantly refused, claiming it was too generous. He didn't know what furniture cost, but it had to be a lot. Cal had already built them a home. Troy would buy his own furniture. Eventually.

But Cal insisted the cabin had been a Christmas gift to Casey, under construction before Troy ever set foot back home. He said the furniture wasn't too generous, considering it was his brother, Jack, causing Troy to lose his job in the first place. Troy had still refused until Casey urged him to reconsider. Raising a baby without a proper home wouldn't be easy. They needed a bed, she needed a crib... If he wanted, Troy could pay him back. At that, the matter was settled. For now, they'd go shopping and furnish the home. When he saved up the money, Troy would pay Cal back for half of it. Cal agreed.

Troy honed in on Casey. "You're not buyin' any frilly, flowery stuff, are you?"

She giggled. "And what if I am? Don't you think Cassidy should have girly things?"

"Don't go makin' a sissy out her. She's gonna be a horse girl." Casey laughed at him. Troy didn't know if she was having fun with him, or making fun of him. "What?"

"You. You're so predictable."

"Is that a bad thing?"

She shook her head. "Not at all. It makes it easy to know what will please you."

Troy liked the sound of that. At the sound of air escaping Cassidy's mouth, he patted her narrow back. "Good girl."

"And you should know better than to think I would make a sissy out of our daughter," Casey went on. "As if I were that kind of woman, myself."

"I don't know about that one." Troy eyed her dress, a floral-printed halter top and skirt that betrayed her denial of feminine taste. "You seem to have taken to girly fashion these days." Which he liked—a lot—though he wasn't gonna tell her at the moment. It would undermine his argument. But he did like it. Casey looked really good when she wore bright colors and prints. It brought out the blue in her eyes, brightened her ivory complexion, kinda like the makeup she was beginning to wear. Not much, but he discovered a touch of colored lip gloss and shimmery blush went a long way on Casey' face. Desire surged. A really long way.

"So that's my grandkid, huh?"

Troy and Cassidy whirled at the sound of a male voice at the doorway.

Jeremiah Ladd strolled in, conceit ingrained in his light brown eyes, the swagger of his blue jeans and ostrich boots. "They told me but I didn't believe it."

Troy pressed Cassidy closer to his body and demanded, "What are you doing here?"

Casey didn't say a word, only stared as her father invaded their hospital room.

"Another girl, huh?" Jeremiah shook his head, short layers of sandy-blond hair greased in place by hair gel as they skimmed over the collar of his lime green pinstriped shirt. "Must be the weak gene pool on your side that can't produce a boy."

Every fiber in Troy's body sprang to ready mode, wanting nothing more than to pounce on this loser. He had no business here. Casey hated him as much as Troy did. Rising from his chair, he stepped forward. "Who let you in here?"

Jeremiah smiled smugly. "Visiting hours don't discriminate."

"You need a pass," Troy objected.

Jeremiah tapped the space on his shirt where the adhesive name tag should have been stuck. "Grandfather of the baby gets family access."

"Well, we don't want you here so I'd suggest you turn around and get out."

Standing near shoulder-to-shoulder with Jeremiah, Troy sensed the hatred pulsating beneath the man's calm exterior. It mirrored that of his own. Jeremiah Ladd was nothing but trouble. He'd caused Miss Delaney grief, Casey, her mother and her aunt Lacy. The man had even been willing go to fists with his old man, and for what?

Land. Money. Jeremiah waltzed into town a year ago claiming Ladd Springs belonged to him. It didn't. Ernie Ladd signed it over to Felicity and she signed half of it over to Casey. Facts Jeremiah was well-acquainted with. The fact that he was here could only mean one thing.

He wanted *revenge*.

# # #

The End

## Deep Dish Sweet Potatoes

3 lbs. sweet potatoes
1/2 cup firmly packed light brown sugar
1/2 cup orange juice
5 TBSP butter, softened
2 tsp finely grated orange zest
1/2 tsp ground cinnamon
1/4 tsp each ground nutmeg, ground ginger
Salt and pepper to taste

Preheat oven to 350°F. Bake potatoes 1 hour or until soft. Cool.

Butter a 2-quart deep dish casserole pan and set aside. Scoop cooked potato from skins and place in a large mixing bowl. Add all ingredients to potatoes and blend until smooth. Adjust for salt and pepper. Transfer potatoes to casserole dish and spread until evenly distributed, creating textured surface. Bake uncovered on the middle oven shelf for about 30-45 minutes or until surface is lightly browned. Serve hot.

The orange-flavored base in this recipe is a great compliment to the sweet potatoes. Variations include the addition/substitution of bacon bits, dried cranberries and walnuts. Let your imagination run wild with this southern staple!

About the Author:

Dianne Venetta lives in Central Florida with her husband, two children and part-time Yellow Lab Cody-boy! An avid gardener, she spends her spare time growing organic vegetables, surprised by what she finds there every day. Who knew there were so many amazing similarities between men and plants? Women, life and love and her discoveries along the way provide for never-ending fun on her garden blog: BloominThyme.com.

You can also find her on twitter @DianneVenetta and facebook.com/DianneVenetta. Plus, learn how you can become a member of her street team, Bloomin' Warriors, where you'll be eligible for special discounts, advance excerpts, author swag and unique gift items throughout the year. For full details, be sure to check out her website, DianneVenetta.com.

Other novels by Dianne Venetta:
Romantic Women's Fiction
The Gables Trilogy:
JENNIFER'S GARDEN
LUST ON THE ROCKS
WHISPER PRIVILEGES

Women's Fiction
CONDEMN ME NOT

Mystery/Romance Fiction
Ladd Springs Series:
LADD SPRINGS #1
LADD FORTUNE #2
HOTEL LADD #3
LADD HAVEN #4
LOSING LADD #5